The Vampire Girl in London

Richard Arbib

HIGHGATE BOOKS®

ISBN-13: 978-0692724910
ISBN: 0692724915
LCCN: 2011944243

For more information, visit:
www.thevampiregirlnextdoor.com

The Vampire Girl in London

Richard Arbib

HIGHGATE BOOKS®

The Vampire Girl in London

Chapter One

As the jet screamed off the runway, I watched the San Francisco Bay Area skyline slowly shrink below us. How beautiful it looked during the sunny afternoon, a sight Sylvia and I would see only rarely.

Sylvia held my hand and smiled fondly. "This is it. The beginning of our future. And we'll have a home in London." Her eyes beamed with pleasure. "And friends, too," she added, nodding her head happily.

"What about Father Callen's friends?" I asked.

She frowned. "Yes, they'll still be after us. But we'll have friends of our own to help us."

The flight attendant came by and asked what we would like to drink, and Sylvia ordered two Perriers. The view of the sunny scene below began to recede, and both of us squinted against the harsh light until I pulled down the shade.

The flight attendant returned with two bottles of Perrier, which Sylvia poured. She handed one of the glasses to me.

"I propose a toast," Sylvia declared, raising her glass.

I raised my glass to meet hers. "What shall we toast to?"

Sylvia smiled broadly, revealing all her teeth. "To an eternity together."

We clinked our glasses together and drank.

An eternity together, I mused. How long it sounded,

1

yet if I had been given a specific amount of time with Sylvia, it couldn't have been long enough, even if it were a century.

I fell hopelessly and helplessly in love with her when I first met her in the hallway of my apartment building only three short weeks earlier—or perhaps I should say three long weeks earlier, since so much had happened since then.

I remembered her introducing herself in front of my door: "I'm Sylvia Martin. You must be my next-door neighbor."

"I'm Mark Sheridan," I said, but I could say no more.

I remembered standing there staring at her, absolutely speechless. She was, quite simply, the most beautiful girl I had ever seen in my life. Her eyes were large and dark, and shaped in a most unusual manner— they appeared to flare upwards at the edges, so that the outside corners were higher than the inside. Her lashes were exquisitely long and thick, and black, just like the long hair of hers that framed her delicate face with soft bangs. That silky hair tumbled over the smooth bare skin of her arms, and came to rest just above her waist—a waist so tiny, it made her hips flare out provocatively. Her long legs gave her the same height as me, and accentuated her daintiness. She stood as still as a statue of a goddess, and I stood as still as an idiot who could think of nothing to say.

After an awkward silence, she said, "Aren't you going to ask me in?" Her face looked at me questioningly, like a little girl locked out in the cold and wanting to come back into the house after playing outside.

How could I possibly resist? That's how it all started. Sure, I felt bad that my good fortune in meeting Sylvia came about because my last neighbor, Harry, had been murdered. And, as much as I hated Harry and his loud stereo, it had still shocked me how he had lost his life so

2

violently, from loss of blood after his throat had been ripped open, right in his very own apartment next to mine. But I came to realize an important truth: if Harry had not been murdered, Sylvia couldn't have moved into his apartment, and she and I might have never met, and that would have been a far more serious tragedy.

As I looked into Sylvia's beautiful and loving eyes staring into mine on the plane, I realized that everything worked out for the best. Sylvia made sure of that.

I glanced around us at the other passengers on the jet. We were seated on the right side of the plane, at the very back. Though almost all of the window aisle rows had three seats, ours had only two because the fuselage narrowed at the end. The last three rows were only two seats across, and we sat at the front of these three rows. Only two rows of empty seats remained behind us. I supposed that the very rear of the plane might not have been as popular with the rest of the passengers, but that suited Sylvia and me just fine. We appreciated the privacy. The only possible intrusion to this was a man sitting in the aisle to our left, just one row back. We happened to look around and he caught our glance, smiled at us, and raised his own glass, as if toasting us. He seemed pleasant enough, and appeared to be in his early thirties like me. Unlike me, he had blond hair and blue eyes. Someone might have thought his smile was specifically intended for Sylvia, but she had the window seat, so I was the one who was closer. If there was any further doubt, it was immediately dispelled.

"I'll bet you're newlyweds," he said in a loud voice, necessary to hear above the loud hum of the engines.

"Not yet, but soon," Sylvia said, flashing her engagement ring with the large heart-shaped diamond.

"I thought you were already from the way you toasted each other. Good luck to you both." He raised his glass again.

3

We raised our glasses to him, then Sylvia and I turned back to each other. The loud hum of the jet gave us a sense of intimate privacy. We could talk to each other in a normal volume without worrying about someone directly in front or behind us hearing our conversation. Because there was no one directly in front of us or behind us, it made our little spot even more intimate. The blond stranger in the aisle one row back had no chance of hearing us unless we deliberately spoke loudly enough.

Sylvia kissed me on the cheek tenderly with her large sensuous lips, then smiled. She had a wonderful smile; it was not the formal smile of a businesswoman where only the mouth moves and the other features remain frozen to keep things from becoming too intimate; nor was it the self-satisfied smile of a beautiful woman gloating secretly as she is being admired without returning the compliment. No, Sylvia's smile radiated warmth as she looked at me because her smile came as much from her eyes as from her lips. Her lower eyelids curved up in their own unique way with the outside edges much higher than the inside, so that the lower eyelids themselves had their own smile that could be seen even if her lips could not. From the very moment I met Sylvia, her eyes had enchanted me. The eyes have been called the window of the soul. If so, here was something more unusual — Sylvia's eyes were black — not dark blue or dark brown — but the darkness that admits no color or light. Upon close observation, it could be seen that the pupils of her eyes were the size of the average person's pupil and iris together, thus the reason for this anomaly. This gave her gaze an unusual intensity. Stranger still was the fact that after Sylvia and I consummated our love, my eyes became as black and dark as hers.

I glanced at the beautiful Patek Philippe white gold watch Sylvia had given me as a gift only two weeks earlier. It said five-thirty, so we had only been in flight for about two hours. Sylvia caught my glance to my watch. "Well, just think, Mark — in only eight hours or so, we'll be in London. And with the time difference of eight hours, we should arrive before ten tomorrow morning. We'll pass the evening on the plane. Not the most romantic setting, but maybe they'll show a good film."

"Anything that would drown out the sound of the engines would be fine with me. This noise is driving me crazy. How in the world do you stand it?"

"Why, I simply tune it out and concentrate only on what I want to hear, like the sound of your voice," she said with a smile. "Here, let's try a little exercise for fun. With practice, you should be able to hear just as I do." She pointed at two businessmen seated halfway between us and the center of the plane. "Concentrate only on their voices. Block out the sound of the engines and all the other voices on the plane."

I tried following Sylvia's directions. As I tried to focus my hearing, the other conversations became a blur, as if I were changing the dial on a radio. At last I honed in on the conversation of the two businessmen discussing "cost overruns." Their conversation was so boring, it hardly seemed worth the trouble to listen to. I told Sylvia.

"All right," she said. "Then try the couple in the front of this section."

Now I had to concentrate even harder, as Sylvia and I both listened to the couple in the front of the rear section, almost in the very center of the plane. They were arguing about the schedule of their holiday. The conversation didn't particularly interest me, and I found the strain annoying.

"This is very difficult for me," I admitted.

"Of course it's difficult for you. You've only been able to do this for a week. It wasn't easy for me my first week, let me tell you. I didn't have someone who loved me by my side to guide me. I was all alone. I had to discover everything by myself."

"I'm lucky to have you," I admitted.

"We're both lucky," Sylvia answered, as she kissed me on the cheek.

I smiled back at her. "I guess we are. It's hard for me to believe how well everything is going. It seems too good to be true."

"Well, believe it. Because it is true. Here, let's try another one." She pointed at another couple, this time in the front section of the plane between the middle and the very front.

We both focused on their conversation, and found that they were newlyweds on their honeymoon. They spoke of their plans for the future and their baby, which was due in eight months. This provided only an instant of innocent diversion for us, for only a second later, her voice changed to one of terror, and both Sylvia and I heard her words: "Oh my God! They have guns!"

Her next words could not be deciphered, for the whole front section of the plane broke out in a verbal pandemonium mixed with several screams.

"Your attention please," came a voice over the loudspeakers of the plane, a voice with a distinctly Middle Eastern accent. "Everyone stay in your seats and no one will be harmed."

Sylvia and I stared at each other, our full attention on the voice over the speaker.

"There will be a slight change in flight plans. This plane is now under control by the Islamic freedom fighters. No one is to move from their seat. If you do as you are told, I promise you will not be shot at this time."

At least two hundred voices all spoke at once now, voices containing questions, panic, and anger. The voices merged together like all voices of the crowd do, becoming like one loud question: "Why is this happening? What will they do to us?" And I heard several people say aloud what I was thinking—on September 11th, the hijackers told the passengers everything would be okay if they cooperated, then they flew the planes into the buildings.

"We are merely going to land in a country that is neutral to our people. Then you will be exchanged for the freedom fighters held by the infidels."

From the front of the plane, Sylvia and I could hear a voice ask, "What if they won't let your friends go free?"

"Pray that they do," came the response of one of the gunmen.

Sylvia's eyes welled up with tears and she balled her delicate hands into little fists. "They can't do this to us. I looked forward to our being together for so long," she sobbed.

The voice came over the speakers again: "At this time, everyone will place their passports in their laps for inspection. No one may leave their seats for any reason."

I looked around and saw people nervously fumbling for their passports. All, except for the blond man behind us to the left, who seemed to move more smoothly and more confidently than the rest. He quickly pulled an American passport and his wallet out of a jacket pocket and slipped them discreetly under his seat. Sylvia leaned over me to see what I was looking at, and then we both saw him open his attaché case at his feet. He withdrew a Walther .380 caliber automatic, complete with silencer attached, and wrapping a newspaper around it, hid it in the magazine pouch on the back of the seat directly in front of him.

"Oh no," said Sylvia. "Is he one of them?"

I assured her that he wasn't.

"How can you be so sure?"

"If he were one of them, he wouldn't be trying to hide his gun—or his American passport."

Just as I finished saying that, he pulled a Canadian

passport from his other jacket pocket and placed it patiently on his lap.

In the front of the plane were two gunmen. One had a beard, and carried a large handgun. He kept looking around, then finally satisfied himself with staying in the front section, while the other decided to join those of us in the rear section. Both men were very well dressed.

The hijacker in the rear section had a moustache and his hair was black like the man in front. He also had a large handgun. Though he was not too close to me yet, I guessed that the revolver might be a .357 magnum, or worse yet, a .44 magnum—the type used by Clint Eastwood in his *Dirty Harry* movies. I knew that such a gun would easily blow a hole through the side of the plane, probably plunging us all to our deaths. But, then a moment later, the gun lost some of its significance as the gunman pulled a hand grenade from inside his jacket.

One of the passengers offered him advice on international diplomacy. "You may as well let us go free now. America never negotiates with terrorists."

The hijacker smashed the man's face with his handgun, breaking his nose and bloodying his white shirt, then pointed the barrel at the man's face. "Don't ever call me a terrorist," he warned.

There was a brief stirring in the seats, as if someone might get up, but the gunman quickly squelched such notions. He swiftly pulled the pin from the hand grenade, being careful all the while to keep the tension on the handle so it wouldn't explode.

Holding the revolver and the pin in one hand, and the delicately held grenade in the other, he strolled through the aisle. "I expect your total cooperation," he explained to the passengers. "If our mission succeeds, you will all live; if it fails, we will all die. We are all in this together. Yes, together we will fulfill our religious destiny."

Sylvia simmered. "I'd like to fulfill my religious destiny right now. I'd like to kill him."

My hand instinctively went to the small quarter-sized medallion around my neck—the same medallion Sylvia gave me just a couple of weeks earlier.

"I don't think you'd want him to die right now," I said. "If he drops the grenade, the plane will crash."

"He can't hold it forever. He'll put the pin back in."

Sylvia was correct. After a few minutes, he grew tired of his display of power, placed the pin back in the grenade and clipped it to his belt. Meanwhile, his friend in front amused himself by brandishing a long curved knife as he inspected the passports of the people in the front of the plane. Occasionally, both men would hit a passenger in the face with a gun if he were to turn around. They wanted things to remain orderly, apparently, and having people look around greatly angered them.

The gunman in our section of the plane began leafing through passports placed on people's laps as he looked for anyone he considered hostile to his cause. Although I felt he was looking possibly for Israelis, I sensed he wouldn't be fond of Americans, and not the British, either. I got my answer to this as he stopped in front of us, and Sylvia handed him her British passport.

"British," he said, passing Sylvia's passport back to her. "We will never forget that your country always helps the Americans to attack our fighters."

"And we will never forget," Sylvia replied, "the London bombings, and all the terrorist attacks in Europe. You cowards think you're getting seventy-two virgins? Dream on. You'll die a virgin."

I placed my hand on Sylvia's. "We better leave politics and religion for another time," I suggested.

The gunman snatched my passport as he threw Sylvia's back to her and tried to ignore her. "I don't like your governments and I don't like the two of you," he said. "Later, you may be sorry you made me remember you so well."

As if to give me one more minor insult on top of everything else, the gunman dropped my passport on the floor. I bent down to pick it up. As I did, the silver medallion on the silver chain I wore around my neck slipped out from underneath my shirt.

"What's this?" asked the gunman, pointing at it.

"A gift from me," said Sylvia. "For good luck and as a symbol of our love."

The gunman's eyes narrowed into slits of hate. "Ah. Jewish!"

"You stupid twit!" Sylvia yelled. "That's a pentagram, not a Jewish star. Can't you see the difference?"

He tried to grab it and I pushed his hand away. He reached for it a second time and as my hand blocked his, Sylvia reached out and grabbed his wrist. He jerked his hand away, but not before her nails carved into his skin, causing him to shriek in pain and grab his bleeding wrist. His reaction was to reach forward and try to hit Sylvia in the face with his pistol, but I moved between the two of them, and the gun struck me across the forehead right above my eye. He tried again to strike her, and as I blocked him again, I felt the gash open up as the pistol ripped my skin open a second time. My hand instinctively went to my forehead and I felt it wet with blood and already swollen. As I did this, his hand jerked the chain from my neck. He held it up as if it were a trophy and sneered at me. "So now I have your Jewish good luck piece." Sylvia's face first registered pity for the deep gash on my forehead, then hatred for him.

"That medallion isn't going to be good luck for you. It's the Baphomet. The symbol of Satan," she said.

The gunman's eyes widened as he looked at the

medallion more closely—at the sign of the goat's head inside the inverted pentagram.

"Satan," he repeated, in awe and fear. "America, the Great Satan."

Sylvia's hate flowed from her eyes to his. "America isn't the Great Satan," she hissed. "I am."

I saw fear and anger in his eyes as he stared at both of us and then the medallion.

"Both of you are Satans," he said, as if this were some kind of revelation. "If the freedom fighters are not released when we land, I shoot you two first."

He tucked the medallion into his front pocket as if he were in shock, then corrected himself before he walked away.

"No, even if the freedom fighters are released, I still shoot you both!"

Chapter Two

I looked over at Sylvia as the gunman walked away. "You must have read Dale Carnegie's *How to Win Friends and Influence People.*"

"I don't want to be his friend," she said. "I want to kill him."

"Fine," I said. "But let's be practical. These guys are religious fanatics. You tell them you're Satan and they think you're serious."

Sylvia's dark eyes met mine. "I am serious."

"They don't have to know that. They don't have to know anything we're going to do. Surprise them; don't warn them."

"I can't help it. I like to tell them first. I enjoy self-fulfilling prophecies. And when I saw him hit you and make you bleed, and then take the medallion away—"

Sylvia began to cry, and I put my arm around her.

"I wore that medallion for many years before I gave it to you two weeks ago. It has a lot of sentimental value. It symbolized a rebirth for me."

"Me too," I said.

Sylvia gazed at me with her large sad eyes. "Oh, I'm so sorry about your head."

"So am I. This really hurts."

"This is all my fault. If I hadn't angered him, he wouldn't have hit you."

"He's hit other passengers for far less. It's not your fault. Anyway, if the plane crashes, this injury won't make much of a difference to me. And if we can somehow get to London safely, I suppose it will heal."

She bent towards me. "Here. Let me kiss it and make it feel better."

"Ow," I said, as I winced with pain as her lips pressed against the open wound.

"I'm sorry."

"That's okay, but you've got my blood on your lips now. "

Her long tongue slowly circled her lips. "Mmm. You're right. I did." She sat there for a moment, her face a picture of tranquility with her eyes closed. Then they opened suddenly as if she had been startled awake after a pleasant dream.

Blood still flowed slowly from the gash above my eye. Sylvia poured the remaining Perrier water from my glass to hers, then used one of the airline napkins dampened with water to clean the blood from my head and stop the bleeding. Apparently, there was quite a bit, for the water in the glass grew a darker shade of red each time she rinsed the napkin in it. Within half an hour, though, I noticed that the pain had ceased entirely. When I placed my hand on my forehead to feel the wound, I could not find even the slightest trace of a cut. The swelling had also disappeared. The only hint that I had been hurt was a small amount of dried blood where the wound had been. Sylvia dabbed it with the dampened napkin, and then my head was exactly the same as before it had been struck.

"Your head looks fine now," she said. "What's the time?"

"Six-thirty."

She opened the shade slightly. The view was total darkness.

"I don't know exactly where we are, but with your watch saying six-thirty, and with us flying into new time zones, it's probably close to seven-thirty or so where we are right here. How do you feel now?"

"I feel fine. I think this is the right time to make our move. Now, if we could only distract them somehow."

"I can do that," Sylvia offered.

"If I could just get that guy's .380 automatic. It's perfect. The bullets won't go through the plane, so it would be very safe to shoot him with it. And the really nice thing is, it won't make enough noise to warn the other hijacker. It's okay as long as we do it when they're apart, and if we can get them before they have a chance to shoot back. Because—their bullets will go through the plane."

"There you go, being practical again," Sylvia responded. "I don't want to shoot him anyway."

I grinned. "Yes, I know what you want."

She smiled back, then said, "How about a compromise? You can shoot one of them. But not this one. I have much better plans for him," she declared happily, then pressed her soft lips against my ear and whispered in hushed but excited tones. Though the whispering was not needed for privacy due to the loud hum of the engines, I made no objection. Her voice at all times sounded like music to me, but especially so when she whispered, when it, not surprisingly, took on the quality of a magical and mesmerizing chant, with the power to lull the listener into an agreeably suggestible state. But such influence was unnecessary at this time, for her plan satisfied both my sense of practicality and her sense of justice.

The hijacker near the cockpit busied himself with the crew in the very front of the plane, while the one who had hit me stood guard in the front of the rear section.

"Excuse me," Sylvia said to me politely as she stood up and squeezed by me to stand in the aisle. She waited a moment until she caught the hijacker's eye.

"Sit down!" he commanded.

She shook her head. He started towards her. One of the passengers began to turn around, and the gunman struck him in the face with his revolver. Everyone else stared forward like obedient children in class.

As he came within a few feet of her, he commanded her once again to sit down. This time no one turned

14

around to watch. Sylvia smiled and shook her head again, her long silky hair brushing back and forth across her shoulders.

"No," she said quietly, in her soft voice, at a volume so low, the other passengers could not hear. "I'm going to use the toilet."

She turned and walked away from the hijacker. He grew furious, commanded her again to stop, then went after her. A few feet before she reached the bathroom in the very rear of the plane, he grabbed her by the arm. She laughed as she jerked her arm free of him, upsetting his balance, as she opened the door and locked it behind her.

The hum of the engines allowed me to follow silently, without him able to hear me until I was within touching distance as he pounded on the bathroom door. My years of Wing Chun kung fu were about to come in handy.

As I reached him, he turned his head towards me. Before he could react, my fists struck his face with three chain punches in a split second. I felt his bones give way with a loud crack. As his head snapped to the side, an explosion of blood spattered the white wall. Yet his problems had only begun. The restroom door opened at that very instant and Sylvia's arm shot out towards him. Her slender fingers with long nails closed around his throat and pulled him into the restroom, jerking him off his feet. He reminded me of a cartoon of some character in an amateur show being yanked off the stage with a long cane for a mediocre performance. I heard a brief muffled scream from inside the door, but it lasted only a short time, and then there was almost silence, though not quite, and I knew that all was well. I also knew that death itself would not come for another minute or two. Despite, or perhaps because of Sylvia's hatred for him, she had the self-control to make sure he didn't die immediately.

I gazed quickly towards the front of the plane. Fortunately, the other hijacker was still in front, but unfortunately, the man with the blond hair was sneaking a glance back at me. I would have to wait for him to turn around towards the front before rushing forward to grab his .380 automatic. I hoped that the hijacker in the front of the plane did not confront us before I had the opportunity to secure the gun. To add to my worries, I realized that the man with the blond hair might have been the one witness on the plane who saw Sylvia and me and the hijacker go to the back. Sylvia and I certainly didn't want any witnesses.

"Sylvia," I called, through the door. "We've got to get the other one before it's too late—before he finds out his friend is missing."

There was no answer, only the sound of running water. I tried the door, but it was locked. The latch suddenly turned and the door opened just a few inches. I could see Sylvia washing her hands in the sink.

She came out and shut the door behind her, then said "Is everything okay?"

"No, it's not. I couldn't get the gun because he was looking. I better try to get it now. Oh, and you better get that blood off your lips."

She ran her tongue around her thick lips, like a little girl licking away the evidence of an ice cream cone.

"How do I look now?" she asked.

"How do you look now? You look beautiful just as you always do. But I think I better try to get that gun away."

We both turned towards the front of the plane to see the second gunman standing right next to where our seats were. He had his long curved knife in one hand. In his other hand, he held his revolver, which, at only twelve to fifteen feet away, I judged to be a .44 magnum after all. He pointed it at my face.

"Do not move," he warned, "or I shoot you both. Where is my friend?"

"Have you checked the front of the plane?" Sylvia asked. "I'm sure we saw him there only a minute ago, didn't we, Mark?"

"Yes," I said, "it was definitely in the front of the plane. I think he's there now looking for you."

He took a step forward. "Put your hands on your heads and don't move." He began to walk slowly towards us.

As we stood with our hands on our heads, the only positive thing I could think of was that if he should get close enough, there might be a chance to get the gun away before he shot a hole through the side of the jet. Our quarters were certainly cramped enough. I stood as close to the bathroom door as I could so that he would have to get next to me and have no room to shoot me from a distance.

"Get away from the door," he said as he moved closer.

We moved back slightly, which, unfortunately, gave him enough room to have access to the door without any chance of me hitting him.

He slipped his long knife into its sheath, then used that hand to knock on the door. When he got no answer, he placed his hand on the knob, turned to us and said, "Now I will see what is inside the door." He made the mistake of looking directly into Sylvia's eyes as he said this.

"No," she said, staring back at him, being careful not to break the eye contact he had inadvertently begun. "*No. You will not open the door. You cannot open the door.*"

He stared at her with the sudden realization and horror that her words were true.

Out of the corner of my eye, I saw the man with the blond hair reach into the magazine pouch for his .380 automatic. Taking advantage of the moment when the hijacker froze at Sylvia's voice and stare, he raised the pistol and pointed swiftly but carefully. There was a zipping sound, audible to Sylvia and me, but certainly not to the other passengers on the plane. The hum of the engines drowned out the sound of the bullet being fired through the silencer, as well as the gasp of the hijacker as his head snapped with the impact from being shot. The man with the automatic rushed up and quickly pumped two more bullets into the hijacker's head just to be sure the terrorist died. The hijacker lay inert on the floor, blood oozing from the three fatal shots. Blood spread onto the carpet. The blond man used his foot to turn him over and looked at his face and nodded knowingly, then sighed. "At last. Finally, at last." He pulled the bathroom door open. Inside was the other hijacker, his lifeless eyes staring vacantly. On his throat were two holes about an inch or so apart. Two small trails of blood had trickled from these holes down his neck and stained his white shirt and his expensive jacket.

The man turned to Sylvia and to me, then bent down over the dead hijacker who lay on the floor of the plane and using a handkerchief, carefully removed his knife from the sheath. He glanced around to see if any of the passengers were watching, but they were still following the commands of the hijackers and kept their bodies facing strictly straight ahead. "We don't want to have to explain those holes in his neck, now do we?" he asked. He then slit the throat of Sylvia's victim, being careful to make the blade obliterate the two small wounds her teeth had made. He placed the knife into the hand of its owner, squeezed the man's fingers around the handle to make an impression of his fingerprints, then let go so the knife would rest on the floor.

"Well, I guess that just about does it," he said. "If you'd like to take your seats, I'll notify the flight crew to resume their normal route to London. When we get to Heathrow Airport, the British authorities may question the passengers, but I know that none of the other passengers saw what you did. So, as far as everyone is concerned, you never left your seats. Do you follow me?"

"You have our thanks," Sylvia said to him.

He nodded at both of us. "And you certainly have ours." He then walked to the front of the plane and entered the cockpit.

As we took our seats, Sylvia noticed the glass filled with a mixture of water and my blood from my head injury. "Your cut is gone, but the evidence of it is still here. We can't have that, now can we?" She glanced around to see that no one was watching, then with a gesture of a toast, smiled at me and said, "Here's to our health, our happiness, and our life together." She drank the contents.

A minute later, a flight attendant used the intercom to inform the passengers that the hijackers had both been killed and that the flight would resume its normal path to London. A cheer echoed through the plane, passengers ordered drinks to celebrate, and things returned to normal in very short order. This was certainly as well, since the majority of our flight still lay ahead of us.

Hours passed, and so did the night. Sylvia and I hadn't slept, of course, so we were able to watch a magnificent sunrise from our vantage point in the heavens. As we passed through these clouds at the end of the flight, the ground below soon became visible. Patches of green and brown could be recognized as farms. We began our descent.

"Where's London?" I asked.

"Coming right up," Sylvia answered.

I searched the scene below. Gradually, industrial sections and suburbs could be distinguished. As the plane dipped even lower, the Thames River could be seen as well, snaking its way through London, and I could see several bridges linking the northern and southern areas divided by the great river.

As we landed at Heathrow Airport, passengers were instructed to stay in their seats until after the local authorities gave permission to leave the plane.

As soon as the main door of the jet opened, two uniformed policemen stationed themselves in the front of the plane, and three men in well-tailored suits accompanied the blond stranger past us to the very rear section. I also noticed several jeeps with soldiers outside the jet, waiting and armed with rifles.

Sylvia and I eavesdropped on the conversation behind us.

"So you shot this one?" one of the men asked.

"Yes."

"What about the other one?"

They opened the door to look at Sylvia's victim.

"My God! What happened to the bloke's throat? He hasn't been shot."

"Oh no," the blond stranger explained. "His throat was slashed by the other man. There's his knife. But be careful. Don't disturb any fingerprints."

"Yes. Quite right. But tell me—why would one kill the other?"

"That's a good question," replied the stranger. "All I know is that they came back here to discuss something. They weren't speaking English, so I don't know what they said, but they were arguing about something. They sounded very angry. Before I knew it, the one with the knife slit the other one's throat and pushed him into the bathroom. I knew that was my one chance, so I shot him."

"Hmm. And so you did. Three times in the back of the head by the looks of him. Did you ever think of trying to capture him? Wound him? Find out who the Hell he was?"

"That was hardly necessary. I know who he was. I've been hoping for this opportunity for years. He's been well known to the agency for some time."

"If only you could have captured him."

"Are you serious?" the stranger asked. "You don't want this man as a prisoner. His friends would demand that you set him free. And if you refused their demands, they would commit all kinds of terrorist actions in London to make you set him free. But now that they're both dead, what can their friends demand? Even they understand you can't raise someone from the dead."

"He has a good point there," said one of the other men.

"How did you shoot him without the other passengers hearing you?"

The stranger pulled his gun out and showed it to the three men.

"This is highly illegal in our country—at least for private citizens."

"Mine, too," concurred the stranger. "But of course there are times when it's necessary for a gun to be quiet."

"Of course."

"That's perfectly understandable," said another. "Especially in light of such a delicate situation."

"It can be a nasty business, can't it?" asked another, rhetorically.

"Quite so," agreed another.

"Well, then. Shall we let the passengers take their leave?"

The four of them made their way to the front of the plane and an announcement was made that we would all be free to depart.

Sylvia sighed. "What a relief," she said to me.

"Oh no," I said, as I put my hand to my throat. "The medallion! They'll find it on the hijacker!"

Sylvia smiled. "No they won't," she said, as she reached behind her neck and undid the chain below the collar of her dress. "It's right here. I took it back from him."

She placed it around my neck and kissed me.

"What would I ever do without you?" I asked.

"That's something I would rather not consider, "she answered. "Perhaps a better question is what will you do with me? That is, once we're home and finally in bed?"

"I can think of a few things to keep us busy for awhile."

"Good. Me, too," she agreed.

We made our way off the plane with the rest of the passengers. Inside the terminal, an immigration agent checked our passports, and saw that Sylvia's was British while mine was American.

"Is this trip for business or pleasure?" she asked, as she handed the passport back to me.

Sylvia gave me a sexy smile, hinting at what we would soon be doing once alone.

"Pleasure," I said, and we went on our merry way, arm in arm.

Chapter Three

Inside the passenger terminal at Heathrow Airport, a man and woman greeted us. The woman and Sylvia hugged warmly as the man stepped towards me and shook my hand.

"This is Susan and Joseph Bentley," said Sylvia. "Susan has been my best friend forever."

"Come now, Sylvia," said Susan, "even I'm not that old. Forever? Not quite. But it has been over a century."

Actually, both Susan and Joseph appeared to be in their twenties. She looked about four or five years younger than him. They both had brown hair and brown eyes, and while they were a reasonably attractive couple, nothing in their appearance was particularly remarkable or exotic. No one would have given them a second look, and indeed, no one did.

As the four of us made our way from the terminal to the parking lot, loaded down with our suitcases, Sylvia summarized the events of our plane flight, including how she killed the hijacker in the bathroom by drinking his blood.

"Well, the two of you have certainly had your share of excitement in the past couple of days, haven't you?" asked Joseph. "I mean, first Father Callen, and then a hijacking."

"Actually, the excitement has been more than just a couple of days for me," I explained. "The excitement started about three weeks ago right around the time I met Sylvia."

"What a coincidence," said Susan with a giggle.

"Hardly a coincidence," I said. "First, she saved my life by killing two of three guys who were trying to mug me in an alley. The following night, she killed the next-door neighbor I always hated, and two days after that she moved into his apartment. By the time I met her, she was already involved in my life and I didn't even know who she was. I didn't know that she was the one who killed them until a couple of weeks later. She told me the truth right after the first time we had sex and right before she turned me into a vampire."

Sylvia looked at me with curiosity. "Do you think I did things in the wrong order?"

"Certainly not," Joseph interrupted. "It's always best to tell the truth after sex, not before."

Susan punched him affectionately in the shoulder and said "My, what an awful thing to say."

"To answer your question," I said, turning to Sylvia, "no, I don't think you did things in the wrong order. As a matter of fact, if I had the power to go back over the past three weeks and change anything that happened, there's only one thing I would change."

"What would that be?" Sylvia asked.

"If I had known what Father Callen was planning, I would have prevented his attack on you."

"You did just fine," Sylvia said to me, smiling. "You saved my life."

Susan gasped. "You mean Father Callen almost killed you?"

"You didn't know?" I asked.

"Sylvia told us that Father Callen was dead," said Joseph, "but of course we didn't discuss the details over the phone."

Sylvia explained. "Father Callen sneaked into our room at the Atlantis Hotel in Reno, and while we were asleep, he drove a stake through my heart."

Susan clapped her hand over her own heart and shuddered. "How awful. What did you do?"

"I didn't do anything. My entire body was paralyzed. But Mark knocked out Father Callen with one blow. Then he slit his own wrist to give me his own blood, and he removed the stake. After I recovered in a few minutes,

Mark helped me up, Father Callen regained consciousness long enough to be fully awake when I hypnotized him to jump off the roof."

"I say—good show!" remarked Joseph.

"But are you sure he's dead?" asked Susan.

"It was twenty-six floors to the parking lot below," I answered.

"Hmm. But you Americans don't count your ground floor as a separate one, do you?" asked Joseph. "Here in England, we would say that Father Callen fell from the twenty-fifth floor because our ground floor would be your first floor, our first floor would be your second floor, and your—"

"It doesn't matter," Susan interrupted. "He's dead at last! Mark, you not only saved Sylvia's life, you made it possible to kill Father Callen. All of us will be grateful to you forever. I'm sure I speak for the others at the house when I say that."

"You can never speak for the others," said Joseph with a trace of contempt in his voice. "Those wretches didn't even join Susan and me when we performed a protective ritual for the two of you after your magical ceremony. You told us Father Callen was after you, so we tried to get the others to join us. They were too busy."

"They didn't join the ritual?" Sylvia asked sadly. "What have we come to?" Her eyes began to mist. "After all these years. And they don't even care!" Sylvia began to sob.

"We care," said Susan. "And so does Mark."

Sylvia nodded and dried her tears with her sleeve. I put my arm around her shoulder as we continued walking through the parking lot.

"Here we are at last," said Susan, stopping.

Joseph reached into his pocket and took out keys and opened the trunk to put the luggage in. The car looked very much like a Rolls Royce, with a similar grill that had the straight vertical stainless steel vanes. The natural wood on the dash and the luxurious feel and scent of the leather interior impressed as much as the exterior.

"What is this?" I asked.

"It's a Bentley Mulsanne," said Joseph. "Similar to a Rolls Royce. The grill and headlights are a bit different, and the suspension is a tad firmer, so it actually handles better."

"What do they cost in American money?" I asked.

"Oh, about three hundred and twenty-five thousand dollars in American money," said Joseph. "Depends upon the exchange rate. Much cheaper than the Rolls Royce Phantom."

"Joseph has a real eye for economy," said Susan.

"And of course," added Joseph, "compared to the Rolls Royce, it isn't quite as ostentatious."

"I don't know about that," I said, laughing. "This will be the most expensive car I've ever been in."

"Not for long," said Joseph, smiling at Sylvia.

Sylvia was about to answer, but just then, a Jaguar F-Type drove up with two men. The horn beeped at us and the driver waved to Sylvia and me, then drove off. It was the blond stranger from the plane.

"Oh no!" said Sylvia. "Now he'll have our license plate if he wants to find us again!"

"Why would he want to do that?" Susan asked.

Sylvia explained who he was as the four of us watched the car drive away. I knew Sylvia was doing the same thing as I was—memorizing his license plate just in case it was necessary. Somehow, I had the strong feeling we hadn't seen the last of him.

The four of us got into the Bentley, its beautiful mirror-like white finish gleaming in the sun. Sylvia sat close to me as I placed my arm around her shoulder. She continued to look in the direction of the Jaguar, even though it was no longer there.

"He better not bother us," she said. "I don't trust him at all."

The Bentley drove out of the parking lot and we made our way onto the M4 Motorway, a freeway, which the British call a "carriageway." At seventy miles per hour, we seemed to be quietly floating on air due to the ride's smoothness.

"So," I said, breaking the long silence, "what kind of car do you have that Joseph implied cost more than his?"

"An Aston Martin DBS V12," said Sylvia, suddenly smiling again. "Daniel Craig drove one in the James Bond movie, *Casino Royale*."

"I knew they were expensive, but I didn't realize they cost as much as a Rolls Royce," I said.

"No, mine would cost about two hundred and sixty-five thousand dollars in American money, so less than this Bentley," Sylvia commented. "We must get you accustomed to English pounds rather than dollars—and of course all the other little differences."

The most striking difference to me at that moment was the fact we were hurtling down the freeway on what would be the wrong side of the road in America. I felt as if I had stepped through the other side of Alice's looking glass and everything had been suddenly reversed.

However, the scenery was beautiful as we drove further past the western suburbs of London towards the center of the city. Sylvia pointed out Osterley Park, which the freeway actually went through, so that we were surrounded by green on the left and right.

"Is it a coincidence," I asked, "that your last names match your cars? I mean since your last name is Bentley, and Sylvia's last name is Martin?"

Joseph chuckled. "As a matter of fact, I do rather like having a car with my last name on it, but I like the car regardless of what you'd call it."

"A rose by any other name—" began Susan. "But if

you and Sylvia get married, then her last name technically won't be Martin anymore."

"If we must be technical," Sylvia said, "we can't use our real names on a permanent basis anyway since we don't age or die. We are always using counterfeit identities."

"As long as you're interested in names and coincidences," said Susan, "do you realize that your initials are the reverse of each other? Sylvia Martin and Mark Sheridan?"

A strange feeling of déjà vu came over me as she said that, but a feeling of déjà vu not for what she said, but rather for what I somehow knew Sylvia would answer.

Sylvia said, "Mark and I aren't just the reverse of each other—we are mirrors."

Her words brought back the memory of other words—those she had spoken only a week and a half earlier in her apartment next door to mine in San Francisco. We stood in front of her large Baphomet on the wall, used for her Satanic rituals. She had explained that there were five dimensions. The first three occupied space, the fourth dimension time, and the fifth dimension was made up of mental activity—all mental activity which took place in the universe—the combined mental activity of all thinking beings. It included not only everything that had been observed or experienced through time, but also anything ever imagined. In this dimension, anything was possible. Past, present, and future coexisted. Because the fifth dimension was made up of combined mental activity, the normal laws of nature did not operate. All kinds of strange beings existed, limited only by an unlimited imagination. Among the beings were demons. Most of these were trapped in the fifth dimension. Some, however, were not. Sylvia had noticed the presence of such a demon within herself many years ago. She found it made her practice of magic much more powerful, but she also found out something else— the demon was more powerful than any one human could absorb, and for over a century it stayed partly in our dimension inhabiting Sylvia, and partly in its own dimension trapped until it could find the other human to inhabit its other half. I was the other half. Sylvia explained to me how she and I were twins, really, born of the same Satanic seed. Born two and a half centuries apart, but still twins on a Satanic level. This, she had explained later to me, was the reason she had moved to San Francisco and searched for me, the reason she saved me from getting shot in the alley and killed my next-door neighbor so she and I could be neighbors, and why both of us were so irresistibly drawn to each other. Most romances are a sort of dance—a game of cat and mouse—advance and retreat. Ours was more like two powerful magnets drawn towards each other with such force and speed that separation would be impossible as well as unthinkable.

The suburbs surrounding the western section of London gradually became denser as we made our way further into the center. The freeway ended in an area of London called Chiswick, which bordered along the River Thames, and from there we travelled down Great West Road which brought us firmly into what I considered to be downtown London. The distances were so great and London so much larger than I had expected, that I wasn't really sure, though Sylvia did her best to keep me informed by showing all the streets to me on a map as quickly as she could. Apparently, London had not been planned on a simple grid pattern on a small piece of land like Manhattan was. No, London grew organically over time, its streets reaching out and growing in a thousand directions, like an octopus with countless tentacles. Magnificent historical buildings were everywhere—the architecture was a sensory overload for the eyes. Roads curved and meandered and disappeared. Here was a city not for the organized and the methodical—but rather for the eclectic and the adventurous.

I immediately fell in love with London—its variety, beauty, and complexity captivated me in a way that a more simple and modern city could not.

We drove along Bayswater Road, and Joseph pointed out Kensington Gardens on our right along with Hyde Park and the Serpentine, a long narrow lake. Susan informed me the lake could be skated on when frozen in the winter and sailed on with boats in the summer, but for now it was not cold enough to freeze nor warm enough for leisurely sailing. The car turned left on Portman Street, then right on Marleybone Road. We crossed the first street and Sylvia pointed out that it was Baker Street, made famous by Sherlock Holmes. Madame Tussaud's Wax Museum stood on our left, and Sylvia said we would have to visit it sometime. Regent's Park also stood to our left, and Joseph turned left at Albany Street so that I could have a nice view of it as we proceeded in a northerly direction away from the center of London.

"You're certainly giving me the grand tour here," I said, my head swimming from all the new visual images.

"It will take years to really see it all and know it well," said Sylvia, "but then we've certainly got plenty of time."

"Speaking of time, how long have the two of you been together?" I asked.

Susan turned around to face me. "Joseph and I met in 1854. We were in love with each other and had planned to marry. Our plans and our destiny were radically changed by another woman—a vampire. Joseph came from a very wealthy family, and this vampire had a proposition for him—marry her so that she would have half his money, and in return she would give him the immortality of a vampire."

"It sounded pretty good to me," said Joseph, "except for one thing—I was in love with Susan. So I said to this vampire, 'How about this: you make me immortal with no marriage, but I'll give you sixty percent of the money instead of half.' Well, that really suited her fine, so we did it and then I made Susan immortal too, and then we married. Even with forty percent of the money left, we were set up pretty handsomely, and it didn't take us that long to build our capital back up."

"We've certainly led a charmed life," Susan agreed.

Joseph continued. "Within a period of only a year, we met three other vampire couples just like us. We decided to pool our money and our business efforts. We found that together, we had great magical power when we performed Satanic rituals as a group. This increased not only our financial security, but our physical security as well. We bought a seven-bedroom mansion. We still live there. Wait till you see it. I think you're going to like it."

"It was thanks to Joseph and Susan that I was found," Sylvia explained. "After a stake was driven through my heart in 1766, I lay inside a coffin in that mausoleum for exactly one century. In 1866, they found me and brought me back to life by feeding me the combined blood of all eight vampires."

Susan laughed. "You should have seen how surprised she was to wake up after a hundred years had gone by! By that time, not only was the railroad operating as mass transportation, the first line of the Underground had been built."

"The Underground?" I asked.

"You Americans call it a subway," said Joseph.

"You mean you had a subway in London back in 1866?" I asked.

"The beginnings of one," answered Sylvia. "It went from Paddington to Farringdon Street. I can tell you it was quite a shock to me. I'd never dreamed of such things in the 1760s. There were lots of surprises to wake up to."

"It looks like I have a lot of catching up to do in order to hear about your life before we met," I said.

"We've got plenty of time," said Sylvia, "but even we don't have enough time for all of it. It's just been too long already. I keep telling myself to look forward or live in the present. My past is too overwhelming, even for me."

The car had left the center of London and we were now travelling north. I asked where we were going and Sylvia said to Highgate, which could be considered a village, but still part of London. The scenery had taken quite a change. The area looked more like a quaint country village rather than part of a metropolis. Rows of eighteenth century houses were interspersed with more modern Victorian architecture from the nineteenth century along narrow streets.

We drove up Holloway Road and it split in two, becoming Archway on the right and Highgate Hill to the left. We took the left hand path. Just a few blocks later, the street changed its name to Highgate High Street. I mentioned this aloud.

"Take a look at this," said Sylvia, showing me her map. "The names of the streets change constantly even though you may still be on the same one."

"Then how do you know where you are?" I asked.

"Sometimes you don't. You just have to look around. Don't look on the street corners for signs like in America because they're not there; they're tacked onto the side of the buildings near the corner. Here's yet another one for you. Remember you said my last name matched my Aston Martin and Joseph and Susan's last name matched their Bentley? The road we were just on, Holloway, is the last name of another couple who live with us. There's no relationship between any of the names and anything."

"Then what's the purpose of a name if it can be

attached to anything?" I asked.

Sylvia smiled. "It gives the illusion of order and meaning in a chaotic world."

"All this talk about names and words and streets and identities and reversals and mirrors and dimensions is making me dizzy," I said. "It makes me think of Alice stepping through the looking glass," I added, as I remembered my train of thought from a few minutes earlier.

Sylvia nodded. "Ah, yes. *Alice's Adventures in Wonderland* and *Through the Looking Glass*. How I loved those stories. I'll have to show you the original manuscript at the British Library of *Alice's Adventures Under Ground*. What beautiful handwriting he had. Poor Reverend Dodgson—in love with young Alice Liddell while she could not understand and return his love. He had to create a fictional Alice that he could love freely. How sad he must have been!"

"But without that love from him, the fictional Alice would never have existed," I pointed out.

"Yes," Sylvia agreed, "but in the end, his love went to a fictional Alice, not the real one. If I were not real and just a fictional character, would you still love me?"

"Absolutely," I said.

"How sad that would be!" Sylvia said. "If that were to happen, then I would hope that you would also become fictional so that we would at least be together."

I thought of Sylvia's words and realized if what she said about the fifth dimension were true—that it was made up of all combined mental activity—then those fictional characters she spoke of existed in the fifth dimension the moment they were conceived.

At the top of the hill, the car turned again, and we drove down narrow meandering streets. Along the side of the road stood a tall straight wrought-iron fence with gold-painted spikes on the top of each bar in the fence.

Behind this lay a slight hill. Through the bars, I could make out a large brick Victorian mansion. Susan reached into the glovebox and pressed a remote control. The massive gates to the driveway opened, then closed behind us as we made our way up the driveway towards the imposing house. A highly decorated archway with another spike-topped iron gate stood in front of the double doors. Extravagant details abounded: gables and towers, pinnacles and slit windows. Joseph stopped the car and we began to walk towards the doorway. In the shadows behind the archway, a female figure stepped forward and unlatched the gate. Two wolves bounded out the gate towards us. Sylvia dropped her suitcase on the ground and held her arms out like she was getting ready to hug them, then bent down, picked one of them up in her arms as if it weighed nothing and kissed it on the top of the head, then set it down and repeated the process with the other one.

"Aren't they nice?" she asked me. "We have them very well trained. They're wonderful as guards and they're so nice and cuddly, too." She stopped in front of the open doorway. "Well, since this is going to be our permanent home, carry me across the threshold as if we just got married. It's tradition."

"Who am I to buck tradition?" I asked, as I picked Sylvia up in my arms and carried her across the doorway into the large front waiting room.

Standing inside was a beautiful young woman, more attractive than Susan, but not dark and exotic like Sylvia. Instead, she had blonde hair and blue eyes. "I'm Yvette Benedict," she said. "You must be Mark." She shook my hand, holding it a little too long as she stared me up and down. "Gee, Sylvia, looks like this one's in pretty good shape." She poked my chest and then my stomach checking to see how solid I was.

"Why don't you just pull up his lips and check his

34

teeth if you're going to inspect him like a horse," Sylvia said to her.

"If I thought he was built like a horse, it wouldn't be his teeth I'd check," Yvette retorted. "Don't worry, Mark. It's all in fun. Sylvia and I are like sisters, you know. We even look alike. Don't you think so?" She spun around like a model, showing off slender legs in a mini-skirt and tremendous cleavage stuffed into a dress that couldn't quite cope with it.

I looked at her and Sylvia. "Actually, I'm afraid I don't see any resemblance at all. I mean, you certainly are attractive, but you and Sylvia are about as different as two women possibly could be. Your hair, your eyes, your heights, your figures. You couldn't be more different."

"Hmm. You know, you're right. I think I have more of the kind of figure you'd see in a magazine like *Playboy*. I could be a Playmate of the Month. Sylvia, on the other hand, is built kind of the opposite of me—not enough on top and a little too much on the legs and bottom if you know what I mean."

"With all due respect to you, I think Sylvia is perfect. Her body is slim, but curvy in the right places like a tall figure skater."

"Thank you," said Sylvia. "That's because I ice-skate."

"I didn't know that," I said. "So do I. We'll have to go together soon."

"It's a date," she answered, smiling.

"Yes, a tall figure skater," Yvette repeated. "You're absolutely right, and oh my God, she's taller than you!"

"No I'm not," Sylvia said. "Mark and I are the same height and you're shorter than both of us."

"You're wrong Sylvia. He is shorter than you. You only appear to be the same height because his curly hair sticks up about an inch. If his hair lay flat like yours, you'd be an inch or two taller very clearly. And you're not even wearing heels. If you were wearing heels, why, you'd tower over him."

"Does this mean I have to go back to San Francisco?" I asked Sylvia.

"Let's send Yvette there," Sylvia said, "preferably in a box by sea mail."

"One problem will be when you're having sex," Yvette pointed out. "When you lie down in bed together, he'll be shorter and that will be a problem."

"When Mark and I lie down together in bed he never gets shorter. He always gets longer. I know because I always check."

Yvette puzzled over Sylvia's remark, then forgot what they were discussing as my Satanic medallion caught her attention. "Hmm. Funny you should have one of those. Sylvia has one exactly like it."

"That *is* my medallion," Sylvia said. "I gave it to Mark in San Francisco."

"Well, then what will you wear?" Yvette responded, but without waiting for an answer, added, "Maybe Mark will get you something nice like this." Her finger tapped at an enormous pear-shaped diamond on a gold chain that dangled around her neck and hung precariously in the soft crevice between her two large breasts. "Like it? Ronald gave it to me for our diamond wedding anniversary. Seventy-five years. Think of that."

"Unthinkable," Sylvia said. "I don't know how he lasted."

"Why don't you ask him?" Yvette asked, as Ronald made his entrance.

He had blond hair and blue eyes and stood about six feet tall and appeared to be in his mid-thirties. "How do you do?" he said formally, as he shook my hand. He appeared as if he had just woken up.

"Look at his eyes," Yvette said to him, as she pointed at my face. "His pupils are just like Sylvia's. He has no iris. His eyes are black."

"Sylvia's eyes are a little different," admitted Susan.

"That's because she's not one of us," said Ronald, with a touch of bitterness in his voice.

"Of course she's one of us," said Susan. "She's just special."

"And so is Mark," added Sylvia, as she put her arm around me and glared back at Ronald. She gave him a cool mocking smile as if she knew something he did not.

Ronald's gaze flitted back and forth, examining Sylvia's eyes and mine. Behind his outward look of menace, I could detect a stronger emotion: fear.

Chapter Four

As Sylvia and I stood in the doorway of the mansion, I wondered what it was regarding the appearance of my eyes that had so unnerved Ronald. Ever since Sylvia had turned me into a vampire only one short week earlier, my eyes became like hers. The iris, previously brown, turned black, like the pupil. Or perhaps the pupil grew to the size of the iris and the iris disappeared altogether. I wasn't sure. What I did know was that since my transformation, the "color" of my eyes was now black, just like Sylvia's eyes. At the time my eyes changed, I assumed that all vampires went through a similar metamorphosis, but now, looking around the room at the others, I could see that their eyes appeared normal.

A door opened and closed from another part of the house, and another man and woman entered the room where we stood. They both had light brown hair and wore long white coats like scientists in a laboratory. Sylvia introduced them to me as Jack and Helen Holloway.

Jack shook my hand, then staring at me, exclaimed to Helen, "Why, take a look at this. He's got the same eyes as Sylvia!"

Helen stepped forward and inspected me. "Well, so they are. Black as Sylvia's soul!"

"What a nasty thing to say," Susan said, scolding Helen.

"Hypocritical, too, I might add," said Joseph, "since neither you nor Jack believe in such a thing as a soul. Or anything else you can't measure scientifically."

"They fancy themselves to be scientists," Sylvia explained to me.

"Mad scientists?" I asked.

Laughter erupted among Sylvia, Susan, and Joseph, and even Yvette suppressed a giggle.

"Mad as hatters," Joseph declared.

Jack and Helen were not amused. "We are serious scientists doing serious research," Jack said. "Since becoming vampires, we have done much work on hematology since vampirism is obviously related to a condition of the blood."

"Jack and Helen think vampirism is a disease," Sylvia said.

"That's correct," said Helen. "A disease we are trying to cure."

"A synthetic blood substitute, to be precise," added Jack. "One which will allow us to live normal lives."

"Who wants to be normal?" Sylvia inquired. "I enjoy drinking blood. Next to sex, it's the most enjoyable thing one can do."

"You're nothing but a savage," said Helen, "content to do nothing but gorge yourself on the blood of others and bang on that damn harpsichord."

"Your stupid cure won't work anyway," Sylvia countered. "The chemical composition of blood isn't what nourishes us, it's the life-force we take from the living."

"What superstitious drivel," Jack retorted.

"You think your science can alter the balance set up by God and Satan?" asked Sylvia. "Don't you see? It's supposed to be this way. We take someone else's life force and it renews us. It's not the blood itself—it's the life within the blood. Your silly scheme won't work. It just wasn't meant to. Why don't you just follow your true nature?"

"What nature is that?" asked Jack. "That of a murderer?"

"That of a vampire," replied Sylvia, with some exasperation. "Sometimes people have to die, but that's the price that has to be paid."

"But you're not paying!" Helen said. "Someone else is paying for you."

Sylvia shrugged her shoulders. "That's okay. Satan doesn't mind. He set it up this way. Why don't you stop trying to be human and just be what you are?"

As Jack and Helen glared at Sylvia, Joseph turned to me, smiled, and asked, "Well, Mark. How do you like it here so far?"

Everyone turned to me, waiting for my reply.

"I don't know. It's not quite what I expected."

Susan laughed. "I can imagine not. Why don't we show you around the house?"

Sylvia suggested that we first bring our luggage to her bedroom. Walking into the large foyer, we came across a large circular stairway. Persian rugs partly covered the hardwood floors. Oak wainscotting covered about the bottom three feet of the walls, the balance up to the tall ceilings being covered with wallpaper of an intricate design. Indeed, intricate designs dominated most of the details of the interior: the corners where the wall and ceiling met, little bookshelves built into the design of the wall, elaborate carvings around the fixtures for overhead lights. Sylvia and I walked up the long winding staircase by ourselves and then down a thickly padded hallway rug. She produced a key and unlocked a door.

"Here we are at last," she said, as we stepped inside.

The bedroom must have measured around twenty feet by thirty feet. A large ornate bed dominated the room. She had a highly decorated writing desk next to the windows, some of which were framed in diamond-shaped panes. Most of the furniture appeared to be French Provincial. Two long and tall bookshelves contained many volumes, but some appeared to be missing. I assumed the missing volumes to be the ones Sylvia had brought to San Francisco, and knew that they would be replaced quickly enough—as soon as the movers brought the rest of our things over.

"When we get our things back, my harpsichord will

go there by the window, though I have another harpsichord in the living room. The only other things I have that will be coming back here will be my clothes and books. So, how do you like it?"

"Fine. It looks large and comfortable. And I think we can use the privacy to get away from the others."

Sylvia nodded and smiled as she placed her arms around my neck. I circled her slim waist with my own arms and drew her towards me, which led to a long, lingering kiss.

As we held each other, I had a strange feeling that eyes were upon us—that we were being watched. And indeed we were.

I looked around to see that along the walls of Sylvia's room, almost completely surrounding us, were dolls—dozens of dolls.

They stood on the floor, up against the wall, most measuring from about a foot and a half to two feet high. They wore the finest clothes of their day, which I presumed to be the Victorian era. As I looked along the entire room, I could see that they took up the floor space along two walls.

"Well, looks like we've got company," I remarked.

Sylvia smiled. "Ah, yes. All my little friends. I hope you don't mind them."

"They're certainly pretty enough, but—"

"But what?"

"They are a bit overwhelming. There are so many of them and they're all staring at us. It will almost feel like we have an audience when we make love."

"Oh, if that's all that's bothering you, I can lay them down on their backs."

"What does that do?"

"It makes most of them close their eyes. Then they can't watch us." Sylvia stood staring at me with a serious expression for a moment, then burst into laughter.

41

"This is a pretty room, " I admitted, "but it does seem to have an overly feminine atmosphere."

"Thank you. I do my best." Sylvia curtsied.

"What I mean is I think we need to strike some sort of balance."

"Balance? What kind of balance?" she asked apprehensively.

"Between the feminine and the masculine, the yin and the yang, the refined and the earthy." I looked around and pointed at a beautifully painted life-size carousel horse in the corner on a pole that ran from the floor to the twelve-foot ceiling. "That's the perfect place."

"Perfect for what?" Sylvia asked, her eyes widening.

"For the moose head." I pointed over at the other corner where Sylvia had several paintings of country landscapes. "Over there would be the perfect place for my fishing plaque. Don't worry. It doesn't smell much."

Sylvia frowned and let out a sigh. "Perfect," she repeated in a low voice, as if in a trance.

Her eyes met mine and I could contain my laughter no longer, then she began to laugh with me.

"I don't have any trophies for hunting or fishing," I admitted, "because I'm not a hunter or a fisherman."

Sylvia clapped her palm to her breast. "What a relief. I would hate to have to change my room so much. It's been this way for over a century and I've gotten accustomed to it. But I would change it if it would make you happy."

"It's fine the way it is. You're fine the way you are."

"Thank you. I'm glad you think so." Sylvia thought for a moment. "You are wrong about one thing, though."

"What's that?"

"You are a hunter. We both are. All vampires are hunters. However, at least we have the good breeding not to put our trophies up on the wall. That would be in very poor taste."

"I agree. But aren't these dozens of dolls kind of like little trophies? Each one representing a victim?"

"Why Mark, what a morbid thought! I love my dolls. Besides, I would never pick a child as a victim. I love children. In a way, these dolls are my children." She stared at them sadly.

I put my arm around her shoulder. "I'm sorry. I don't want to make you feel unhappy."

"You never make me feel unhappy. It's the dolls. I love collecting them, but sometimes they remind me how much I would like to have a real child."

"You never mentioned children before."

"There was no point in mentioning them. Vampires can't have children, of course. Imagine what it would be like if we could. Would we watch our child gradually grow older than us and finally die of old age? Or would we decide to stop the aging process at some point by creating another vampire? If we did that, what age would that be? No, it's better the way it is. I don't have to make such complicated decisions."

I observed Sylvia as she stared at the dolls surrounding us. All were dressed in the finest clothes, hair perfectly styled, faces meticulously formed and painted to convey childlike beauty in its ideal form. As Sylvia contemplated them silently, I felt guilty about my remark comparing them to little trophies of victims. I apologized to her.

She shook her head and placed her hand on my shoulder. "No need to be sorry. I know you didn't mean to make me sad—and you didn't. It's the dolls themselves who do that. But here, you must meet them."

She pulled me by the hand and started to explain them to me. "Most of these are French, made between the 1860s and the turn of the century. About half of them are Jumeau dolls, like this one here." She picked one up and handed it to me. It wore a dress made of silk and lace, and appeared to be a young girl in miniature. Sylvia picked up another with almond-shaped brown eyes and dark brown hair. "She's one of my favorites. A Bru doll, probably the finest of any made at the time." She pointed at another, this one with an adult face and a more womanly body. "This one is a Gaultier, a fashion doll, dressed to show off Parisian fashions in the 1880s."

"They're all works of art," I said.

"Yes, they are," Sylvia concurred. "And the thing about them that I like so much is that they are more human than any other work of art. A painting is flat and two-dimensional. A statue is made of stone or metal and does not have realistic coloring of the skin, hair, or eyes. A fictional character has personality, but exists only in the minds of the writer and readers. But a doll is as close a representation to the original person as one can possibly obtain. Why, some of these can even walk and talk! Owning a doll is a little bit like owning or possessing a real person. A doll is made, and the image of the person is immortalized and captured. It's sort of like a three-dimensional photograph you can pick up and hold in your hands."

"Speaking of photographs, when I first met you, you didn't want me to take your picture. Remember?"

"Oh, that." Sylvia dismissed it with a wave of her hand. "It's not that I didn't want you to have my picture, I just didn't want anyone else to see it—for security reasons. When you're a vampire and you don't age, it's not a good idea to have lots of photos floating about. People could come to conclusions about that. If you remember, I refused to pose for you before I made you a vampire. You can have a photo of me now if you like. But if you shoot film instead of digital, don't have it developed in a commercial photo lab."

"How will we develop it, then?"

"Since you like photography so much, we can put a

darkroom in here at the house. We have room for it."

"That sounds great. I'll have to take lots of pictures of London, too, now that I'm here for the first time. You can give me a tour."

"Of course I will. That will be a real pleasure. There's so much to see here. Speaking of tours, though, I should show you the rest of the house."

Sylvia led me by the hand back through the hallway and down the stairs to an enormous living room. The ceiling was even higher than the one in her bedroom. It appeared to be about sixteen feet in height. Sylvia's other harpsichord, a French, with a double keyboard, stood at one end of the living room. A large chandelier hung from the ceiling, and that, combined with a velvet-textured wallpaper, gave the room elegance. Next to the harpsichord was Sylvia's Bosendorfer piano, with the 97-key keyboard she had told me about before.

The others were seated in couches and chairs around the living room as we came in. Susan looked at us, then at the rest of the group, and said, "I think Sylvia has an important announcement to make."

"I do?" Sylvia asked.

"About Father Callen?" said Susan.

"Oh yes, you're right," said Sylvia. "How could I have forgotten to tell you all? On Sunday morning, I killed Father Callen."

"Killed Father Callen?" asked Ronald. "How? Where?"

Sylvia summarized how Callen burst into our room at the Atlantis Hotel and Casino in Reno, Nevada, just two days earlier, how he drove a stake through Sylvia's heart, how I knocked him out and revived Sylvia with my own blood, and how she hypnotized him to jump from the roof twenty-six floors to his death.

"That's wonderful!" said Yvette, smiling at me. "He's been after us for years. I'm so glad you and Sylvia got rid of him."

"Let's not forget who was responsible for the existence of Father Callen's vampire-hunting cult in the first place," said Jack as he looked at Sylvia accusingly.

"And who ultimately bears the responsibility for their most recent actions against us," added Helen, as she rose up against Sylvia, too.

"That's not fair to Sylvia," Susan said.

"What are they talking about?" I asked.

Sylvia then explained to me in front of the group, how Father Callen's group originally came into existence:

In 1685, while Sylvia was 19 yeas old and not yet a vampire, witch hunters came to her family's small farm and killed her family while she was out in the field. She was forced to watch their murder, unable to help, for they would have killed her, too. Although she fled and escaped, Sylvia was attacked by a vampire who transformed her into one also. She ran away from the vampire later and used her new powers to kill all the villagers who murdered her family. Father Callen's group formed in response to Sylvia's revenge on the villagers.

"But you were justified in what you did," I said.

"Thank you," said Sylvia. "I think so, too. But Helen is partly correct. If it hadn't been for Callen's group, there would be two more of us here right now." Sylvia stared at the floor in sadness.

"About a year ago, Father Callen and his group took revenge against us," Ronald explained. "One of the other couples who had been here in the house with us for many years was murdered by Callen's group."

"But that's crazy," I said. "You mean that they took revenge over three hundred years after Sylvia killed the villagers?"

"I'm afraid so," said Ronald. "That's why we must be careful. In the past, they didn't know where we lived. But if Callen was able to find you in America, they must know

46

more than we thought they did."

"I hate to sound paranoid," I said, "but here's something else to worry about." I looked at Sylvia, Joseph, and Susan. "That guy who drove by in the Jaguar when we were in the parking lot—I'm sure he took down your license plate and had it traced."

"Why would someone do that?" Ronald asked.

Sylvia then had to summarize the events of the plane hijacking to the group.

"So this man in the car, who you say carries a gun with a silencer, and shoots hijackers—this man has the license plate of a car sitting here in front of our house?" Ronald placed his palm over his forehead as if experiencing a headache. He shook his head as if the news were too bad to be believed.

"He's probably not a vampire-hunter," I said, to reassure the group. "I'm sure he's just a CIA agent or something."

"Just a CIA agent?" Ronald said sarcastically. "Well," you can't imagine how pleased I am to know that a man who can trace Joseph's car to this house, who can tap our phones and spy on us, is just a CIA agent. I don't know if Sylvia bothered to mention this to you, but as vampires, there are occasions when we might bend the law. Nothing more serious than murder, of course, but still enough to upset people who work for the government." Ronald stared ahead blankly, apparently engaged in serious thought about the matter.

"If Mark and I had done nothing on the plane to the hijackers, we wouldn't be here right now. We'd be hostages or dead. "

"If you hadn't gone to America, you wouldn't have run into Father Callen or the hijackers," Helen remarked.

"Then I wouldn't have met Mark!" Sylvia protested.

"So what?" asked Jack. "What good has that done?"

"Aside from the fact that Sylvia and I love each other

47

and are happy, if we hadn't been on the plane, all the passengers might have died."

"I wonder if the CIA agent will take that into account if we're all arrested for murder later on?" Ronald asked.

"We have his license plate number as well," Sylvia pointed out. "Perhaps we can find him first."

Ronald nodded and tried to regain his composure. "Perhaps we can."

"Enough of this gloom and doom," said Yvette. "Ronald, show Mark and Sylvia their engagement gift."

Sylvia looked at Yvette with some surprise. "You bought us an engagement gift?"

"Actually Ronald picked it out and paid for it, but it is from both of us. I know you're going to love it."

As Yvette momentarily left the room to fetch the present, Sylvia gave me a look that registered her suspicion over receiving a gift from them. I just raised my eyebrows and shrugged my shoulders.

When Yvette returned, it was with an ornately gift-wrapped box, covered with shiny blue and red aluminum foil wrapping, similar to what sometimes holds a bouquet of flowers. Silk ribbons were tied around the box, which must have measured about a foot around and three feet long.

"I hope that you will like this, too, Mark," said Yvette, "but as I'm sure you just discovered from Sylvia's bedroom, she collects dolls."

"Another one?" I asked Sylvia quietly.

"This was especially made for you by Pierre," said Ronald.

Sylvia turned to me and brightened. "Pierre is a famous French doll maker here in London. He sells rare collector dolls, but also makes excellent reproductions himself. They're quite costly."

Ronald nodded in agreement. "They certainly are. Particularly this one."

Sylvia smiled happily as she began to unwrap the box, lifted off the lid, revealing an adult doll, realistically sculpted, wearing a mini-skirt, but lying face down. Sylvia simultaneously lifted her out of her confines of the box and turned her over to face us.

The doll was Sylvia in miniature, and perfect in every way, even down to the finest details of her eyes.

"It's two feet, ten inches tall," stated Ronald, "exactly half of Sylvia's height of five feet eight. It was made perfectly to scale."

"It certainly was," agreed Yvette. "It's even anatomically correct, unlike other dolls. You'll see when you take her clothes off."

I looked on the doll with delight, even love; Sylvia stared at it in horror.

"Why, oh why have you done such a terrible thing?" she asked.

Everyone in the room gawked at her in shocked disbelief.

"I don't want to be photographed or drawn or created in sculpture or dolls or written about," she said.

"But Sylvia," I protested, "this is a beautiful present. The artist has captured your beauty and recreated it."

"But I don't want to be captured or recreated. Don't you understand that it steals my image from me?"

"You're still as beautiful as before," I said. "It doesn't take anything away. If a work of art could possess someone's soul, then why did you paint a portrait of me before we ever met?"

Sylvia stared at me intently with her large and melancholy eyes for an unusually long silence, then finally answered, "That's exactly why I painted your portrait."

"Your portrait of me was unnecessary to possess me. I loved you the moment I saw you." I picked up the doll and held it towards Sylvia. "And I love this doll, too, because it reminds me of you."

"You don't need a reminder," she said. "You have me."

"But whenever we're away from each other, I can look at this doll and think of you."

"Whenever we're away from each other?" she asked. "I never want us to be away from each other. Never!"

Across the room from me, behind Sylvia, sat Yvette. She looked at me, crossed her eyes, twirled her finger around in circles pointing at her head, then pointed at Sylvia, letting me know she thought Sylvia was acting crazy.

Sylvia immediately noticed the eye contact and turned around to catch Yvette in the middle of her mime act. Under Sylvia's glare, Yvette's finger went down and her hand dropped as if she were a little girl caught holding something forbidden.

"Perhaps Pierre would take it back," said Ronald. "He told me he got several offers for it before I picked it up. Generous offers, I might add."

Sylvia gasped in horror. "Sell a doll of me to strangers?" She reached for the doll, which I already held. "Not a chance. Now that it's been made of me, it mustn't be sold or destroyed."

"What a stupid waste of money," muttered Helen. "You almost could have bought an economy car for the price of that silly doll."

"Why would Sylvia want an economy car when she has an Aston Martin?" Susan asked. "I think I understand why Sylvia feels so strange about it, though."

"Why is that?" asked Ronald, as the rest of the group looked at Susan.

"Because being involved in magic as we all are," explained Susan, "means that we are more conscious of symbols, and this doll is certainly a lifelike symbol of Sylvia. I can understand her feeling vulnerable. She identifies so much with the doll that she is afraid she will lose her own identity."

"Thank you, Sigmund Freud," said Jack.

"I think it's just beautiful," I said, and Sylvia smiled weakly and handed the doll to me.

"I never said I didn't like the way it looks," Sylvia explained. "It's just such a shock to see a doll that looks exactly like me."

"But your reflection in the mirror doesn't shock you," Joseph pointed out.

"It might if it left the mirror and became three-dimensional like this doll," Sylvia said.

Everyone in the room was finally at a loss for words. The drama of the doll seemed to have played itself out.

"Sylvia and I haven't slept in over twenty-four hours," I said. "This may be a good time for us to go to bed."

Sylvia nodded as we left the room. With one arm, I circled her waist, with the other, I circled the waist of the Sylvia doll, and the three of us made our way up the circular stairway.

Chapter Five

"Alone at last," she said with a sigh. "We're finally here. After surviving Father Callen, the terrorists on the plane, and finally the insults of Yvette and the rest of them, after going without sleep for over twenty-four hours—now we finally have some privacy."

I set the Sylvia doll down on Sylvia's bed, allowing her head to rest upon the pillow. She did not close her eyes.

"Look," I said, pointing to her. "She doesn't seem to be tired at all."

Sylvia looked at the doll on her bed. "Hmm. Fixed eyes. They stay open all the time. Some of my other dolls are like that, but they're not quite so unnerving."

"Unnerving?" I asked.

"Yes, unnerving. Don't you see? It's a bit like being forced to look in the mirror all the time."

"Is that so bad? With the way you look, I'd think you'd be delighted to look in the mirror."

"Perhaps my soul is in the mirror and I don't want to see it. Or maybe I just don't like the way I look."

"You've got to be kidding! You're the most beautiful woman I've ever seen in my life."

Sylvia attempted a smile. Her large full lips drew back, revealing the slight prominence of her canine teeth. "Really? As beautiful as Yvette?"

"Certainly. Yvette is beautiful, but in a standard way. She looks like a lot of other beautiful women—models or actresses. You don't look like anyone else."

"No," Sylvia admitted. "I definitely don't look like anyone else. My eyes are very different."

"So are mine since you turned me into a vampire."

"That's not what I mean. I'm not talking about the fact that our iris appears to be black instead of brown or blue, though that is a little odd. Even the others have

52

normal colored eyes. What I'm talking about is the shape of my eyes. People stare at me sometimes. They think I'm strange." Sylvia stood her doll against the wall.

"They stare at you because you're beautiful. You're not strange. You're exotic."

"Exotic?" Sylvia mused. "Do you know what exotic means?"

"Of course. Enticing—beauty that is rare and unusual."

"It means strangely beautiful," Sylvia emphasized, as she slipped off her shoes. She turned her back towards me and pointed at the zipper at the top of her dress, motioning for me to unzip her, which I did. "I've always felt strange. Different from the others, and certainly less attractive than Yvette."

"She wanted you to feel that way," I said, as I began to remove my own clothes. "The way you feel about yourself has nothing to do with the way you look. It has to do with Yvette trying to make you feel bad about yourself so that she can feel good about herself."

Sylvia stood in her bra and panties, and began to slowly remove her panties, pulling them over her long legs, standing gracefully on one leg at a time like a crane, never losing her balance. "She said I'm too tall for you. I thought we were the same height."

"You may be an inch taller." I smiled. "It's all in your legs. And your legs are much better than Yvette's— they're longer and shapelier."

Sylvia smiled. "You don't mind then, that I'm taller than you? "

"Why should I mind? You're someone I can look up to," I punned.

Sylvia slipped off her bra and panties. "I like that. Someone you can look up to," she mused. "Could you look up to me and go down on me at the same time?"

"Why, certainly," I answered, as I lay down on her

53

bed and invited her to join me.

Sylvia moved onto the bed and her smooth thighs straddled my face and squeezed together affectionately. "Ah, yes," she said happily. "This is one position where you can look up to me and go down on me at the same time. I even have the best seat in the house to watch it all from."

I almost laughed at Sylvia's puns, but she pressed her fragrant dampness against my lips, her fingers entwined themselves into my hair, and her hips moved around in a circular motion. As I began to lick her, she began to smile. Though we stayed in this position for a long time, her eyes kept contact with mine for every moment, unblinking, and our souls were one.

Later, after we finished making love, we lay side by side, our arms around each other.

"I feel very close to you when we make love," I said. "It's almost difficult to describe."

"Try," said Sylvia, smiling.

"It's as if there were no you or me involved, just us. Not two separate people with two sets of feelings or two sets of sensations, but one being with the same feelings and perceptions. It's as if I can feel everything you are feeling and you can do the same with me."

"We can and we do," said Sylvia. "It's true. When we make love, we can feel everything the other feels to the point where there is no actual other, just us."

"Almost as if we were just one entity," I said.

"We are just one entity." Sylvia smiled.

We lay in bed, facing each other, our eyes on each other, and eventually, we fell asleep, though I didn't remember when it actually was. I didn't remember actually closing my eyes or seeing Sylvia's eyes close, and when we woke, I didn't remember opening my eyes or seeing Sylvia's eyes open. We were just both awake again. Our eyes were on each other, our arms were around each other, and our bodies were in the same deliciously tangled position that we had slept in.

We kissed, then disentangled ourselves and looked at the clock.

"Hmm. Nine o'clock in the morning," Sylvia observed. "I never wake up at this time. How strange. We slept for sixteen hours!"

"It must be the lack of sleep we had, plus the change in time zones. Our bodies are still on San Francisco time, which is eight hours behind London."

"I feel wonderful, though," said Sylvia. "So rested. None of the others will be awake for about another six hours or so. Why don't we go out and enjoy the day?"

I stared at Sylvia with some surprise. In San Francisco, she avoided going out during the daytime. Her fears of Father Callen killing her during vulnerable daytime hours were partly the reason, of course, but she had also explained how the sun could rob us of energy—energy which could replaced by the drinking of human blood.

"You're surprised I mentioned a daylight excursion, aren't you?" Sylvia asked.

I mentioned her reluctance to go out during the daytime in San Francisco.

"This is different. We may need a little more blood than normal if we are to go out during the day than at night because of the energy it requires, but some of that energy can be made up just by sleeping longer—as we just did. Also, here in England, there are very few guns as compared to America. Consequently, there are fewer murders. Of course, we could get hit by a car or have some type of accident, but no matter how serious it was, when nighttime came, we would recover. Even if we were shot dead during the daytime, we would recover during the night. Best of all, Father Callen is dead."

"That's great that Father Callen can't go after us

anymore," I admitted. "But I'm sure he's got friends. And surely you're not saying that we can't be killed under any circumstances, are you?"

"No, but those circumstances are very limited. If our bodies were totally destroyed during the daytime, then we could not be revived. If we were to be burned to ashes, blown up in an explosion, or otherwise destroyed so that there was no possibility of reviving, then yes, we could die permanently. But there's really little chance of that happening."

"What if one of Father Callen's friends were to come here?" I asked.

"They don't know where we live, or else they would have acted long ago."

"Then how did Father Callen know where we lived in San Francisco? And how did he know which hotel room to find us in when we were gambling in Reno?"

Sylvia thought for a moment and frowned. "I don't know. That's something we must find the answer to."

Just a little while later, we set out on foot. Sylvia explained that Highgate was small enough for us to see the main sights without resorting to a car. The morning was sunny, something Sylvia explained as unusual for a winter day, but the temperature was brisk. After about fifteen minutes of walking hand in hand down quaint side streets, we arrived at the corner of South Grove and Highgate High Street.

"This is the main street in town," Sylvia said, pointing along Highgate High Street. "Further down the hill just a few blocks, it becomes Highgate Hill."

We stood on South Grove, the street branching off to the side of Highgate High Street.

"This is Pond Square." Sylvia pointed at a large open area, which might have been a park, but was covered with concrete instead of grass. A few trees grew through the concrete, and the area did look like a square of sorts,

56

only it was shaped more like a triangle.

"Where's the pond?" I asked.

"They were filled in back in the 1860s. However, this is still the center of the town."

A beautiful gray church stood before us on South Grove, its four tall narrow windows rising to points, and filled with ornate stained glass composed of warm colors. Next to it, at 11 South Grove, was a brick building with arched windows, a white door, and a black wrought-iron fence atop a small wall around the front. Over a large arched window, a sign read: The Highgate Society. On the wall next to the door, another sign read: Highgate Literary and Scientific Institution. Sylvia led me by the hand through the doorway.

A small group of people stood and talked in the front room. Two middle-aged women recognized Sylvia and greeted us. One said, "How nice to see you, Sylvia. Are you going to introduce your young man to us?"

"This is Mark Sheridan. We were just engaged in San Francisco a week ago."

"How nice," the other remarked. "You must stay for coffee."

"I thought one stayed for tea here in England," I said.

"One does," the woman answered, "but we serve coffee here every Wednesday morning from 10:30 to 11:30. You're in luck."

"I'll say you are," remarked the other. "How did you ever meet such a lovely girl as Sylvia?"

"We were neighbors in San Francisco."

"In San Francisco?" The woman looked puzzled. "But Sylvia doesn't live in San Francisco. She lives right here in Highgate."

"I was just visiting," Sylvia explained.

One of the women looked at our hands, noticing Sylvia's engagement ring.

Sylvia caught her glance. "How do you like my new

engagement ring? A flawless, heart-shaped diamond, three point three three carats."

"Wise decision," said one, as both of them nodded their heads approvingly.

Sylvia explained that the Highgate Literary and Scientific Institution and the Highgate Society put on a number of interesting cultural programs—lectures, exhibitions, plays, film shows, and dances. They also had a library of over 20,000 volumes, some that Sylvia had donated.

"I think it's important to be involved in one's community," she commented, as we left for my tour of the rest of Highgate.

"It certainly strikes me as strange," I told her, once we were outside, "that here you are friends with the respected conservative people in this town and they don't seem to suspect you're a vampire."

"Well, remember, I'm respectable, too. Being a vampire certainly doesn't take that away from me. One must have self-respect, regardless of one's station in life."

"But how do you keep it secret?"

Sylvia gave me one of her sly smiles as we walked, hand in hand, down South Grove towards Highgate High Street. "First of all, I go out during the daylight, and of course, the people here know from the films they've seen, that vampires don't do that. I dress like most normal people, and again, the vampires in films don't. I give money to the local charities. I'm involved in civic activities. My practice of Satanism is kept secret from them, and most importantly, I never kill anyone in Highgate. Neither do the others. It's a very strict rule with us here. After all, these are our neighbors."

"But what if a vampire outside the group should move in and start killing people?" I asked.

"They better not. We'll kill them if they do. We've done it before. No, we won't have any of that here. It's a nice peaceful community, and we intend to keep it that way."

We turned right at Highgate High Street and began our slow descent down the hill. On the left, Sylvia pointed out a bookstore, Fisher & Sperr, where she bought her used and collectible books, and further down the street stood Highgate Bookshop, where she bought her new books. Many of the buildings on the street were done in brick, though some were wood on the ground floor, with large curved bay windows.

"The architecture here is a combination of the eighteenth and nineteenth century," Sylvia explained. "Just like me."

Actually, the resemblance went beyond that. Sylvia was a microcosm of London in several ways. Beautiful, quaint, with a long history behind her, complex and multifaceted—she was easy to fall in love with at first sight, but it would take a lifetime to know her fully.

About a block further down Highgate High Street, we turned right, into one of the entrances for Waterlow Park.

The sun shone on all of us that sunny day. People walking their dogs, children playing, mothers pushing baby carriages, and of course, the two of us—all were enjoying the serenity. We passed a grassy hill, then came upon tennis courts. Sylvia told me that all the others at the house played there, sometimes doubles. Exiting the park, we walked down Swain's Lane, which bordered on Highgate Cemetery. At the corner of Swain's Lane and Chester Road, stood a group of eight quaint houses all in the same style. They looked like smaller versions of the mansion Sylvia and the others lived in. I mentioned that to her.

"Yes, you're right. We had an architect copy the style, right after it was built in the 1860s, only make it bigger. Holly Village is well known, but the public hasn't seen our mansion because it's hidden behind the gates."

"The movers should be here today," Sylvia said, changing the subject. "I want to get my books and my clothes back, and of course my harpsichord."

"I love listening to you play, especially the fast ones."

"Ah, you like the Bach Partitas, and 'Fandango', by Antonio Soler. It's nice to have someone to play for. The others don't particularly like it, except for Susan and Joseph, naturally. Jack and Helen care only for science, not art. Ronald is only concerned with business and money, and Yvette is only interested in spending money faster than Ronald can earn it. That's quite an accomplishment for her because Ronald is very business-minded and so there's loads for her to shop with."

"I think your talent on the harpsichord is more significant than Yvette's expertise in shopping. You should be giving concerts. Other people need to hear you."

Sylvia brightened. "Do you think so? The others always objected. They say the exposure would be dangerous for the group."

"Exposure? What's dangerous about you playing a harpsichord in public? It could be done at night if you're worried about the danger. The others are keeping you from living up to your full potential."

"You're right," said Sylvia, nodding. "I'm going to do it. I'll arrange a concert and play whether they like it or not."

This issue settled, we continued our stroll along a path through the rolling hills. Weeping willows circled two ponds upon which sailed ducks and swans coexisting, the ducks unaware of the beauty of their elegant feathered neighbors, with the result that they seemed to have no jealousy or animosity.

At the southern end of the park, we crossed Swain's Lane, the dividing line between Waterlow Park and the west side of Highgate Cemetery.

"Back there is the east side," Sylvia said, as she pointed in the opposite direction. "But we shan't be going there. It's much more modern, and not nearly as interesting. It's mostly famous because Karl Marx is buried there."

"Karl Marx?" I asked, somewhat surprised.

"Quite ironic, isn't it?" Sylvia commented. "I mean the Industrial Revolution he detested so much started here in London, and now he's surrounded by the elite of society that he rebelled against. Highgate is one of London's most exclusive areas, after all. Funny that he should end up here, of all places. What's more amazing is how much influence his ideas have had upon the world, but then, people are basically stupid, aren't they? If each person gives according to their stated ability and receives according to their stated needs, what's to keep one from lying about either one to receive the most for doing the least? And if one cannot state what he or she may do or need, then who will make the determination for them? It all leads to lack of incentive and lack of freedom. Both mediocrity and repression are built into the system. No, he's certainly not my favorite philosopher. I much prefer Adam Smith and Friedrich Nietzche."

Sylvia led me away from the east side and towards the west side. On the other side of the narrow hilly road called Swain's Lane, was a gray stone wall with massive wrought-iron gates, perhaps seven or eight feet high. Instead of the usual spike-topped decoration, above the gate was a long horizontal bar, about a foot higher than the top of the gate. The bar had spikes sticking out in all directions, and rotated, if one were unlucky enough to try to climb over the top. To the sides of the gate, barbed wire was strung.

"My God! What are they afraid is going to try to get in?" I asked.

"Or out?" Sylvia responded, with a wide devilish smile, which revealed the slight prominence of her canine teeth. "Superstitions die hard, sometimes, even here. But actually, there are good reasons for the gate. This cemetery has quite an unusual history, as you're about to find out."

Fortunately, the massive gates to the west side of Highgate Cemetery were open, so it was not necessary to deal with the rotating spikes or the barbed wire at the top of the gate. As we walked through, we saw a beautiful chapel on our left, which was in the process of being renovated. Sylvia explained that I would see renovation of historical buildings throughout London. Monuments were not allowed to succumb to the elements and crumble away; the past and heritage of Britain was to be preserved. A small folding table had a sign saying "Friends of Highgate Cemetery." This was a group of people dedicated to saving the cemetery as an important piece of history. They oversaw the renovation of the chapel, repaired monuments, planted flowers, and gave guided tours of the west side of the cemetery, which we now stood in, the older section.

A group of about twenty-five of us followed a guide up a dirt path that was soft and beginning to turn to mud in some spots. The path, or road, was just wide enough to accommodate one car. But other paths grew too narrow for vehicles, and required one to be on foot. The stark gray of the tombstones and monuments contrasted sharply with the wildly overgrown greenery that engulfed the cemetery. It was as if life had somehow been nurtured by death.

The guide pointed back towards the gates and told us that there existed, an underground tunnel, linking the east and west sides, so that coffins would not have to cross Swain's Lane after the burial service. He also told us the history of Highgate Cemetery, which opened back in 1839, and was one of the earliest of London's cemeteries. Covering thirty-seven acres, the east and west sides together held 166,000 people buried in 51,000 graves. As we walked north on East Boundary Path, making our way through the dense greenery, the guide pointed out various monuments to the group.

At the same time, Sylvia put her lips to my ear and whispered her own tour of the cemetery just for me. "When I came here to Highgate in 1866, this section was much more barren. Many of the grave sites still hadn't been purchased, and there were very few trees."

We turned right at the next path, and the guide pointed to the right and told us that Stephen Geary was buried there, the founder of Highgate Cemetery.

"Mr. Geary died twelve years before I came to Highgate," Sylvia informed me quietly.

I smiled as I wondered what the rest of the group would have thought about the "private tour" I was receiving from Sylvia, but of course they heard only what the guide told them.

Along the path, we saw a tombstone further along, which had this inscription:

"TIS A BEAUTIFUL BELIEF THAT EVER ROUND OUR HEAD ARE HOV'RING ON ANGEL'S WINGS THE SPIRITS OF THE DEAD."

"Perhaps they're speaking of us," Sylvia said to me with a smile. "Only we haven't any wings."

I returned Sylvia's smile, then noticed her expression changed as she regarded two men who also seemed to notice the same tombstone.

One of the men, the older one, appeared to be in his fifties, and nodded his head knowingly. The younger one, perhaps in his late twenties, looked at the tombstone and at the older man. Like the other tourists in the group, they carried cameras, and photographed parts of the cemetery as they went along.

"I have a feeling about them," Sylvia said to me, "and it's not a very good feeling; I can tell you that."

I nodded. "You're right. I don't know why, but I feel something wrong about them, too."

"Your psychic ability is starting to grow," said Sylvia. "It will get stronger as time goes on."

"Perhaps we should make sure we don't appear in any of their pictures."

"That's exactly what I was thinking," Sylvia said. "Even better would be if we could photograph them."

"No problem. I always carry a camera."

"You do? Where is it?"

I reached into my jacket pocket and pulled it out, and began to take pictures of the two men. By placing them between us and the scenes of photographic interest, I was able to get the two men in the corner of every picture, while appearing to be only a tourist.

Sylvia nodded her approval at my technique, and I could see that while she still regarded the pair with suspicion, she seemed greatly relieved that they were in our pictures, while we were not in theirs.

Indeed, they took no notice of us at all, or any of the others in the group, for that matter. They seemed primarily concerned with Highgate Cemetery itself.

As we continued walking north, we walked straight into Egyptian Avenue, an entrance into the catacombs. A massive archway, flanked by two columns on each side as well as an obelisk on each side, marked the entrance to the catacombs. As we walked past the rusted iron gates, the tunnel came out into the sunlight again as we entered the columbarium, named the Lebanon Circle. This strange circular collection of catacombs lay beneath ground level, yet we were still in view of the sun. The inner walls held the catacombs, and the curvature of the walls gave the feeling of being inside an unusual mausoleum with no roof. In this almost subterranean atmosphere, the guide led us.

"Is it true that people have seen ghosts and vampires in Highgate Cemetery?" asked one of the tourists.

Sylvia whispered into my ear: "There were lots of reports of vampires and ghosts in the late sixties and early seventies. Father Callen was one of the crazy vampire hunters who took part. That's why the authorities sent him to prison. He and his group dug up coffins and drove stakes through corpses. Ironically, none of them were vampires. There never have been any real vampires in this cemetery."

Another tourist repeated the first one's question to the guide. "Yes, what of the stories about ghosts and vampires?"

"They're nonsense, of course," said the guide, dismissing the notion with a wave of his hand.

The first tourist persisted. "But in the book, *Dracula*, Lucy is seen in this cemetery."

"For God's sake, man," answered the guide with some annoyance in his voice, "that was only a novel."

"Perhaps it was only a novel," a loud voice agreed. The voice belonged to the older of the two men who had aroused Sylvia's suspicion. "But what about the articles in the *Hampstead and Highgate Express*? The *Evening News*? The *Finchley Press*?"

All the tourists in the group turned to face the man and his younger friend. They eagerly gave all of their attention to their "new" guide, even if that position was a self-appointed one.

"Indeed, there have been vampires in this cemetery," the older man declared to his audience. "My friend here and I have both seen them."

"I knew these two men were trouble," Sylvia said to me quietly.

The older man now had the crowd's undivided attention.

"What did they look like?" someone asked.

"Were they walking around or in coffins?" asked another.

"I think you're a phony!" yelled a teenager.

"If you saw a real vampire, why would it let you live to tell about it?" asked another tourist.

"It was asleep in its coffin," replied the older man.

"Are you one of the nut cases that vandalized our cemetery in the 1970s?" asked the guide. "If you are, then I insist you leave at once before I call the police."

"We are not breaking any law by being here now," the younger man retorted.

"Our religious order has worked to protect you, the public, from vampires," the older man explained to the crowd.

The guide's anger grew. "Are you the loony who desecrated corpses here in the 1970s—the one who was sent to prison?" he yelled.

"It wasn't me," the older man answered. "It was our leader—Father Callen."

Chapter Six

Sylvia gasped. "Oh no! Two of Father Callen's men! What do we do now?" Her eyes conveyed her fear.

My own reaction was not fear, but anger. I had only to remember back three days to Sunday, when I woke to Sylvia's scream as we lay in the hotel bed, and I saw Father Callen's hand holding a hammer high, readying for a second strike to drive the stake deeper into Sylvia's chest. It came back to me in slow motion, like a terrible nightmare: the stake piercing her chest, the blood spreading across her breasts and running down towards her stomach, but worst of all her scream, and the horrible way her eyes stared vacantly at the ceiling. A swipe of the back of my hand sent Father Callen across the room, bouncing him off of the wall and knocking him unconscious. Then, in an attempt to join Sylvia in death, I slashed my wrist across her sharp canine teeth, which had grown to their full length due to her ordeal. But as my own life force began to leave me, it dripped into Sylvia's mouth. Miraculously, my blood revived her. I removed the stake, gave her more of my blood, and she recovered in a matter of seconds. The wound in her chest healed itself before my eyes. Father Callen woke just a few minutes later and made a futile attempt to ward us off with his white plastic crucifix, but she snapped it in half, saying, "You don't need this. You're not a Christian. Christians don't go about trying to kill people. Jesus never killed anyone. He had the power. He used it to help those who suffered, not to kill those he felt were wrong. Since you don't follow Christ, perhaps you want the moral freedom of a Satanist. After all, you don't mind killing your enemies. Beware! A Christian who plays the game of life by Satan's rules has neither God's mercy nor Satan's power, and must die at one of their hands. And you know who I am." At this point, Sylvia put Father

Callen into a hypnotic trance and had him jump off the roof of the hotel as we watched his brief flight of twenty-six floors from the parking lot below. Because we removed both Father Callen's identification papers and cards from his person before his fall, and the hammer and the stake before we left the hotel room, he appeared to be just a suicide that could have jumped from any floor, and who could not be immediately identified.

As I stood in Highgate Cemetery now and looked at these two men who were, doubtless, part of Father Callen's plan to murder Sylvia, I had to control the anger that raged within me.

"What do we do now?" I asked, repeating Sylvia's question. "We kill them. That's what we do."

"They could kill us, too," Sylvia said.

"Not here. Not now. No one's going to kill anyone in front of all these people. But we're going to get these two later. I promise you. Right now, we're going to talk to them."

"Talk to them? Mark, have you gone crazy?" Sylvia's voice was incredulous as she stared at me in shock.

"They don't know who we are. I'm sure of it. They never gave us a second glance or tried to take our picture. They may not even know that vampires can go out during the daytime."

"Father Callen knew. He saw us at Dave and Gail's wedding at Grace Cathedral, and that was in the afternoon."

"Hmm. You're right about that. But have you ever seen Father Callen in the daytime before that afternoon in the church?"

"No, I saw him give a couple of lectures to groups in the evening. He had too many people around, so I couldn't do anything to him."

"As far as you know, had Father Callen ever seen you either during the day or night?"

"Not that I'm aware of—not until that afternoon in church."

"Then that leads me to two conclusions and one question. First, the group may have never known that we can go out during the daytime, and if Father Callen did not contact his group between the time he saw you at the wedding on Saturday afternoon a week and a half ago and the Sunday eight days later, then they probably do not know that we can go out during the daytime. Second, to your knowledge, Father Callen did not know what you looked like until you saw each other at the wedding at Grace Cathedral in San Francisco. My question is this: how did he learn that you can go out during the day, and more importantly, how did he know what you looked like?"

"I don't know," Sylvia admitted.

"How did Father Callen know you were in San Francisco at all? At Grace Cathedral that particular afternoon? Living at the same apartment building as I was in San Francisco? And how did he know that you and I were in a particular hotel room on the twenty-sixth floor of the Atlantis Hotel and Casino in Reno, Nevada?"

"I don't know," Sylvia said, looking flustered. Her eyes showed her distress and anxiety. For a moment, she appeared as if she were about to cry. Her large melancholy eyes revealed her despair as she implored me, "What are we going to do?"

"We're going to get the answers to these questions—all of them."

"They would never tell us willingly," Sylvia pointed out, "and we can't get it out of them by force or hypnotism in front of all these people."

"You're right," I agreed. "I have a different idea. Follow my lead and try not to look nervous."

With Sylvia at my side, I approached the two men and smiled at them. "Hi. I'm Jeff Fowler from the

National Enquirer," I lied. "Perhaps you've heard of our American paper—'for enquiring minds.' I think you have a fascinating story, and I'm sure it's one our readers would be interested in."

"So you do believe us," said the older man.

"Let's put it this way," I answered, "I think I have a more open mind to the subject than our guide over there."

"I'm glad to hear that," said the older man. "Why, the way he talked, you'd think our beloved Father Callen was a murderer. Imagine that."

I didn't have to imagine Father Callen as a murderer; I needed only to remember my horror three days earlier when I thought for several minutes that he had actually succeeded in killing Sylvia. "Regardless of what the guide said about your Father Callen, I think I can safely say that in the end, true justice prevails, and that Father Callen will get the treatment he justly deserves."

"Well said," remarked the younger man, "and kind of you to say so."

Sylvia smiled at the double meaning of my statement, and I could see she had lost her nervousness, which now had given way to amusement in this little cat and mouse game.

The two of them now turned their attention to her, as the older one asked, "Are you with the same American paper?"

"No," explained Sylvia, "I'm writing for the *Daily Mirror*, but the two of us are working together right now."

"But wouldn't you two be competitors?" inquired the younger man.

"No. We're not competitors. We're partners. We work well together," Sylvia said, smiling.

"Our papers may be similar," I clarified, "but they really reach different markets. This way we cut our research time in half."

"What would you like to know for your article?"

70

asked the older man.

"I have so many questions," I said, "and I don't know if this is the right time and place for an interview. Besides, it would be great if we could interview your leader, Father Callen, as well."

"That's not possible." The younger man shook his head. "He's in America right now."

"How interesting," remarked Sylvia. "What is he doing there?"

"He's on the trail of a vampire right now whilst we speak," said the younger man.

"My goodness, how frightening!" exclaimed Sylvia, feigning shock.

"Yes, quite," agreed the older man. "The last time we heard from him was on Sunday. It was morning there and late in the afternoon here. He said he was on his way to destroy the vampire."

"And did Father Callen destroy him?" Sylvia asked.

"The vampire was a woman," the younger man said.

"A woman!" said Sylvia with surprise in her voice. "My, how interesting. I didn't know they had vampires who were women." She pointed at me. "You better be careful of strange women!"

"This is no joke," the older one explained. "We're worried about Father Callen. He should have called us on Sunday after destroying the vampire. We still haven't heard from him and it's Wednesday."

"He couldn't have been killed," the younger man assured him. "In his wallet and his passport, he carried letters explaining his mission. If he had been killed, the police would have found the letters and contacted us."

"That was very clever of him," Sylvia commented, and I knew that in her mind, she was remembering how the two of us had taken those letters along with the rest of Father Callen's papers.

"When do you expect to hear from him?" I asked.

71

"We don't know," said the older man, looking worried, "so if you're in a hurry, you may just want to interview the two of us."

"What about the rest of you?" Sylvia asked. "Surely you don't perform such dangerous duties by yourselves."

"On the contrary," answered the younger man, "it's not necessary or desirable to have large numbers of people involved in this. It's a matter of security, you understand."

"I'd like to know more about this female vampire you say Father Callen is after," said Sylvia, quickly adding, "I'm certain it would be of interest to our readers."

"Yes, for starters, what is her name?" I asked.

"Her name is not important. She has many names," the older man explained. "The vampire I speak of has quite an interesting history behind her. But I'm afraid the story will have to wait for another time." He glanced at his watch. "When would you like to speak again?"

"Well, my partner and I have some work to do this afternoon," I said, "so how about this evening, say around eight o'clock?"

"I'm afraid we won't be free this evening," said the younger man. "Why not tomorrow morning?"

Sylvia shook her head. "We'll be busy tomorrow morning. Why not eight o'clock tomorrow night?"

They both agreed to Sylvia's schedule, and I could see that Sylvia was as pleased as I was that we would be seeing the two of them at the peak of our powers. We would learn everything we possibly could about them, their group, and Father Callen's past before we killed the two of them.

"We prefer doing it during the daytime," said the younger man.

"That's a shame," I said, "because we both have lots of other work during the day. I can promise you this, though—it will be worth an evening. If we get to run the

72

story on your group, you'll get great publicity. Probably an offer from a book publisher and an appearance on television. It could mean a lot of money to you."

When the older man heard the word "money," his eyes lit up with desire, but then he quickly regained his composure and said, "Of course, the money is minor."

"But of course," I agreed. "However, it would certainly help your cause. And I'm sure you must have other charities you give to."

"Our fight against evil uses all our money," he answered. "We don't have anything left for charities."

"One must set priorities, mustn't one?" Sylvia said.

"Yes, quite so," said the older man, not seeing the sarcastic irony in Sylvia's question. He then wrote down a telephone number and above it, his name, Father Clifford, and his partner's name, Brother Phillips. "Call me tomorrow late in the afternoon and we'll decide where to meet at eight o'clock."

"How about your place?" Sylvia asked.

"No, it wouldn't be safe," Father Clifford answered. "We must keep it secret for security."

"Your secret is safe with us," Sylvia reassured him. "We would have no reason to divulge it to anyone else."

Father Clifford shook his head. "No, not under any circumstances. We'll meet you tomorrow in some public place where no one can follow us."

With that, the two of them took their leave of us. I looked around and saw that the tour group had already walked off without us. Father Clifford and Brother Phillips started towards them, and we followed, so that all of us were moving in the same direction—towards the gate where we had originally entered. As the tour group gradually slowed their pace before reaching the exit, Father Clifford and Brother Phillips caught up with the group and we caught up with them, with the result that everyone left together. All of us started walking up

Swain's Lane, the road dividing the East Cemetery from the West Cemetery we had just left.

"I wish I had brought my car. It would have made it easier to follow them," Sylvia remarked.

"We may not need a car to follow them," I said.

This turned out to be the case, for as the group reached the top of the hill, all of us turned to the right and boarded one of the red double-decker buses. Father Clifford and Brother Phillips climbed the stairway to the upper section of the bus and sat in the very front. Sylvia and I took our seats in the very rear of the upper section where we could keep our eyes on them but still keep out of sight. The view from the upper part of the bus was great as the bus rolled down Highgate High Street and Highgate Hill. We passed Waterlow Park, where we had just visited, as we made our way to the bottom of the hill. Further down, the bus stopped, and the two men along with about half of the other passengers started to leave the bus.

"They must be going to Archway Station," Sylvia said, "which means they'll be taking the Underground. Most likely south towards the center of London."

"Then let's follow them," I suggested.

Sylvia nodded, and we kept our distance from them, but since there were many others on the bus who were now entering the front of Archway station, we would not have looked too suspicious to Callen's men—at least not at this point in the journey.

"If we should come into contact with them on the Underground, we should tell them we're on our way to Fleet Street. There are many newspaper offices there."

"How far can we follow them before they realize the truth?" I asked.

Sylvia shrugged her shoulders. "I don't know. I don't want them to know we're following them, but all we have now are some photographs you just took of them and a phone number we haven't been able to check out. I'd hate to let them slip between our fingers."

By boarding the train car next to theirs, we kept them within our sight for the entire ride. At Tottenham Court Road Station they left the subway and we followed from a safe distance. As they rode up the escalator, Sylvia and I noticed that for the first time since we left Highgate, they were engaged in conversation. We strained our hearing to the limit to try to pick out their voices against the backdrop of many others along with the noise of the trains below us and the street traffic above. We both heard small snatches of conversation.

"What do you think of them?" asked Brother Phillips.

The escalator reached the top and they were walking out onto the sidewalk as Sylvia and I heard Father Clifford's reply: "I think that we should —"

But here his answer was cut short by the noise of a large truck driving by. I could see from Sylvia's frustrated expression that she didn't hear the answer either. We now stood only twenty or thirty feet away from them as we stepped onto the sidewalk, too. Traffic passed us travelling up Charing Cross Road and on through Tottenham Court Road. More traffic zoomed by on the corner along Oxford Street. The contrast between Highgate and this corner was quite striking. I judged us to be in one of the busiest sections of downtown London.

Father Clifford raised his hand. A taxi immediately stopped for them. Sylvia and I looked for another taxi, but the closest one was a half a block away with many cars in front of it and waiting for a red light to turn green.

We watched as Callen's men in their taxi slipped away.

Sylvia looked at me and sighed with disappointment. "I'm afraid we've lost them."

Chapter Seven

"Cheer up," I said. "We haven't really lost them. Look on the bright side. I took several pictures of them, and we have their phone number."

"Maybe it's their phone number; maybe it's the number for the weather or the time," said Sylvia. "Who knows?"

"We'll just call them later and see what happens."

Sylvia pointed up Tottenham Court Road and we crossed the street amidst a snarl of traffic. We quickly found a phone booth, quaint in its red wooden frame. Sylvia dialed the number and a woman answered. With the receiver an inch from Sylvia's ear, I could easily hear the entire conversation.

"Is Father Clifford there?" Sylvia asked.

"Not in now," the woman answered.

"We have a package to deliver," Sylvia explained, "but the address on the label is illegible. Where do we deliver it to?"

"I wouldn't know," the woman said, "we're only the answering service."

"What company or organization is your answering service answering for?" Sylvia inquired.

"They never gave me a company or organization name," the woman replied. "They're never at our office. Their calls are just forwarded here if they don't pick up their own phone. Would you like to leave a message?"

"No thank you. I'll call back later." Sylvia hung up the phone. She looked me in the eyes and pleaded with me. "What do we do now?"

I explained we could find it on the Internet through companies that sell such listings. "A long time ago, you'd look it up in directories in the library."

"That reminds me. We're only a few blocks from the original British Library!" Sylvia said, suddenly excited. I have to show it to you. She grabbed my hand and started to pull me along the street.

We walked along Great Russell Street just a few blocks till we came to the entrance of the British Library, which Sylvia explained was part of the British Museum. The gate and fence surrounding the museum was identical to the one that surrounded the mansion at Highgate; it was wrought iron, over twelve feet tall, with sharp gold spikes at the top. It was comforting to realize that if an intruder should be impaled, it would be done with a certain amount of class. Plain black spikes just wouldn't do.

The entrance to the original British Library and Museum was a magnificent work of classical architecture with pillars supporting a building that might have been equally at home in ancient Greece or Rome.

Sylvia wanted to show me the Reading Room.

"I shouldn't have left school in the middle of the semester," I mentioned to Sylvia. "I only had a few more credits left to get my master's degree."

"You can always go back and get it later," Sylvia replied. "I have a number of different degrees from all the time I've spent in school. Of course, I can't ever use them."

"Why not?"

"Imagine how I would look presenting a diploma that is thirty or forty years old when I appear to be in my twenties. No one would believe that it is real. When I get a diploma, I can only use it for about ten or fifteen years. After that, it doesn't match my apparent age. It may be nice to acquire the knowledge, but then, I can always get that by going to the library, which is where I've received most of my education. Much of what I know I learned right here in this very building. I've spent thousands of hours in the Reading Room. It opened back in 1857. My first 'higher' education occurred when I graduated from a women's college in the 1870s. I'll have to show you the diploma sometime. I still have it, even though the paper turned yellow. After all, it is over a hundred years old."

"How will I ever catch up?" I asked.

"Simple. Read everything you possibly can for the next hundred and twenty-five years or so, and make sure that I don't read anything else during that time."

For the next few seconds, I thought about what Sylvia had said, and realized the incredible futility of it.

"Don't worry about it, Mark. Of course you can't catch up. I've lived and read too long. But it doesn't matter. No one's keeping score on the number of books we've read, and you've got all the time you could possibly want."

"You don't mind the gap in our knowledge? That I know less than you?"

"What else could we do? If I had some kind of prerequisite for marriage that my husband had to have more knowledge than I, then I would always be alone. If you use your gift of eternal life to read and study, then one day you will be one of the most intelligent people in the world."

"Just like you?"

"Yes, just like me." Sylvia smiled shyly. "Are you trying to make my head swell up? If you build me up to be any bigger, I'll never get through the door."

We got to peek inside and the Reading Room took my breath away. The large round blue room boasted three levels of bookshelves that curved all around. The dome, which Sylvia told me was 106 feet high by 140 feet in diameter, had tall arched windows 27 feet high which surrounded the room. The result was an interior lit by natural sunlight, but at the same time, a crowning achievement to the labor of man.

"Hope you don't feel like we wasted time on that one."

"Not at all. I'm glad we came. I love this place."

Sylvia smiled. "Good. We'll come back again. Charles Dickens used to come here towards the end of his life. I saw him when I first started coming here. George Bernard Shaw came here for years and years. I saw him here many times."

We quietly left the Reading Room, but I took another look around before we left. Here, with a single glance, I saw more books at one time than I possibly could anywhere else. As I looked at these books and then at Sylvia, I could not help but think how she was like a microcosm of this great place of learning; behind her beautiful face was stored the memory of so many of these books. It was a wonder how the books from such a vast collection could fit inside her head.

"There's something else I want to show you," Sylvia said. "You remember while riding in Joseph and Susan's car, how we spoke of *Alice's Adventures in Wonderland*?"

"How could I forget? Ever since I met you, life has been one unusual adventure after another. I feel like I'm living in the sequel to *Alice's Adventures in Wonderland* right now."

Sylvia laughed. "You couldn't be. The sequel was *Through the Looking Glass*."

"Yes. I think I must have stepped through the looking glass when I met you."

Sylvia nodded in agreement. "I helped pull you through. As soon as both of us existed—that is, once you were born—the mirror was always in existence with us; we just couldn't find it. Once we met, we saw each other in that mirror and you crossed over the line to meet me. As I said before, I existed in both the third dimension, which you call reality, and the fifth dimension, which could be considered thought, mental activity, dreams, and spiritual activity. You existed only in the third dimension. I'm helping to pull you through to the fifth dimension as well." Sylvia sighed. "Anyway, the original manuscript of *Alice's Adventures in Wonderland* was here, but now it's at the new British Library. Would you like to see it?

The next thing I knew, we were back outside and on our way to the new British Library on Euston Road, near Regent's park. We found the Treasures of the British Library exhibition, which also included the Magna Carta, Gutenberg's Bible, Shakespeare's First Folio, and handwritten lyrics by The Beatles. And there was the *Alice* manuscript.

She pointed at a glass case. Inside, a small sign read:
Lewis Carroll (Charles Lutwidge Dodgson)
(1832-1898)
Alice's Adventures under Ground
Next to this was the original manuscript, opened, so that the viewer could see a picture of Alice leaning her elbow on a table with her head tilted to the side. This was on the left page along with the text. On the right page, was a picture that took up the entire page. In it, Alice was lying down, squeezed into the frame so tightly because she had just begun to grow to unusually large proportions.

"This is the book that Reverend Dodgson wrote about and for young Alice Liddell," Sylvia said, then pointed at the book. "It's all written by hand—and what beautiful writing he had. He even did the drawings. Most people haven't seen these drawings. They're only familiar with the ones Sir John Tenniel drew for *Alice's Adventures in Wonderland*. Tenniel's drawings are very nice, but this is the way Lewis Carroll wanted his fictional Alice to look— very much like the real Alice who inspired it." Sylvia stared at the book for some time, and her eyes grew misty as she reflected. "I feel so sad when I look at this, so nostalgic. He wrote this in 1864, just two years before I woke from my century-long sleep. About the time I came to life again in 1866, *Alice's Adventures in Wonderland* was published. It became quite popular. I think about how he loved young Alice Liddell, but couldn't get her love in return. He transferred that love into this book, with his own hands, and now here we are looking at it over a century later. Lewis Carroll and Alice Liddell are gone, but the book remains."

"If you can appreciate a work of art that is a representation of someone real, then why don't you feel the same way about the doll that was made of you?"

"That's different. Pierre's craftsmanship went into that doll, true, but I'm not just referring to Lewis Carroll's aesthetics. This book has love inside it. It was inspired by love — his love for Alice."

"If I were to write such a book about you, how would you feel about it?"

Sylvia's expression brightened. "Oh, I would like that very much!"

"You would?" I asked, somewhat confused. "But when Yvette gave you the doll, you said that it stole your image from you. You said you didn't want to be sculpted, drawn, photographed, or even written about. You said you didn't want to be recreated. Remember?"

"Yes, but that was different. As I said, Pierre did not create the doll out of love, no matter how skillfully he put his talents to work."

"But why was the doll frightening to you?"

"When art imitates life, it takes on a life of its own, so whoever creates art, also creates life."

"But that doll doesn't have a life of its own."

"All art has a life of its own," Sylvia said. "All art that is a representation must steal its essence from its original subject. Did you ever read the short story, 'The Oval Portrait,' by Edgar Allan Poe?"

I nodded. I remembered it well. In "The Oval Portrait," the narrator of the tale spends an evening in a gothic mansion, recuperating from a sickness or injury.

His room is in the most remote part of the mansion, shut off from the outside. The walls are covered with paintings, and by moving his candelabrum slightly, an indentation in the wall is revealed that had been previously hidden in darkness. In it is the portrait of a beautiful woman, so lifelike that the narrator almost mistakes it for a real woman. After gazing at it for a long time, he happens upon a book that gives the history of the paintings. He discovers that the subject of the painting was the wife of the artist. Shut away in a remote room (perhaps like the narrator's) the artist worked away for many days on the portrait until he was able to recreate her likeness perfectly. At the very last brushstroke, he cries out, "This is life itself!" and turns to his wife to see that she has died, her life essence transferred to the portrait.

"Yes, I remember 'The Oval Portrait', by Poe," I said. "But the artist was more obsessed with the artistic representation itself than with its subject."

Sylvia nodded in agreement. "Artists often are. They paint a flower, only to find that when the art is completed, the flower has already withered away."

"But at least the painting is permanent," I said.

"Yes, but during the painting of it, the artist could have smelled that flower while it was still alive."

"You're different, Sylvia. You will never wither or die. I could recreate you through photography or writing, and your beauty would be as permanent as the art."

"Photograph me or write about me if you wish, but never forget that I am not permanent. I can die if I am killed, and even though I may be less vulnerable as a vampire, I can still be killed. You met two people today who would gladly murder me if they had the chance. Please keep that in mind. Enjoy me as much as you can today, for I may be dead tomorrow."

I put my arm around Sylvia and held her tightly to

me. "Don't say that. I couldn't live without you."

"You may not have to," Sylvia said. "You and I are always together. If they were to kill me, they would probably kill you at the same time."

My fear of losing Sylvia caused a rising panic. With all the unanswered questions I had about Father Callen's group, and how they had learned so much about Sylvia when we knew so little about them, they were a terrible threat.

"No one is ever going to kill you," I promised Sylvia, as I felt my anger turn to fear. "We're going to find the members of Father Callen's group and kill them first. No one will ever take you away from me."

Sylvia smiled weakly at me and placed her arm around my shoulder. My arm circled her slender waist, and the two of us left the British Library holding each other a bit more tightly than we had when we walked in.

Chapter Eight

As Sylvia and I descended into the Underground, it had already grown darker. The sun of the morning and afternoon had given way to the grayness of twilight. London's subways were far under the ground; the escalators were longer and steeper than any I had ever seen. A child experiencing these escalators for the very first time might logically conclude the trip to be a one-way journey to the center of the earth; a religious child could see the escalators as a convenient conveyance to Hell.

I mentioned this to Sylvia. She laughed. "You don't need to take an escalator. I have your soul already and I'll never give it back." She placed her hands over her heart as if holding my soul inside, then smiled as she looked at me out of the corners of her eyes.

We took our seats on the train and began to look through the pictures on my camera of Highgate Cemetery along with those of Father Clifford and Brother Phillips. The photos came out razor-sharp. This would enable us to make suitable blowups of the men individually.

Right after we took our seats, the train filled up quickly as it was close to rush hour. Apparently, Tottenham Court Road Station was not only a transfer station, but was also close to many businesses. As I looked around, I noticed how different this subway was from the one that ran inside San Francisco. While this one was far older with darker walls, no graffiti had been sprayed there. Instead of a dozen teenagers with stereo headphones turned up loud enough for everyone to hear, there was almost silence, punctuated by the rustling of paper as businessmen read *The Times*. Here in the subway as in the library, the rule of the day was order.

I glanced at the names of each station as the train stopped. As we passed Kentish Town and Tufnell Park, I expected us to exit at Archway, where we had originally got on after leaving the cemetery. Instead, we went on one more stop to Highgate Station, which, Sylvia explained, was closer to the mansion.

We emerged from the Underground to total darkness. Even though it was only six o'clock, the winter meant that the sun set early. This suited Sylvia just fine. Since our powers peaked during the darkness, the winter gave more hours of useful time.

"Whenever I travel during the day, I try to use the Underground rather than the bus or my car," she explained. "That way, I conserve my energy. After all, you know what happens if the daylight takes away our energy."

"I remember," I answered, and I only had to remember back four days, to Saturday night. Sylvia and I had won about $100,000 playing twenty-one in the casinos in Reno. As we left the casino, a limousine pulled up with three men inside. They requested the pleasure of our company at gunpoint. We went along for the ride to a deserted spot where they had planned to kill us and steal the money. Then we drank their blood and left them out there. It had now been four days for me. Sylvia had renewed herself when she killed the hijacker on the plane on Monday night. Even so, we had been through an emotional ordeal on the plane, had spent quite a bit of time out in the sun, and had lost sleep due to the change in time between San Francisco and London. All of these factors conspired together to create both the need and desire for more blood.

But the thirst had not come upon us yet. How soon it would come and how strong it would be was still unknown.

As we reached the mansion, the gates were open, and a moving van was in the driveway. Men were carrying boxes of our things, which had been sent from San

Francisco. The front doors stood open, and Joseph and Susan, along with Yvette and Ronald, watched the procession of boxes, which were all brought to the hallway upstairs, right in front of Sylvia's bedroom.

We watched them for a few minutes and didn't speak until they left.

"Guess who Mark and I saw today?" Sylvia queried.

"Prince William and Kate?" Yvette looked excited.

"Not quite," revealed Sylvia. "We met two of Father Callen's men."

"Met?" asked Joseph. "You mean 'met' as in 'Hello, it's a pleasure making your acquaintance'? That kind of met?"

"Something like that." Sylvia then gave a detailed account of our entire morning and afternoon, starting with our tour of the Highgate Society, Waterlow Park, Highgate Cemetery, our conversation with Callen's men, how we tried to follow them, and finally, our trip to the British Library.

"Mark and I have an appointment to interview them tomorrow night," Sylvia said.

"That's wonderful," Susan remarked. "Now you can find out all about them—how many of them are around, who the leader is now that Father Callen is dead, and many other things."

"I have some questions of my own I want to ask them," I said. "For example: How did Father Callen know what Sylvia looked like? How did he know she was in San Francisco? Living in my apartment building? How did he know which hotel room we stayed in?"

"Don't be a fool!" Ronald yelled. "They're not going to tell you that!"

"Not willingly," I conceded. "We'll start with simple questions first, ones that don't seem threatening. When we get to the important questions, we'll rely on hypnotism or force."

"You'll bring about our destruction with your recklessness," Ronald said, as he pointed an accusing finger at me.

"On the contrary, I'll help ensure our survival. I already lived through the experience of seeing Father Callen drive a stake into Sylvia. That will never happen again."

"We've done just fine without you all these years," Ronald said.

"No you haven't," I responded. "Two of your friends were killed and Sylvia was almost killed and Callen's group is still wandering around free. You're not doing fine at all."

"When are you supposed to see them?" asked Joseph.

"Sometime tomorrow night," said Sylvia. "Probably at eight o'clock. But we have to call them first to confirm it."

"Susan and I were going to drive downtown tomorrow anyway," Joseph said. "We can drop you off, pick you up later, even follow behind for safety if you like."

"Oh, we'll be safe," Sylvia assured him. "We made certain to arrange to see them after dark so that we can't be killed. No daytime appointments for us."

"We were going to stay downtown part of the day and part of the evening," Susan explained, "but of course you and Mark can come with us. And you can see Father Callen's men whenever you want."

Ronald scowled at Susan.

"Good," Sylvia said. "Then everything is settled."

Jack and Helen entered the living room, wearing white coats.

"What's settled?" Jack asked.

Sylvia and I explained, once again, everything that had transpired and how we were to meet with Father

Clifford and Brother Phillips tomorrow evening.

"I think it's too risky," Ronald said to Jack and Helen.

"I agree," said Jack. "What if it's a trap?"

"That's the chance we have to take," Sylvia said.

"You're not taking all the chances," declared Helen. "You are forcing all of us to take the risk with you. Even if they killed you and Mark tomorrow night, do you think that would be the end of it? No. They would then be able to find the rest of us much easier."

"This is a democracy here, isn't it? Let's vote on it," suggested Sylvia.

Joseph and Susan voiced their approval of our plan, while Jack and Helen disagreed.

"I think this is the most stupid and dangerous idea Sylvia has come up with yet," Ronald announced, "and I know I speak for Yvette, too, when I say that." He stared at her waiting for her agreement.

Yvette turned her eyes away from Ronald's intense stare. Her voice was softer and quieter than I had heard before. "I'm afraid I have to agree with Mark and Sylvia this time."

Ronald glared at Yvette. I got the impression that any disagreement from her was not only rare, but also very irritating to Ronald.

"I'm sorry," Yvette said, as she turned to face Ronald, "but something has to be done about Callen's men. Look at what happened to Sylvia because of Father Callen. If it hadn't been for Mark, she'd be dead now. We've already lost two of our number. How many of us have to die before we do something?"

Ronald had no answer to this, so Sylvia and I excused ourselves from the group so that we could unpack our things, which had just arrived from San Francisco by the moving van. Because we had everything shipped by air rather than by sea, we did not have to wait long. We had arrived in London early Tuesday afternoon, and here it was early evening on Wednesday and we had everything already. Much of the boxes contained books, both Sylvia's and mine. One of the larger items was Sylvia's harpsichord, the English bentside spinet she had in San Francisco, much smaller than the French harpsichord in her living room. The top part was not attached to the legs, as the legs were on a separate stand. As I went to lift the harpsichord and carry it, I was struck by its incredibly light weight.

"Is this as light as I think it is or am I just that much stronger from becoming a vampire?" I asked Sylvia.

"Both," Sylvia answered. "It's much lighter than a piano, but you're also much stronger."

"I guess that would be a real advantage if I were to go back to lifting weights in a gym."

"That's not necessary. You don't need to exercise in a gym to keep your strength up. That's one of the advantages of being a vampire."

"I count my blessings every day."

"Don't be sarcastic," Sylvia said as she playfully punched me in the shoulder. "Do you want us to wind up like Yvette and Ronald?"

"We'll never be like them," I assured her. "Even though I wasn't around last century when they met, I'm certain they weren't like us when they first married."

"You're right about that," Sylvia laughed.

I set the harpsichord down in Sylvia's bedroom, near the corner, so she could look out of the diamond-shaped windows as she played.

"I was surprised to see Yvette vote against Ronald," I said.

"Me, too," admitted Sylvia. "She doesn't do that very often. In spite of her joking mood, she's really afraid of him. He's really not much fun. Neither are Helen and Jack."

"I felt the same way about them right away. But then why do you stay? I know you like Susan and Joseph, but considering the problems you have with the others, is it worth the trouble?"

Sylvia stopped replacing the books on her shelves and turned to me. "Sometimes I ask myself that very question. And now that you're here, that changes things."

"How do you mean?"

"Now I'm more likely to leave here if we should have too many problems with them. In the past, I would have put up with it because I didn't want to be alone. But of course, there were other reasons for staying here besides liking Susan and Joseph and not wanting to be alone. It's much safer for me to live here. There is strength in numbers. And I like the mansion here. I've lived here for over a century. I like my room, the view of the garden and the yard outside my window, the serene and peaceful atmosphere of Highgate. I enjoy walking in Waterlow Park, looking at the ducks and swans, watching the children and the dogs play. I enjoy Tweedledee and Tweedledum—"

"Who?" I interrupted.

"My pet wolves."

"Where are they now?"

Sylvia pointed outside the window. The two of them sat on the lawn looking like regal guards at a palace.

"Is it legal to have wolves as pets here?"

Sylvia laughed. "That should be our most serious legal worry. Finding victims when we need blood is much more of a problem when it comes to the law. Ronald creates legal problems, too. He has some rather shady business dealings going on along with the more legitimate ones. That's why he was so worried about the man on the plane with us—the one who's probably a CIA agent."

"Actually, it would be a good idea for us to try to trace the license plate of the Jaguar he drove. We may be able to find out more about him."

Sylvia nodded in agreement. "We've got to trace his license, then the phone number of Callen's men, then find the three of them and discover what they're up to. When we left San Francisco to come here, this isn't what I had in mind. I thought we'd be able to relax."

"That's what I'm going to do right now," I said, as I slipped off my shoes and lay down on the bed.

"Sounds like a good idea." Sylvia joined me on the bed, then lay on top of me. "Alone at last," she said, as we began to kiss.

A knock on the bedroom door interrupted us. Sylvia groaned, then asked who it was.

"Can I come in?" Helen asked.

"No," Sylvia answered.

"We have something important to ask the two of you," Jack said through the door.

"I hope this won't take long," Sylvia told me as she rose from the bed.

She opened the door, but Jack and Helen stood in the hallway as if they were trained to stay out of Sylvia's bedroom because it was a forbidden zone for them.

"We were wondering if Mark would be interested in seeing our laboratory," Jack asked.

"Right now?" Sylvia asked in disgust.

"There's something else," admitted Helen. "We'd like to find out how much Mark is like you—and how different he may be from the rest of us."

Sylvia regarded Helen warily.

"You both have the same large pupils with no irises," Jack said.

"All the better to see you with," Sylvia answered.

"We think there must be some reason for that," he continued, "just as your blood is different from ours."

"Are you saying you want to give us blood tests for your damn experiments?" Sylvia asked, with some annoyance.

"Well, yes," replied Helen. "Out of scientific curiosity, of course."

"Is this test necessary for consummating our relationship?" I asked.

"If it is, they're a little bit too late," said Sylvia. "They missed us last night—and every night for that matter. Except, of course, the night on the plane. I remember that we didn't make love on the plane on Monday night."

"If we could get you two to just stop thinking about sex for a few minutes, we could contribute something of value to science," Helen said.

Sylvia rolled her eyes up and sighed. "Let's get this over with quickly then. The test, I mean, not the sex."

We descended the stairway down to the main floor, then travelled down a hallway to a door. It looked like the rest of the mansion, which had been built about a hundred and fifty years earlier. But when Jack opened this door, another one lay directly behind it. Unlike the wooden door that faced the hallway, the door behind the door was metal. He opened it with a key, and it slid sideways into a space between the two walls, then shut again after we had stepped past it. We now stood on the landing of a stairway. Descending these stairs, we came to another doorway, but this one had no knob or keyhole. To the left of it was a small digital keyboard. Helen punched in the combination with her fingers and this door opened for us and we entered the laboratory. The metal door closed behind us.

I judged the room to measure perhaps fifty feet wide by seventy feet long. There were filing cabinets, chemicals in beakers, banks of computers, medical equipment and technical gadgets I had never seen and had no name for. There were also black tables in the center of the large room. Upon each of these tables lay cadavers, in various stages of dissection.

"This is where we do our medical research," explained Jack. "We hope to make important contributions in the advancement of medical science."

I couldn't help staring at the cadavers on the tables.

"We do this so that we might benefit humanity," added Helen. "What do you think of our laboratory?"

"Well," I began, as I tried looking around but found my eyes always being pulled back to the tables in the center with the partly dissected cadavers, "I suppose your lab is properly equipped—if one goes in for this sort of thing."

"It makes me want to throw up," confessed Sylvia. "After I'm finished drinking someone's blood, I certainly don't want their body lying about if they're dead. And if I've only taken a small amount of blood and left them alive, I always hypnotize them so that they can't remember what has happened to them. That way they can just go about their business as usual. As a matter of fact, that's what I usually do. I usually don't kill my victims."

This revelation of Sylvia surprised me. Though I had only known her for two and a half weeks, and had only been a vampire for one week, what she now said went contrary to what she did when I first met her. In the past three weeks, she had gone through many victims. Two occurred days before we met. She killed two muggers in an alley who were about to shoot me. The following night, she killed my next-door neighbor, Harry, whom I had always hated, and she moved into his apartment two days later. A week after that, a British housing developer named Graystone, who had been staying in San Francisco, was murdered. I later found out that Sylvia did it. Then, a few days later, after Sylvia turned me into a vampire (thus taking my human life away), she and I shared the blood of a knife-wielding robber in another alleyway, a young woman sleeping in her apartment, and finally, three apparent mobsters in a limousine who drove us out to a deserted road to kill us and steal the $100,000 we had won playing twenty-one in casinos and got more trouble than they had bargained for. Of all these victims in only three weeks time, only one of these killings had been a "mistake," that of the young woman in her apartment. Sylvia and I had meant to take only enough blood to survive, but since she had been my very first victim, I didn't realize that I had gone too far. I had felt pangs of guilt afterwards, which Sylvia tried to soothe by explaining that we needed blood to survive. That part was true, yet we did not have to kill to survive, not if we were able to get enough blood on a regular basis. To be fair to Sylvia, though, most of the other victims, such as the muggers in the alleys and mobsters in Nevada, deserved to die. While my neighbor, Harry, may not have deserved to die, I couldn't honestly say I was disturbed by his death. The only one I found hard to judge was Clark Graystone, the millionaire housing developer. I didn't know why Sylvia picked him specifically.

"You usually don't kill your victims?" asked Helen. "That's news to me. I know Jack and I rarely do."

"Are these victims still alive?" Sylvia pointed at the cadavers.

"Of course not," replied Helen, "but they served a useful purpose. Not only did their blood sustain Joseph and me, but now their bodies are being used for medical research that will someday benefit all of humanity."

"My, aren't you and Jack the altruistic ones!" remarked Sylvia. "But you could say the same for me. The blood of my victims sustains me and allows me to continue creating wonderful art and music—art and music that will someday benefit all of humanity."

Helen sneered at Sylvia's parody of her own speech, but I knew that Sylvia had spoken the truth. Her ability at painting was just as remarkable as her ability to play the harpsichord. While I wasn't sure whether either of these talents would benefit all of humanity, it would doubtless benefit the intellectually elite who could appreciate it fully. The majority of humanity who could not understand or appreciate Sylvia's genius was of no concern to her. She had explained that to me before.

"Now you and Mark have an opportunity to benefit humanity in a medical way, too," said Jack. He asked permission to draw small samples of blood from the two of us, then smeared a drop of each on glass slides and looked at them under a microscope. "Take a look at this!" he declared to Helen.

"This is incredible!" she exclaimed.

"Can you imagine having your fun this way?" Sylvia asked me with a sigh. "I'd rather be upstairs playing my harpsichord. Or better yet, if you hadn't interrupted us, by now Mark and I would be —"

"Never mind what you would be doing," interrupted Helen. "This is much more important. Take a look at this."

Both Sylvia and I looked at the slides. Our blood seemed similar to each other. Nothing particularly remarkable struck me about it, and I made that known.

"Then take a look at this," said Jack, as he placed another slide under another microscope.

I looked at it and had to admit that they looked quite different, though my lack of medical knowledge could not explain what the difference was.

"That was the blood of a normal human," he clarified to us.

"So our blood is different than a normal human. I'm not that surprised," I admitted.

"Then look at these," Jack said, as he placed six more slides under microscopes.

All six looked alike, but they matched neither the human blood nor that of Sylvia and me. If there were a way of differentiating them, it could be said that the six looked as if they were in a stage that was partway between human and that which Sylvia and I were.

"Those six samples are from the rest of us here," Jack explained. "You can see the difference between the blood of a human and the rest of us here—excluding you and Sylvia. Just as there is a qualitative difference between the blood of a human and that of a vampire, there is the same difference between the blood of the six of us and the blood from the two of you."

"Are you saying Sylvia and I are not vampires?"

"On the contrary," Jack replied. "You and Sylvia are even more so than the rest of us."

"How can that be?" I asked.

"We told you that Sylvia was different from us when we saw your eyes. Sylvia's eyes are different from ours."

How could I forget such a thing? I looked into Sylvia's beautiful eyes every chance I got, and I certainly got a lot of chances. But of course, he was referring to the blackness of the color of her eyes, not her beauty.

"She made the color of your eyes like hers," Helen pointed out. "It happened from transforming you into a vampire. None of us have eyes like that. Our eyes are normal. You and Sylvia are not only different from humans, you are different from us."

"There's no disagreement from me on that point," Sylvia said.

"Sylvia needs more blood than the rest of us," Helen explained. "So will you. Her blood is more vampire-like than the rest of us. So is yours. She has all of her vampire powers in a more powerful way—her hearing, her night vision, her strength, and above all, her power to hypnotize with a glance. You will now have these same highly developed vampire abilities just like her."

"The part about the increased power sounds fine to me," I admitted.

"Me, too," agreed Sylvia.

96

"But of course, we already knew all that," said Jack. "None of it comes as a surprise at all to us."

"Then why were you so excited when you looked at the sample of our blood?" I asked.

Jack took out another slide and put it under the microscope, explaining that it had been taken from Sylvia just a month earlier. We looked at it and Sylvia gasped. She looked at her early sample, then at the new one.

"It's different! What can this mean?" she asked.

"It means that after you and Mark drank each other's blood, you precipitated a new change," Jack said. "Your blood is different now. You are different now, and you're both changing. Evolving."

"Evolving into what?" Sylvia asked.

"Even more of a vampire," explained Jack. "You will become even more powerful, perhaps take on a new ability that the rest of us don't have."

"What kind of ability?" Sylvia asked.

"We don't know yet," admitted Jack. "Whatever it is, I'm sure you'll like it—and you'll know about it first."

Sylvia looked at me and smiled until her voluptuous lips drew back to reveal the slight points to her canine teeth.

Chapter Nine

There could be no doubt about it. Things were getting better all the time. Sylvia and I had found two of Father Callen's men and we would discover everything we needed to know about them the very next night. We would all be much safer and more secure with them out of the way. To make our day even happier, we had just learned that the power that Sylvia and I shared would now grow to even greater proportions. Our vampire powers would evolve into something even better. We would have new abilities that we were not yet even aware of. Everything was going right.

Though Jack and Helen wanted to perform more tests, Sylvia and I felt we had enough of their laboratory for one day. The four of us walked upstairs to tell the news to the others.

"How interesting," remarked Susan as we explained the results of the test.

"What kind of powers are these?" Ronald asked.

"We don't know yet," Jack said.

"There may actually be several different powers," Helen said. "And they may not all occur at the same time."

"Whatever it is," said Joseph, "this can only help to make all of us more secure. Any type of psychic or magical ability will mean that we can eliminate Callen's men."

"That's right," agreed Susan, as she sat next to Joseph on one of the sofas in the living room.

Ronald stood up and began to pace back and forth in the middle of the room on a large Persian carpet that covered the hardwood floor. "Then why not delay your meeting with Callen's men until after you find out what these powers are? Wouldn't that be safer?"

I shook my head. "We'll be seeing them tomorrow

night at eight o'clock." I looked at the beautiful gold watch Sylvia had given me two weeks earlier. "That's just twenty-four hours from now."

"Nice watch," Yvette remarked. "Is it a gift from Sylvia?"

Sylvia smiled and nodded. "It's a Patek Philippe Calatrava with a white gold case."

"How much did it cost?" Yvette inquired.

Susan gave a disapproving glance to Yvette.

"Eighteen thousand, nine hundred dollars," Sylvia explained. "I saw the same model on one of my victims in San Francisco almost two weeks ago."

"He must have been very rich," Yvette said.

"He certainly was," agreed Sylvia. "I'm sure you've heard of him — Clark Graystone."

"You killed Clark Graystone?" exclaimed Ronald amid a stunned silence in the room.

"Yes, I did," Sylvia answered. "The Friday before last, if you want to be precise about it."

"Ha ha!" Ronald yelled with joy. "Break out the champagne! It's time for a celebration!"

"I don't drink champagne," Sylvia said.

"It's only an expression." Ronald turned to Sylvia. "Well, you've certainly made my day. I knew that deep down, you had to be good for something."

"I resent that," Sylvia said.

"Please don't," Ronald said. "Take the remark in the good spirit in which it's given. What I meant is that all your harpsichord playing and your art may be nice, but it does nothing for the rest of us —"

Sylvia glared at Ronald.

"Nothing in a real material way," Ronald continued. "Even though your artistic talent is certainly something to be proud of, it doesn't add any money to our collective efforts. But this, on the other hand, this will make all of us richer. Quite a bit richer, I might add."

"What are you talking about?" Jack asked with annoyance.

"I've wanted Graystone out of the way for some time," Ronald said, gloating.

"Then what a lucky coincidence this was," Yvette said. "Just imagine, of all the people Sylvia should pick as a victim, she happened to pick someone you hated. Thousands of miles away, no less. It must have been Sylvia's psychic ability guiding her."

"Psychic ability, Hell," said Jack. "Ronald put her up to this. Are we going to make contract killers of each other now?"

"Sylvia and Ronald cooperating with each other on a murder?" asked Helen. "What strange bedfellows you two make."

"Bedfellows!" yelled Yvette. "You mean the two of them are going to bed with each other?"

Sylvia sighed, shook her head, and rolled her eyes up in exasperation at Yvette's charge.

"Because if you are going to bed with each other," Yvette countered, "then I think it's only fair that I get to go to bed with Mark."

Everyone in the room looked at Yvette, then at me for my response.

I stifled a laugh. "'Strange bedfellows' is only a saying," I explained.

"Yes, they're saying that my husband and your fiancée are strange bedfellows," Yvette responded.

"It's only an aphorism," I replied. "It means that Sylvia and Ronald make unusual partners—in this case, business partners."

"Oh," Yvette said, her voice so low and soft with embarrassment that it would have been inaudible, except for the sensitive hearing of everyone there and the silence that filled the room.

"As to you offering to sleep with Mark so that

Ronald and I could sleep together," Sylvia remarked, "that's an arrangement which would only benefit you and Ronald, certainly not Mark or me." Using her finger pointed at Yvette for emphasis, Sylvia continued, "And if you did ever go to bed with Mark, I'd kill you—and that's not just a saying or an expression."

"Enough of this nonsense!" yelled Ronald. "No one's going to kill anyone here, and no one is going to bed with anyone."

"That's for sure," Yvette replied with contempt as she stared at Ronald. "It's certainly been awhile, hasn't it?"

Ronald glared at Yvette. The two of them stared each other down for several seconds until they were interrupted.

"So why did you have Sylvia kill Clark Graystone?" Joseph asked.

Ronald then explained how Graystone, a British housing developer, had set up competitive bids for a multi-million dollar construction project. One of Ronald's many businesses, a construction company, was about to lose a project that would have been extremely profitable. Since Ronald managed the combined assets of all the vampires in the mansion, everyone stood to gain if he could secure the project; if Graystone had won, they would all lose.

"We're not talking pennies here," Ronald said. "The profit is in the millions." He looked at me. "Probably between eight and ten million of your American dollars in the next year or two."

"That doesn't make the murder morally right," Helen pointed out.

"It certainly makes it more right than if there would be no financial gain," Sylvia countered. "Right and wrong are not black and white. They're mostly shades of gray. If we stand to gain five million pounds by his death, then surely it's more morally right than if I killed him for nothing. If a hunter kills an animal and eats it, isn't he more morally correct than a person who hunts an animal just for the fun of shooting it?"

"Bravo," declared Ronald. "I couldn't have said it better myself."

"That's why I said it," Sylvia remarked.

"It's still wrong," Jack said.

"I needed the blood anyway to survive," Sylvia said. "It's not wrong to survive. All creatures have the right to survive — vampires, humans, and animals."

"That's why Helen and I are working on a cure for vampirism," Jack said. "If our cure works, it will make blood unnecessary for our survival."

"If your cure should work, would we remain as we are except with no need for blood?" I asked. "Or would we become human again?"

"I'm not sure," Jack admitted. "We might become human."

"How stupid!" said Ronald. "You think we would want to weaken ourselves? We have more power as vampires."

"What?" cried Sylvia. "Lose my special abilities and talents? Watch Mark and myself grow old?"

"Grow old?" Yvette gasped in horror as she put her hands to her face as if she were trying to imagine what wrinkles might feel like. "Why, I'd never take such a step. You two should be locked up in a nuthouse for even suggesting such a thing!"

Ronald chuckled. "If the two of you are so disturbed by the blood money, perhaps your consciences would be clear if you were to forfeit your share of the money. That way you would also forfeit your share of our collective guilt. Is your conscience worth over a million pounds?"

Jack and Helen sat in silence.

"Well, is it?" Ronald asked, but he received no answer. "I didn't think so. But be happy. Just think what each of you will do with one-seventh of the money."

"One-seventh?" Sylvia asked. She placed her arm around my shoulder. "There are eight of us here."

"Eight!" protested Ronald. "Mark wasn't even with you then."

"Yes he was," Sylvia replied. "I met him a week earlier. Now there are eight of us here, not seven. Four couples. So the money should be divided equally among the four couples. And remember it was the murder committed by me that brought the money. You needed it done that night during your business meeting here in London so that you would have an alibi. It was the perfect murder for you. You could imply responsibility for it to keep your adversaries in line, but deny blame since you had the perfect alibi. So the money gets split eight ways, not seven."

Ronald rolled his eyes up, sighed, and threw his hands up. "You win."

"No," Sylvia retorted. "We all win."

Ronald turned to me. "How does it feel, Mark, to be a millionaire? You already have a nice place to stay, so you can spend quite a bit on investments or toys. You could buy any car in the world and still have a nice amount of change left over."

Visions of Lamborghinis danced through my head.

"A penny for your thoughts," Sylvia said to me.

"You can afford more than a penny," Yvette pointed out. "Besides, you can probably read Mark's mind anyway."

"I was thinking about what Ronald said and wondering what kind of car I would buy," I answered.

"Any kind you want, of course," Sylvia replied. "But there's no hurry in the next day or two. We all have cars here. You've already been in Joseph and Susan's Bentley. Ronald and Yvette have a Rolls Royce. Helen and Jack, being the stuffy, sensible types that they are, have a

Mercedes. And being the type I am, I have an Aston Martin DBS V12. If you like, we can drive downtown in it tomorrow night."

"I thought you were going to ride downtown with us tomorrow night," Susan said.

"Yes. You're right," agreed Sylvia. "The four of us will ride in the Bentley tomorrow night." Sylvia turned to me. "Do you mind if we wait a couple of days before we take my car?"

"Not at all. Maybe we can go for a long ride over the weekend."

"Every day is a weekend," Sylvia declared. "I don't work. I just create my art in paintings or I play my harpsichord. All days are the same to me."

For some reason, this struck me as strange. How could one know how and when to have a good time if there was not time allotted to be bored and miserable, such as one experiences at work? If all days were totally good or totally bad, would it eventually become impossible to distinguish one from the other? More importantly, were people the same way?

Jack and Helen stood up to make an announcement. Jack turned to us. "We'd like the two of you to help us with our experiment by testing out our new formula. This is our ongoing research to not only find a cure for vampirism, but also to be able to give some of the vampire's youth and resistance to disease. We may be able to cure cancer, heart disease, and even the aging process. We need to test the formula on vampires before humans. Would you let us test it on you?"

I turned to Sylvia. "What do you think? Is this safe?"

Sylvia turned to Helen. "What will it do to us?"

"We think it will result in temporary unconsciousness or paralysis. For a few minutes, or longer, you may be temporarily human, but then it would wear off quickly. We want to see how long it lasts."

"Why don't you test it on yourselves?" I asked.

Jack looked at me. "We already have. On us, it had the results Helen described. Since you and Sylvia have even stronger vampire powers, we want to see if it works the same. We were back to normal in about ten to fifteen minutes."

Sylvia sighed. "All right. We'll try it if this won't take more than fifteen minutes and you've both tried it. What do we do?"

Jack produced a plastic spray bottle. "I just spray you in the face as you breathe. The effect is immediate, then wears off within fifteen minutes."

Sylvia and I agreed. Jack and Helen approached the couch where we sat together and sprayed us with the bottle. I immediately lost consciousness, but that may have only lasted seconds. Then I felt paralyzed and couldn't move or speak. Sylvia didn't move, either. But after just a few minutes, she regained movement and speech.

"That was strange, wasn't it Mark?" she asked me.

I couldn't answer or move, though I could see and hear her.

"I was unconscious until just a few seconds ago. How long was I out?" she asked everyone.

"About ten minutes," Helen said.

Sylvia turned to Yvette. "Help me get Mark to my bedroom. He can wake up in my bed instead of down here with everyone gawking at him."

Sylvia took hold of my wrists while Yvette grabbed my ankles as they carried me upstairs. Apparently, Sylvia could not hear or see while she was under the influence of the drug, so she assumed I was in the same condition.

"This really presents me with a golden opportunity," Sylvia said as they carried me through her doorway and laid me on her bed.

"I hope you're not thinking what I think you're

thinking."

She looked at Yvette. "You can help me get Mark into my bathtub."

"If you're going to try to wake him up, you could just wait a few minutes and it will wear off like it did with you. But if you absolutely insist on putting him in your bathtub, we better take his clothes off first."

"I don't want to wait until that antidote wears off. I want to take advantage of the situation I have right now. You know about my sexual preferences. When I turned Mark into a vampire a couple weeks ago, I drank his blood, then forced him to drink my blood. Then he passed out for three days. Right after I drank his blood and I made him drink mine, I carried his body into the bathtub and washed the blood off by peeing on his face and in his mouth."

"Are you sure Mark can't hear us?" Yvette asked.

"No, he can't. I couldn't hear or see anything until I woke a few minutes ago. Anyway, Mark already knows what I did right after I drank his blood."

"Oh my! How did he find out?"

"I told him afterwards."

"Why would you do something stupid like that?"

"Because I think it's wrong for couples to have secrets. Honesty is the best policy. Besides, it was so much fun, I didn't want to do it just once. I want to do it all the time. Every day. After all, we have sex every day. So why not golden showers every day?"

"And what did Mark say to all this?"

Sylvia sighed. "Unfortunately, he does not share my interest. I hope I can eventually persuade him to change his mind. But for now, this is my only chance."

"You'll make an awful mess if you leave all his clothes on."

Sylvia nodded. They both removed my shoes and socks, and then unbuttoned my shirt.

"This is a great idea," said Yvette. I've got to get some of this antidote to use on Ronald. I'll do the same thing and get him into our bathtub. He'd never agree to the golden showers, so I would never tell him—and don't you ever tell him I said so. If he found out, he'd probably kill me in my sleep."

"Mark and I have no secrets. I'll tell him about it later. I'm sure he'll forgive me—again. He's a wonderful man. I'm lucky to have found him."

"That's good to know," I said, suddenly finding my voice.

They both screamed together.

"Oh my God! How long have you been conscious?" Sylvia asked.

"Since the two of you carried me from downstairs." I sat up on the bed.

"Oh, this is awkward for me. I think I'm going to leave you two lovebirds alone. You have lots to talk about." Yvette laughed as she walked out the door.

"Yvette is right. This is awkward. I don't know what to say. Now you're probably mad at me—again."

"Well, nothing happened since I was finally able to speak again. But what if I hadn't woken up?"

Sylvia sighed. "Then right now you would be in the bathtub with your clothes off and I would be the happiest vampire girl in London."

"I'll try to find some other ways to make you happy. How about flowers or chocolates?"

Sylvia shook her head. "Nice intentions, but that's not a proper substitute. There is no substitute. I will just patiently wait until you change your mind. Eventually, your desire to please me will win out. I have all the time in the world and so do you. And once you agree to indulge my fantasies, I won't want to do the golden showers in the bathtub anyway."

"You won't?"

"Of course not. I'll want to do it in bed, where we can both be more comfortable."

"Wouldn't that be even more of a mess?"

"There's no mess at all if you swallow. That's how it's supposed to be done. The bathtub is just an initial compromise — like learning to ride a bicycle using training wheels. Never let it be said that I'm unwilling to compromise."

"What did you do in relationships before you met me? I can't imagine this wasn't a problem in the past."

"It never was a problem. Believe it or not, some men like the golden showers. You and I both like it when I sit on your face. This is the next logical step. I'm sure you realize I haven't been celibate for three whole centuries! In the past, if a man didn't want to do the golden showers, I could always put him in a trance and have him drink it anytime I felt like it. I never had to argue or negotiate with a sex partner — I just told them what to do and they always did it. Maybe I should have waited a few months before turning you into a vampire. Then I could have put you into a trance every time we had sex and you would just have done what I asked each time. Of course, since I'm in love with you, I'd prefer that you did it to please me and also because you enjoyed it too. But don't worry. No one is more patient than I am."

"It's been quite a day," I said, changing the subject, as both of us began to undress. "Things seem to be going well. That is, as long as we can get rid of Callen's men. How can they do the things that they do and still belong to a church?"

"They don't belong to a real church," Sylvia explained. "They're part of a cult. Of course, that's not the reason they do the things they do. Look at what the real church did during the Inquisition. How many innocent people were executed? Hundreds of thousands? Millions? I was around near the end of it; my family was murdered because of the superstitions of the people in our village. And that was in 1685, just one year after the last official execution of witches in England. Neither America nor England executed any witches in the 1700s. The Germans and the Spanish did, though, right on through the middle of the eighteenth century. I wouldn't have wanted to live in either of those countries back then. They certainly had wonderful music, though! How about Antonio Soler from Spain?"

With that, Sylvia sat down at her harpsichord and played Soler's masterpiece, "Fandango," an incredibly intricate piece that started off slowly, but gradually built up more and more speed until it ended in a crashing climax. Listening to it with the sensitive hearing of a vampire was something like getting on a rollercoaster that gradually picked up speed, then got faster and faster with incredible highs and lows, and finally ending at the highest speed, the tallest height, and abruptly, as if flying off of the track. The piece was so long, it took Sylvia over ten minutes to play it.

"That's great." I clapped my hands as she stood up and curtsied. "But I hope that if you play it in public, you won't do it in your bra and panties."

Sylvia looked down at her nearly-naked body, then back at me. "I suppose you're right. This is concert attire for the bedroom only."

Our eyes met each other, then our bodies followed. We held each other, then began to kiss.

As we stood in our underwear, holding each other, a knock sounded as Yvette opened the door, entered, and said, "Can I come in?"

Sylvia froze for an instant, then shook her fist at Yvette. "Are you trying to kill our mood?"

"Kill your mood? I think you did that just a little while ago! How was I to know you two were almost undressed? I heard you playing the harpsichord while I was in the hall. I just assumed you'd have your clothes on. Besides, it's only around nine o'clock. What are you doing with your clothes off so early?"

"What do you think?" Sylvia fumed.

Yvette stared at us, taking a particularly long look at me. "I've seen you undressed before," she told Sylvia, "though this is the first time I've seen Mark." She smiled and winked at me. "I hope it won't be the last time."

"Get out!" Sylvia yelled, as she rushed towards Yvette.

Alarmed, Yvette ran into the hall, slamming Sylvia's door shut as a barrier between the two of them. The wall shook for a brief instant, and Sylvia and I both turned towards the other side of the room just in time to see the awful result. Perched on her tallest shelf stood one of her dolls, which now tipped over. Sylvia and I both raced to the shelf on the other side of the room in a desperate attempt to save her before she could hit the floor. As the doll eluded our hands, it landed on the carpet with a soft crack. Sylvia let out a gasp of pain as if she were the one who had been hurt instead of the doll. Carefully, she kneeled down and picked up the doll, cradling the body with one hand and the little doll hand in Sylvia's other hand,

"I bought this doll back in 1885," Sylvia sobbed as her eyes welled up with tears. "One of the best Gaultier dolls made."

I looked at the doll and at Sylvia. "Perhaps your friend Pierre can put the hand back on. He did such a good job on the doll he made of you, I'll bet he can fix this so you won't be able to see any cracks." I had no idea whether what I said was true or not, but it sounded reassuring, and I couldn't bear to see Sylvia in pain.

"I guess you're right." She stood up and laid the doll on the shelf.

As I looked at it on its back, its fixed eyes open, I

could not help but think for a second that it was a real person who had just died.

"Damn Yvette!" Sylvia clenched her fists.

"I'm sure she didn't mean for this to happen, but we certainly get interrupted here a lot. It's hard to get any time alone. Maybe you should have your pet wolves stand guard outside your door to keep them all away."

Sylvia shook her head. "It wouldn't work. Tweedledum and Tweedledee only guard against strangers. They never warn against the enemies within our midst."

"I think we're safe now. I doubt anyone else will interrupt us tonight."

Sylvia nodded. "You're right. Let's go to bed."

After Sylvia and I made love, we lay on our sides facing each other, our arms locked in embrace just as our eyes were. To be able to gaze so freely upon Sylvia's hypnotic beauty without her looking away or even blinking was a feast for the eyes. Yet there was something else — something unusual — perhaps even slightly disconcerting. I had only seen Sylvia's eyes closed a few times — when I woke — and when I looked at them, they instantly opened.

I told her this as we lay next to each other, though in a light manner, and wondered aloud whether she ever really slept.

"Don't you like to see my eyes?" she asked.

"Of course. Your eyes are the most beautiful I've ever seen. They draw me into you. They cast a spell on me."

Sylvia kept her eyes on mine. "Call them beautiful if you like. Say they draw me towards you if you will. But please don't say they cast a spell on you. It's not true. I can cast a spell with my eyes. I did it with the hijacker when I made him freeze. But I would never do that with you — even if I could — and I can't."

"You can't? Why not?"

"Because we're both vampires," Sylvia explained. "If you were human, I could. But since we're both vampires, we both have the same powers and abilities, the same strengths and weaknesses."

"We do? I don't feel like I can do all the things that you do. I couldn't have made the hijacker freeze the way you did."

"Yes you could," Sylvia said. "You just don't realize your potential yet. Your abilities are a mirror of mine. That's why Ronald is so jealous of you. He's never really liked me. He's treated me with a healthy respect mixed with jealousy and distrust. With you here, now there are two of us. I'm surprised he bought the doll for me. Actually, I'm shocked."

"It's a beautiful present. It looks so much like you, I just love it."

Sylvia's eyes looked upon mine with apprehension.

"Not only does the doll look like you—you look like the doll."

Sylvia appeared more alarmed. "What do you mean, I look like the doll? I'm the one who's real here; the doll is just a work of art—an imitation of life. Don't turn me into a work of art."

"I'm sure you've heard that art imitates life."

"Yes?" Sylvia asked suspiciously.

"Sometimes it works the other way. Life imitates art."

"How perfectly dreadful!" Sylvia proclaimed. "I don't want to be a work of art."

"It can't be helped," I explained. "Your beauty preordains it."

"Then art could make someone less than human, couldn't it?" Sylvia asked.

"Or more than human," I answered.

Sylvia smiled. "Well now. I like that a little better. As a vampire, I'm already more than human."

"So you don't mind that I like the doll so much? You understand that I like it because it's a representation of you?"

Sylvia seemed to be in deep thought for a moment, as if a thought had just come to her or she had just recognized some truth which had slipped not only her notice, but mine as well. "You're right, Mark. I do understand now. I just remembered that I..." But here Sylvia changed to "I mean I just realized how you must feel. Actually we're more alike than either of us realized." She laughed softly to herself, but in the laugh was the slightest note of irony.

Sylvia smiled at me. We gazed in each other's eyes, and as we did, I could not help but think that, yes, she and the Sylvia doll did look alike. I know that we fell asleep at some point, but I could not tell when it was. I remember our eyes on each other. Wide open. Just like the doll.

Chapter Ten

I woke, the next morning, to Sylvia's loving eyes gazing into mine. We lay next to each other, side by side, in a tender but pressing embrace, our faces just inches from each other.

"Don't you sleep?" I asked, returning her smile.

"I slept for a hundred years. Maybe I'll stay awake for a hundred."

I stared at her in shock.

"My goodness, Mark. I was only kidding. Don't take that seriously."

"But you told me that when you were staked inside the coffin, you slept from 1766 to 1866."

"Yes, that part is true," Sylvia admitted. "But I'm not going to stay awake for another hundred years to make up for what I missed while I was asleep. I do need the rest."

"I wasn't sure. I really don't know. Sometimes I wonder if you ever sleep. I almost never see your eyes closed. I know this sounds strange, but—"

"Yes?" Sylvia questioned, her eyes probing mine.

"Sometimes I have this strange feeling that you never sleep—that if I were to open my eyes at any time, your eyes would be open, looking at mine."

"Hmm, what an interesting idea. Yes, I like that. How romantic you are. But it's not true, I'm afraid. I close my eyes when I sleep, just like you."

"You mean you just wake up earlier?" I asked.

"No, actually you wake first. Your mind wakes up right before your eyes open, and my eyes open the instant your mind wakes up. My eyes open and I wake in response to your mind."

"That's incredible," I said.

"Wonderful," Sylvia corrected. "Our minds work in tandem. And it will be even more so as time goes on. You heard what Jack and Helen said about us in their laboratory."

I remembered, and wondered aloud to Sylvia just what new abilities we would discover as part of our mutual evolution.

"Helen and Jack don't really understand," Sylvia explained, "Their materialistic, scientific philosophy can only conceive of a physical change. They're wrong. It's not physical. It's mental. It's magical. We're already changing. I can feel it. Can't you?"

"I don't know if I can always recognize what is magical," I admitted.

"Sometimes it's right in front of your face," Sylvia said, her eyes smiling into mine, her face just inches away from me.

I pulled her closer to me and we kissed, then made love, joining our bodies, minds, and souls together as one.

Around noon, we looked out from the diamond-paned windows of Sylvia's bedroom, surveying the immaculately kept grounds of the mansion. The thermometer outside the window said 58 degrees Fahrenheit and 14 degrees Celsius, and the sun shone brightly with scarcely a cloud in the blue sky.

"Take a look at this." Sylvia observed the same scene, as if we were looking out of one set of eyes. "It's almost sixty degrees out there! And look at the sun! This is a rare winter day for London, let me tell you. Too nice to spend the entire day inside. Let's wake everyone up and get them outside."

"Are you sure they'll want to get up now?" I asked, as we got dressed. "They're not living in California time the way our bodies still are. They may not be used to these odd hours."

"We're not living in California time either. We're eight hours ahead here in London, not eight hours behind. In San Francisco, we were waking up around five or six in the afternoon. That would be one or two in the morning in London. Instead, we've been waking up at nine or ten in the morning here, which would be like waking up at one or two in the morning in San Francisco, something we never did. Everything has become reversed, including our time."

"Along with everything else, now time itself has become reversed," I said. "First, there are your streets with the traffic reversed, then the names of the cars that match the owners' names, then the names of the streets which change even though the street is still the same, and then there is the connection between us, which you say is not a reversal, but a mirror—and I don't understand how one can be one without also being the other—and then there is the matter of identities, and nothing can be identified because the names have no meaning, and even your identity, which you change frequently with false papers, would seem to be several people, and then there is the doll which is a perfect representation of you which you say has stolen your image, and at first you said you did not want to be written about, because all art steals its essence from its subject, but then you said it would be nice if I were to write about you because it would be done out of love, and now, not only have our space and identities become all reversed and tangled, but you say time has become reversed as well."

"That's quite a mouthful," Sylvia replied. "As far as the reversal of space is concerned, Kant believed that spatiality is not a characteristic of things-in-themselves, but only of things as we perceive them. I believe that, and I also believe that things-in-themselves do not change just because they have been relabeled or renamed. I do not change because of having several identity cards. But my essence is stolen by the doll, even though I haven't lost it."

"What?" I cried. "How can your essence be stolen

116

from you without you losing it?"

"How can one lose one's temper and yet still have it?" Sylvia queried. "But to get away from semantics and back to metaphysics, if such is possible, the image of me is stolen by the doll. That is clear. It could not have received my image without me. But once the doll was completed. I was no longer necessary."

"You're necessary to me," I protested.

"But not necessary to the doll. It exists apart from me, not needing me. I gave it birth—unknowingly and unwillingly—it could not have existed without me. Now it has a life and existence of its own. To a certain extent, it has replaced me. Whatever is copied is diminished."

"How can this be?" I asked. "I see the reverse of this. Something must have value first, or else someone would not have made a copy."

Sylvia shook her head. "Let me give you an example. There are two paintings, equally beautiful, equally valuable. Both hang in museums and can be viewed there. One is also reproduced many times in posters that anyone can buy for a few dollars. The other is not allowed to be reproduced. Given that the two are of equal beauty and value to begin with, which of the two will attract the most people at the museum? It should be the one which cannot be reproduced, because it can't be seen anywhere else. The other painting can be owned as a cheap poster, so no one needs bother to see the real thing."

"But what is the real thing?" I asked. "Is it one of those two paintings you described? Or is it the subject of the painting? If all art is representation, then you could say that art itself is not real; only the subject is real."

Sylvia smiled. "Perhaps art is both a representation, and real within itself. And perhaps the subject of the art is not only real within itself, but also a representation."

"That's a very strange thought," I observed, as I prepared to open Sylvia's door.

Walking out that door, and into the hallway, Sylvia said, "Now I will show you how to reverse time, not on a metaphysical level, but right here in this house, as I wake everyone up. It will seem reversed for them."

Indeed, Sylvia was correct. It was a reversal for them, and Ronald, Helen, and Jack especially let her know, without mincing words, just how much of a reversal and inconvenience it was.

After Sylvia had them all awake and assembled downstairs in the living room, they stood around sleepily and stared at Sylvia and me.

Ronald looked at his watch. "It's a little after noon," he announced to Sylvia. "I hope you have an excellent reason for waking all of us up so early."

"But of course," Sylvia agreed cheerfully. "I thought that with such a beautiful sunny day, we could all go outside and play croquet."

Ronald glared at her in stunned silence. His eyes blinked a couple of times as if in disbelief, then without saying a word, sat down on the couch. He stared at the floor and shook his head. "I cannot believe that you woke us up for this," he said, looking up at Sylvia. "This must be a nightmare. Tell me that I'm only dreaming."

"Play croquet?" asked Helen. "What a silly waste of time."

"It's never a waste of time to enjoy oneself; it's a waste of time to be bored," Sylvia pointed out. "Besides, why are you so concerned with time? Do you plan to die soon?"

Helen, Jack, and Ronald all walked off in a huff. Susan, Joseph, Yvette, Sylvia, and I went out upon the lush green lawn of the mansion's grounds and began to play croquet in the sun.

Sylvia turned to me. "Have you ever heard anything so ridiculous? We've all been here over a century, none of us are aging, and they're worried about wasting time!

Time is hardly passing."

I looked at Sylvia with some surprise, since I clearly remembered that it was only the previous afternoon in the British Library when she had told me how I should enjoy her as much as possible now because she could be killed the very next day by her enemies, and that time was precious.

"I know what you're thinking," Sylvia said, looking into my eyes. "You think I may be contradicting myself by saying today that time is hardly passing when I told you only yesterday how precious time with me was because I could be murdered anytime."

"Murdered?" asked Yvette. "Don't be so morbid. Why would anyone murder you?"

"Ask Father Callen," Sylvia replied.

"I can't," Yvette said. "You already killed him. Maybe you should have asked him."

"He tried to kill me because he didn't like vampires, but then a lot of people don't. Believe me, Yvette, he wouldn't have liked you either." Sylvia turned back to me. "Anyway, what I was trying to explain was how time could seem to be standing still and precious at the same time. Time stands still for me because I don't age, yet time is precious because I could be killed."

"I won't let that happen," I said. "I stopped Father Callen. The others won't ever get another chance like the one he had."

Yvette held her mallet tightly to the middle of her chest, as if embracing it, causing her sweater to pull even more snugly across her pointed breasts. "My, how romantic," she said, smiling.

As we continued to play croquet on the sunny lawn, the two wolves followed us around the grounds. They carefully eyed the five of us, as if they were circling in on their prey. They watched as Sylvia hit the ball with her mallet, their gaze moving with the ball. Then they stared at Yvette momentarily before looking straight into Sylvia's eyes. Sylvia broke their gaze by glancing at Yvette, and the wolves' eyes followed Sylvia's, glancing at Yvette, then back to Sylvia. Sylvia nodded her head at them but once, and they rushed forward towards Yvette, one of them scooping up her ball and running off.

"Hey! Come back with that!" Yvette yelled.

The wolf dropped the ball for a second, then the other grabbed it in its teeth, and the first one chased after it.

Sylvia let out a high musical laugh as she watched the two wolves chase each other playfully.

"That's not fair," Yvette told Sylvia. "Make them give it back."

"Stop," Sylvia commanded them. They froze, waiting for her next instructions. "Show how nice you are and give the ball back."

On hearing these words, the wolf trotted over to Yvette and laid the ball at her feet.

Yvette picked it up to replace it in its former position, but immediately dropped it. "Oh, yuck." She crinkled her face into a grimace. "It's all slimy."

Sylvia looked at the wolves and at me and suppressed a giggle.

"Why are you being so nasty to me by making the wolves steal my ball?" Yvette asked.

"Revenge for last night," Sylvia explained.

"Just because I walked in on you and Mark?"

"Not only that," Sylvia said. "When you slammed the door, you made one of my Gaultier dolls fall down. Its hand broke off."

Yvette's voice dropped lower. "Oh. I'm sorry. I really am. I know how much you like your dolls. Maybe I can make it up to you. Why don't we all go downtown together today and pay a visit to Pierre's Doll Shop. I'll pay to have it fixed or I'll buy you another one. It's up to you."

Sylvia agreed to have it fixed.

"Then you forgive me?" asked Yvette.

"Yes, still friends." Sylvia nodded.

After finishing our game of croquet, we returned to the mansion to explain our slight change of plans to the others: that Yvette would come with the four of us in the Bentley that afternoon to the doll shop and would return with us after we "interviewed" Callen's men in the evening.

"You intend to take Yvette with you to see those two religious fanatics?" asked Ronald. "You want to expose her to danger as well?"

"My, how romantic you are!" Yvette proclaimed, smiling. "How nice it is to see you so concerned about me." Yvette turned to the rest of us. "Underneath his tough shell, he's really soft and tender."

"Sort of like a crab?" queried Sylvia.

Ronald glared at Sylvia. "It's not enough to contact the same people who want to kill us. You have to drag Yvette along with you."

"I won't be meeting them anyway," Yvette protested. "I'll be waiting in the car with Joseph and Susan."

"That's right," agreed Joseph. "We'll be waiting close by just in case they decide to bring friends."

Sylvia shrugged her shoulders. "Let them bring an army of religious zealots. I don't care. We'll be seeing them at eight o'clock—well after dark. They can't do anything to hurt us then. During the afternoon, we'll be seeing the sights downtown, going shopping, and having my doll fixed at Pierre's. How dangerous can that be?"

"You win again," declared Ronald, "as always."

"Don't worry," Yvette told him as we left. "We'll be back later tonight, probably around ten." She gave him a light kiss on the lips as his expressionless face watched us leave.

As Joseph and Susan drove the Bentley through the gates of the mansion and onto the road, I had Sylvia on my left and Yvette on my right. The four of them took turns pointing out attractions in London.

"We're getting close to the British Library where we were yesterday," Sylvia told me, but the area didn't look familiar to me. "Things change quite a bit from one block to the next," she explained.

"There's the University of London," Joseph said.

Within one more block, I saw the original British Library and the British Museum. Joseph turned off Bloomsbury Street onto Great Russell Street, where Sylvia and I had walked only the day before. It was comforting to know that in this massive city, I could feel that something was already familiar. We drove past the gates of the entrance of the British Museum. Yvette pointed out Bloomsbury Square on the corner to our right, a small block-sized park. Joseph turned left on Montague Street. Just one block up, Susan pointed out the other side of the University of London on our left, and Russell Square on our right. This square was about twice the size of the previous one, and had several footpaths. The road around it was a one-way street, so we circled the square.

We began heading south on Southampton Row, and Sylvia pointed towards the left. "Just a few blocks past the Children's Hospital there, is Charles Dickens' house."

"What a beautiful area this is," I said. "What is it called?"

"Bloomsbury," Sylvia answered. "Keynes, the economist, lived here. So did a lot of writers: Virginia and Leonard Woolf, George du Maurier, T.S. Eliot, Bertrand Russell, and D.H. Lawrence."

"Did their characters live here, too?" I asked.

"Characters live inside their creators," Sylvia said, as she nodded her perfectly created head and looked at me.

"I don't know about characters living here," Yvette added, puzzling over our remarks, "but Sylvia has a beautiful flat here. Do you want to see it?"

"We can't do that," Sylvia explained. "People are living there already. I've been leasing the flat out for years. I doubt they'd like us to drop by uninvited."

"I didn't realize that you had your own flat," I said, somewhat surprised. "I would have thought it something you would have mentioned yesterday—"

Sylvia's eyes widened in alarm and she clapped her palm over my mouth and shook her head. She apparently knew what I was thinking: I remembered our conversation yesterday afternoon in her room when I had asked her why she didn't move away from the others earlier.

"Why should Sylvia have mentioned it yesterday?" Yvette asked me.

Sylvia answered for me. "We were only a few blocks away from here."

"I'm sure you were if you visited the old British Library," Yvette answered, "but why is that so much of a secret?"

To Yvette's annoyance, Sylvia ignored her question. While I could understand how Sylvia might not want the others to know that we had even discussed moving out, I also believed she would have been better off confronting her problems with the others directly. But I also knew that I could wait to tell her that when we were alone.

Next, we drove through Soho, a district that included many theaters on Shaftesbury Avenue. Sylvia promised that we would return soon to watch a play.

"There's quite a bit to do here, especially at night," Sylvia said.

"That's for sure," agreed Yvette. "I spend most of my time down here when I go out. We're only a few blocks from the Hippodrome. I went dancing there years ago when it was a disco."

"Do you and Ronald go dancing?" I asked. Somehow, I couldn't picture him on a dance floor having a wild time.

"Ronald dancing?" Yvette echoed. "He'd never dance."

"Whom do you dance with then?" I asked.

"Anyone nice-looking who asks me. There's not exactly a shortage of men. I meet more men than I possibly know what to do with."

"I don't know about that," Susan said. "You certainly know what to do with them."

"Doesn't Ronald get jealous?" I asked.

"Jealous? We've been together for over a century. If you and Sylvia should last so long do you think you'd still be jealous? You'll probably be bored to death with each other long before then."

"Don't count on that," Sylvia said. "Mark and I are different than you and Ronald."

As an awkward and angry silence ensued between Sylvia and Yvette, I wondered how two totally mismatched people such as Ronald and Yvette could have ever gotten together—and more incredibly, stayed together for all those years.

The silence didn't last, however. Soon, we approached the Westminster Bridge, and everyone in the car started to point out the places of interest: the clock of Big Ben atop the tall tower adjoining the Palace of Westminster containing the Houses of Parliament. The Bentley pulled over to the side of the road on the bridge and we got out of the car to take in the view.

I looked around and noticed that we were the only car that had stopped right on the bridge, but traffic just drove around us with not a single driver beeping a horn.

"Aren't we in the way?" I asked Joseph. "Won't you get a ticket?"

Joseph laughed. "They'll see the Bentley parked there and assume that we're important."

"We are important," Sylvia said.

Sylvia's announcement had a cheering effect on Yvette. She smiled proudly, and seemed to walk with her head and her nose a little higher as she strolled along the sidewalk by the railing.

"Joseph and I haven't been out in the daylight like this for awhile—aside from giving you two a ride from the airport," Susan said. "It certainly feels different—playing croquet on the grounds on a sunny day, touring the center of London in the middle of the afternoon. Sort of daring, actually. What time is it, anyway?"

I looked at my watch. "Two o'clock."

Sylvia caught my lingering gaze at my watch and guessed correctly at my thoughts. "You're thinking about what Jack and Helen were saying about Graystone's murder, aren't you?"

"Yes," I admitted. "Yes. I remember you said Graystone had the same watch."

"They can't accuse me of stealing his watch. I'm not a thief." Sylvia put her arm around my shoulder and pressed her face against mine. "I needed blood to survive, so I was morally right in drinking his blood. His death brings us millions, which makes it even more right. What should I have done so that I could be morally right?" Sylvia held her hands out, palms up, as if she were a preacher asking for the word of God.

"I don't know," I answered. "I'm hardly a moral authority."

"We're all moral authorities," Sylvia said. "Every last one of us. All of us and none of us."

"So what should I do so that I won't feel guilty about the watch? I feel a little guilty that you were inspired to buy it after killing someone that had the same model of watch."

"There's only one thing to do." Sylvia said, pointing at my watch. "I can throw it off the Westminster Bridge here. Then all the guilt will be gone."

"Why would you do that?" I asked.

"Because the watch makes you feel guilty. I want your conscience to be clear."

"My conscience is clear. You bought the watch. You didn't steal it."

"I'm glad you like the watch," Sylvia pointed out. "All watches will bring on memories. The memory is in you, not in the watch."

"You're right, there's no getting away from it. Though I'll probably even feel guilty about you spending the money on a watch for me."

"No you won't. My diamond engagement ring cost one hundred and eighty thousand dollars, so the watch was much less money. I like to go shopping."

Yvette laughed. "Isn't that the truth! Sylvia may not be an expert on morality, but she certainly knows how to shop. Take it from me. We've been out shopping together many times. She loves to spend money."

"As do we all," Joseph remarked with a chuckle.

"This is the warmest, sunniest day I've ever seen in the winter," observed Susan. "It almost makes me feel like going out during the daytime is worth the risk."

The Bentley turned around and headed north again over Westminster Bridge. I looked over to our left as we passed the Houses of Parliament. We pulled over and Joseph took a photo of Sylvia and me standing on the bridge with Big Ben and the Houses of Parliament in the background. Sylvia remarked that since we now had a photo of us there during the day, we should come back some evening and take a nighttime photo with a full moon. I agreed.

Joseph informed me that we were on our way to Pierre's Doll Shop. Although Susan explained that we would be going back in the same direction we came from when we were near Sylvia's flat in Bloomsbury and the original British Library, we did not drive quite so far, and I could not recognize any of the streets.

Though I tried to trace our movements on a small map, I found too many little streets meandering unnamed among the larger ones. Somewhere between Cambridge Circus, the hub where Shaftesbury and Charing Cross Road met, and Covent Garden was where we now found ourselves. I remembered that Shaftesbury Avenue was where so many theaters were and that Sylvia told me that Charing Cross Road had the world's largest bookshop, Foyles. Covent Garden had many fine shops and restaurants. As before, I realized how difficult it was to define where one was without the use of the name or label. All I could use by way of definition was to situate myself between two or more relatively known labels, but this was still a matter of defining oneself by stating what one wasn't.

We drove down a narrow one-way street barely wide enough for two cars to pass each other if one parked partly on the sidewalk. With our left side of the car almost flush with the brick wall of the building next to it, we all had to exit from the right, the driver's side.

On the opposite end of the street stood an early Victorian faded brick building with large bay windows. Displayed in the windows were many fine dolls, mostly attired in Victorian fashions. A large painted wooden sign hung in front which read "Pierre's Doll Shop."

As the five of us entered the store, we were surrounded by dolls in all directions—old dolls, new dolls, dolls in Victorian dress and in modern clothing, celebrity dolls, baby dolls, girl dolls, adult dolls— hundreds of eyes stared at us in unblinking silence.

"Sylvia!" a voice declared from the back of the shop. A small elderly man with a moustache came towards us with his arms open in welcome. "I haven't seen you here in months." He looked at Yvette, Susan, and Jack. "I see you've brought your friends." He then shifted his attention to me, smiled, and looked back to Sylvia "Is this the lucky man? Your boyfriend?"

Sylvia nodded. "This is Mark Sheridan. My fiancée." Sylvia held out her hand, showing off her engagement ring.

Pierre appeared puzzled. "You just got engaged? I must have misunderstood. Somehow, I thought it had been months ago. I guess it was when you met that I was thinking of, not your engagement."

"That's not possible," I pointed out. "Sylvia and I just met each other. Actually, less than a month ago."

Pierre looked even more confused. "How can that be? Sylvia showed me the portrait she painted of you. That was months ago."

"Months ago?" I asked, as I remembered the strange events of several weeks ago regarding the painting. Less than three weeks earlier, Sylvia presented me with a portrait she had painted of me. It wasn't just the fact that the portrait was preternaturally lifelike that disturbed me at the time. An artist friend explained to me how Sylvia would have had to spend months painting it, and another few months would have been required for the oil to dry sufficiently. In all, she would have needed to start the painting a minimum of six months before we ever met. Sylvia later explained that because she and I were spiritual twins, born of the same Satanic seed, she had actually sensed a connection to me even before I had been born. Within a few years of our meeting just a few weeks ago, she had already been able to clearly visualize what I would look like, even though we had never met. Perhaps the most startling thing about the portrait was that my eyes were black like hers—the way my eyes looked after she turned me into a vampire. Yet she painted the portrait

128

while I was still human. In effect, it became a self-fulfilling prophecy.

Once again, life imitated art.

"Yes, Sylvia brought in the portrait months ago," Pierre said. "So of course you must have met before then. In French, we call it 'déjà vu'. But in any case, it's a wonderful likeness, no?"

"Absolutely," I agreed. "Sylvia is a fantastic artist."

"Sylvia?" he questioned. "Oh yes, of course she is. But I was referring to me. The likeness I created."

I had to suppress laughter. While the man was clearly an artistic genius, his lack of modesty was amusing. "The doll you created of Sylvia is absolutely beautiful. It couldn't be more perfect."

"Thank you," he said, with a low bow, "but actually, I was referring to—"

He suddenly stopped in mid-sentence as he saw Sylvia, slightly behind me, shaking her head. I started to turn my eyes in her direction, but her gesture immediately stopped. For some reason, she did not want him to finish his sentence. It felt strange to realize that she was trying to keep some kind of little secret from me. I resolved to ask her about it after we got home, where she might feel more comfortable about it. Sylvia had always been honest and direct with me, never telling me a lie. The only exception to this was when we first met, she didn't reveal that she was a vampire or that she intended to turn me into one. But she had explained to me later that if she had told me the truth at the time, I might not have liked it.

Sylvia broke the silence by placing the cardboard box on his counter. "Pierre, I hope you can help me with this." She opened the cover of the box.

As we all crowded around the box with the doll inside, I could not help but think how it seemed like a person lying in a coffin, and how we were all waiting for Pierre, creator of dolls, to take on the role of a necromancer, and perform a ritual for her revivification.

Sylvia pointed with her finger to her hand, and the injury she had received.

"How did this happen?" Pierre inquired with concern.

Yvette hung her head in shame, like a dog feeling guilty.

"It fell down," Sylvia said.

Yvette let out a soft sigh of relief at not being blamed in public.

"Don't worry," Pierre assured Sylvia. "When I get done, she'll be as good as new."

The front door burst open, and a little girl, about seven or eight years old, came running inside. An older woman, who looked as if she could be her grandmother, followed in much more slowly.

"Sylvia!" the little girl cried, and went running up to her.

Sylvia turned, smiled broadly, and swept the little girl up off her feet, giving her a big hug and kiss. She did it with as much ease as if the girl had been a doll.

"This is my little girl," Sylvia said. "My adopted girl, Lilly." Sylvia pointed me out to the little girl. "And this is Mark, my fiancée."

"Does that make him my adopted Daddy?" Lilly asked.

"It certainly does," Sylvia agreed.

I then learned that the older woman was the girl's grandmother, and that Lilly's parents had both died in a car accident when she was only three years old. She had met Sylvia in Pierre's Doll Shop two years earlier. The grandmother, who struggled to support them both, had tried to find a doll she could afford to brighten a dreary and destitute Christmas. Sylvia had seen her dilemma, and paid for one of the finest dolls, a brand new reproduction of a Jumeau doll. One thing led to another;

Sylvia formed a friendship with them. They invited her over. She took pity on their poverty and helped them with their bills. Lilly considered Sylvia to be her adopted mother, the grandmother explained. "But she is more than that," the elderly woman declared. "She is an angel, sent to us from God."

"I wouldn't go quite that far," laughed Sylvia. "I'm certainly no angel. And God hasn't sent me. I've come on my own. "

Pierre returned to us after a short trip to the back of the shop. He opened up a long box and pulled a beautiful doll out, like a magician pulling a rabbit out of a hat. "The Bru reproduction is finished," he said to Sylvia. "How do you like it?"

Everyone turned towards the doll in admiration. Lilly's eyes opened wide and her mouth opened in an expression of awe. Sylvia's eyes caught Lilly's reaction. She walked over to Pierre and picked up the doll, admiring it as she turned it around in her hands.

"Would you like to hold it?" Sylvia asked Lilly.

Lilly's eyes opened even wider in surprise as she nodded eagerly. Pierre tried to disguise his reluctance to the idea of a small child handling such an expensive bisque doll that could easily be broken when he had vinyl dolls made for the less careful hands of children.

Lilly picked up the doll and held it carefully, admiring its beauty.

"Do you like it?" asked Sylvia.

"It's very pretty," Lilly said, as she held the doll out to Sylvia, while at the same time, pained to part with it.

"Merry Christmas, then," Sylvia said.

"But it's not Christmas," the little girl said with some surprise.

"Sure it is," Sylvia said. "It's Christmas whenever one wants it to be."

Lilly hugged the doll, then reached out for Sylvia,

who bent down towards the little girl. Lilly kissed her on the cheek and said, "Thank you, Sylvia."

Lilly looked like a doll holding a smaller doll and kissing a larger doll. Her dress had the same touches of luxury and extravagance that the doll's dress had. I guessed that Sylvia had bought her the clothing as well. It made me feel good to see the purity of Sylvia's love in action.

Sylvia paid Pierre, then waved good-bye to him as all of us walked out the door.

Joseph and Susan started for the car as Yvette, Sylvia, and I stood in front of Pierre's speaking with Lilly and her grandmother.

I noticed two men, apparently foreign businessmen by their accents standing close to Susan and Joseph by their car.

"A beautiful car," said one. "A Rolls Royce."

"Actually, it's a Bentley," said Susan.

The other man shrugged his shoulders. "It doesn't matter."

They both walked off and Joseph started the car. Susan got inside with him, but after a minute more of our conversation between Sylvia and the grandmother and Lilly, Joseph got out of the car and walked towards us. Susan followed. The car sat parked against the wall of the building opposite us, the door open, the engine idling quietly.

"Won't that waste gas?" I asked.

"It's all right," Joseph said. "We can afford the petrol."

For a moment, I thought how marvelous it was that such a luxurious car with an enormous engine could idle so quietly. A moment later the smooth sound was interrupted by a tiny click.

Suddenly a burst of light exploded. A loud boom ripped through my ears. A shock wave blasted all of us to the ground as if we were nothing more than dolls from the shop.

I felt pain, but it seemed to come from everywhere. My head spun. I tried to focus my eyes and turn around.

"Sylvia!" I yelled. Somehow, there was something terribly wrong with the sound of my voice. I could barely hear it even though I yelled. A ringing sound echoed through my ears. I put my hand up to my head and it was wet with blood. I tried to push my face and my body up off of the street.

In the corner of my eye, the skeleton of the Bentley sat in flames.

I reached out for Sylvia and felt my hand grasp hers. Her hand was covered with blood.

Chapter Eleven

Moments after the explosion from the car bomb, time seemed to have changed. Everything around us appeared to be moving very fast. I could hear screams; people were running towards us surrounding us, staring down at us from a curious circle of onlookers above. Simultaneously, time had slowed down: I could barely move, and did so languidly amidst pain all over my body. My hearing had been impaired. The sounds around me were all muffled and dampened by a ringing in my ears.

I felt Sylvia's hand in mine, but could feel it was wet—wet with blood. A sickening feeling came over me, a sense of dread.

"Sylvia," I yelled again, my voice not sounding loud at all to my ears.

To my relief, her hand squeezed mine. I tried to lift my head from the street to look at her. A wave of dizziness hit me and my head fell to the pavement. I lifted my head again and turned my face towards Sylvia.

Her eyes opened and as she looked at me, I saw her lips move. Even though I could not hear her words, I could read the movement of her lips as she called out my name softly—too softly for me to hear.

I became aware of people and sounds around us. Red lights flashed and sirens wailed. Sylvia and I were being lifted up on stretchers, being carried towards an ambulance. Susan and Joseph and Yvette were being helped to their feet. Out of the corner of my eye, I could see little Lilly being rushed onto a stretcher and into a waiting ambulance. Sylvia's eyes followed mine, and I could see them filled with tears.

The two of us were silent in the ambulance on the way to the hospital. An odd sense of calm filled us—or maybe we were just numb. We looked into each other's eyes as the ambulance sped through London, bouncing up and down, with its siren screaming through the afternoon traffic.

Once at the hospital, Susan, Joseph, and Yvette rejoined us. They had small bandages over small cuts caused by flying glass and bits of metal. I reasoned that they must have been directly behind us at the time of the blast—just as certain as Lilly was directly in front of us.

It turned out that Sylvia and I had lost almost no blood. Enough to alarm me when I felt her hand, but we discovered that was caused by a cut to her wrist—a cut that was easily bandaged. The cut to my head was also bandaged, which stopped the bleeding. It was the actual shock of the blast that had injured both of us. Sylvia and I could no longer hear normally, let alone hear as acutely as we had been used to. But the damage to our ears went beyond our hearing.

Apparently, the blast had done something to our inner ears, affecting our balance. Neither of us was able to stand up.

"How are you?" she asked me, as they wheeled both of us into a hospital room with Susan, Joseph, and Yvette following behind us.

"I could be worse, I suppose. How are you?"

"I'll get better." She tried to smile with some effort, then grew suddenly alarmed. "What about Lilly and her grandmother?"

"They were brought in here at the same time as you," answered one of the doctors. "They were still alive." His eyes looked down at the floor momentarily, then back to Sylvia. "However, they may not be as fortunate as you. We'll have to wait and see what happens."

Sylvia began to cry. "This is all my fault. If Lilly hadn't walked out of Pierre's at the same time with us, this wouldn't have happened to her." She began to wipe her tears away with the sheet around her. "First her parents were killed in a car accident, and now this happens." Sylvia turned to the doctor. "When can Mark and I go visit her and her grandmother?"

The doctor appeared shocked. "Visit her? She's in critical condition. She can't be visited until she improves. Besides, you two have to rest. Neither of you are in any shape to visit anyone. You don't seem to realize your condition. Neither one of you are going anywhere for awhile."

Sylvia looked at me. "We're going to miss our eight o'clock appointment with Callen's men."

"I think we already had our appointment with them," I answered. "I think they just moved the time up a few hours."

"I'd forget about any appointments for now," the doctor said. "You both may require surgery on your inner ears to be able to walk without losing your balance."

"Surgery?" Sylvia asked. "No thank you. Mark, what time is it?"

I held up my wrist in the air as she looked over at me.

"I'm glad you still have your sense of humor," she said.

"It's after four o'clock," I said. "And the sun will be setting pretty soon if you know what I mean, and I think you do."

"Do we have to be in separate beds?" Sylvia asked the doctor. "We're engaged. We want a double bed."

"You don't seem to understand the gravity of the situation," the doctor explained. "The two of you can't even stand up until we do something about your balance. You can't walk or sit in a chair. You can't do anything yet. I don't want to sound harsh, but do I make myself clear?"

"What time is it?" Sylvia asked a few minutes later.

"It's almost four-fifteen," said the doctor with some exasperation. "Just forget about any appointments. You're both going to be here for a while. As soon as you're feeling a little better, you'll be getting a visit from Scotland Yard."

"Scotland Yard?" Sylvia exclaimed.

"Of course," the doctor said. "They want to catch the people who did this to you."

"Yes, they must be caught," Sylvia agreed.

"They wanted to question your friends here immediately," the doctor said, "but I told them they'd have to wait a couple of hours."

"We appreciate that very much," said Joseph.

"They're waiting out in the hallway now," the nurse told us.

I glanced at Sylvia and saw her anxiety over this piece of information.

"We'll be bringing dinner by for you in an hour," the nurse said. "Buzz us if you need anything before then."

She and the doctors left the room.

"Scotland Yard!" Sylvia exclaimed. "We have enough troubles without them! We've got to get out of this place."

"Won't the doctors have a field day testing our blood and discovering all about us?" I asked.

"That does it. We're leaving right now." Sylvia tried to sit up, almost losing her balance, then put her hand to her head as if dizzy.

"I think you better wait a little longer," Susan remarked. "I'm sure you'll both feel better soon."

Susan was correct. Sylvia and I did feel better soon. As a matter of fact, it was very soon. Before five o'clock it had grown dark outside. Sylvia looked out the window at the darkness and saw us reflected in it. She peeled the bandage away from her wrist and both she and I noticed that while the dried blood still remained on the white gauze, the cuts had already healed. I felt the cut on my head and it had also disappeared along with the ringing in my ears.

"Checkout time!" Sylvia declared, standing up.

I stood up, too. Considering my rapid recovery from the gash on my forehead from the hijacker on the plane, I was not particularly surprised to find that our balance had returned and that our cuts had healed once it had grown dark.

The four of us left the room and began walking down the hall towards the elevator. In the hallway, we came across the two doctors and the nurse who had been in our room less than an hour earlier.

"My God!" one of the doctors yelled in shock. "What are you doing out of bed walking around?"

"Yes," answered Sylvia. "That's exactly what we're doing."

"We've decided to go home," I explained. "We're feeling better now."

"But you can't leave so soon," one of them protested.

"Why?" asked Sylvia. "It's not against the law, is it?"

"No, of course not. But we still must make some tests."

"I don't think so." Sylvia shook her head.

Two men in suits came up to us. One of them asked the doctors whether we were the ones who had been bombed. The doctor nodded.

The two men explained that they were from Scotland Yard and showed us their identification.

"We're glad to see you up and about," one of them remarked. "According to your doctor here, you were in no shape to talk to us only an hour ago." He glanced suspiciously at the doctors.

"That's true," one of the doctors explained. "They couldn't stand up. I don't understand it."

"A miraculous recovery," said the second of the two men, "but what we would like to know is why someone would try to blow up your car. People just don't go planting bombs for a pastime. There's usually some kind of reason: political, criminal, perhaps..."

"We have no idea at all," Sylvia said.

"I'm afraid we must insist on getting to the bottom of this," the first man told us.

A phone rang at the nurse's station about fifty feet away from us. The nurse answered, then called out for the two men from Scotland Yard. One of them walked to the phone while the other stood by us regarding us with suspicion. Sylvia and I listened attentively to the man on the phone. Even at that distance, he lowered his voice so he wouldn't be heard. We heard him anyway.

"What?" he said, incredulous. "You expect me to just let them go right now? I've got to ask them a few questions. What do you mean, I can't ask them a single question? By whose authority are you giving this order?" The expression on the man's face changed from anger to shock as he paused for the answer. He swallowed nervously, glanced back at us, then spoke as quietly as he could. "Yes, I'll tell them. No, I won't ask them any questions. No, not any questions." He set the phone down slowly, as if he had just experienced a great personal defeat.

He left the nurse's station and walked over to us. "I don't know who you are and I'm not going to ask who you are. You must have friends in high places. Very high places. You're all free to leave. No questions asked. At least not for now."

"Do you mean that Scotland Yard will be contacting us later?" Sylvia asked.

"I don't know about Scotland Yard," he answered, "but someone may—someone from a different government agency."

With the thought of that ominous possible appointment with the representatives of the law firmly in our minds, we took our leave of them.

Once outside, Joseph asked, "Now what do we do?

I've lost my car. We don't even have a way home."

Susan turned to Sylvia. "What about your appointment with Father Clifford and Brother Phillips? Maybe we can still find out if they were behind this."

Sylvia agreed that we should call them again and try to still keep our eight o'clock appointment with them. The rest of us stood by close to Sylvia as she held her cell phone away from her ear so that we could all hear the conversation. The same woman answered the phone.

"Is Father Clifford there?" Sylvia asked. "We have an appointment with him and Brother Phillips for an interview this evening."

"I'm sorry," the woman replied. "You just missed him. He was expecting your call earlier in the afternoon, but he said you could call him back tomorrow if you like. He mentioned he has some free time tomorrow afternoon."

"I'll bet he does," I said to Sylvia, as I remembered how he seemed to prefer a daytime interview when we spoke to him at Highgate Cemetery.

Sylvia informed the woman that she would call back tomorrow, then she turned to us. "I suggest we go home. I want to call the hospital and find out how Lilly and her grandmother are doing." She looked at Joseph. "And I suppose you will want to call your insurance company."

Joseph groaned. "Now we'll have to get another car. No doubt we'll have to pay some kind of deductible amount for replacement."

"Are you out of your mind?" Yvette yelled. "We almost got killed! Who cares about your damn car?"

"I care," Joseph said calmly. "I'm a caring person. Caring and sharing. That's my motto."

"Let's not fight among ourselves," Susan said. "Let's save our anger for our enemies. Apparently there's no shortage of them."

"What do you suggest we do?" taunted Yvette.

"I suggest we perform a Satanic ritual," Susan replied. "A destruction ritual — aimed at whoever tried to kill us."

"A wonderful suggestion," agreed Sylvia. "I think that's the very first thing we should do when we get home. And while we're on the subject of magical rituals, I also want to perform a compassion ritual — to heal Lilly and her grandmother."

Everyone readily agreed with Sylvia on both rituals.

While I certainly thought both were fine and noble aims, I admitted aloud that my lack of experience in magic could be an impediment, but Sylvia assured me that sincere intentions were more important than esoteric knowledge.

"Should we call the house and tell the others what happened to us?" Susan asked.

"Let's surprise them," suggested Yvette, as if showing up at the mansion with blood on our clothes would be some sort of practical joke she could play on Ronald.

We found a taxi and went straight to Highgate. Yvette's objective, if I read her correctly, proved true.

Ronald's eyes practically popped out of his head when he opened the door and saw us.

"My God! What's happened to you?" he shouted as he saw the bloodstains on our clothes.

Yvette hugged Ronald as Joseph explained to him and to Helen and Jack how the car was bombed.

Ronald pulled Yvette away from his body and held her at arms distance looking into her eyes. "Didn't I warn you that this would be dangerous?" he said, as if he were a father scolding his little daughter for playing in the street. "Didn't I tell you that you shouldn't go with them?" He turned to the rest of us. "I hope you're satisfied. You practically got Yvette killed along with the rest of you. I told you that Father Callen's men were dangerous."

"It may not have anything to do with Callen's men," I pointed out.

"Nothing to do with them!" Ronald yelled. "Who do you think was behind this?"

"It could have been Callen's men," I admitted, "but then again, it could have been someone else. Right before the bomb went off, there were two men near Joseph's car. They were looking at it. I noticed that they spoke with a foreign accent. They could have been related to the terrorists on the plane. Then again, there could be a relationship between these two men and the CIA agent on the plane."

Ronald considered this idea thoughtfully, then nodded his head. "That's right. You said the CIA agent probably had Joseph's license plate number. That's all he would have needed to trace you. But why would he have tried to kill you?"

"Perhaps to cover up his shooting of the other hijacker on the plane," Sylvia offered. "But I really don't think that's it. Since I killed the other hijacker, I certainly wasn't about to shout to the world about the killing the CIA agent committed."

"Anyway, if there's one thing I feel certain of," I said, "it's that those two men carried out the bombing. Whether it was ordered by Father Clifford, the terrorists, or the CIA agent—that I don't know."

Ronald nodded. "For once, I must agree with you, Mark. Your explanation is the most logical. The bombing must have been ordered by one of those three—Father Clifford, the terrorists, or the CIA agent. The question is: who did it?"

Chapter Twelve

As the eight of us stood in the hallway for a moment, pondering who was trying to kill us, Sylvia broke the silence. "Regardless of who it was, one thing is certain: we must seek revenge."

"Haven't you had enough trouble for one day?" Helen asked.

"You know what Nietzsche said," Sylvia remarked. "That which doesn't kill me only makes me stronger."

"Perhaps," said Joseph, "but he died of poor health at only fifty-six."

"And that which does kill us will not make us stronger," Susan added.

"Let's not go chasing phantoms till we find out who's behind this," Ronald said.

"I'm talking about performing a Satanic destruction ritual," Sylvia explained, "aimed at whoever is responsible."

"We've already agreed to that," Susan said.

"Helen and I haven't," Jack stated. "We don't care for religion."

"All religions make use of a focused energy-force," Susan explained. "Christians use prayer, Buddhists use chants, and Satanists perform rituals."

"So why are you Satanists?" I asked. Even though I wore the Baphomet, the symbol of Satan, around my neck since Sylvia had given it to me a few weeks earlier, I still knew little about the practice of magic.

Sylvia was only too happy to explain. Her tone was always instructive, never defensive. "Given our lifestyle, which sometimes results in our taking others' lives— though usually accidental—it would not be possible for us to be good Christians. We can pursue our goals more freely as Satanists because there are no restrictions against sex, material wealth, power, or vengeance—all those things we enjoy so much."

"But can't you pursue all those things as an atheist?" I inquired. "It doesn't seem as though it's necessary to be a Satanist."

Jack's eyes lit up. "Precisely my point. All this hocus-pocus is a waste of time."

"Please don't fill Mark's head with your own doubts," Sylvia pleaded. "You'll ruin things for us. I don't want you sapping his power."

"I couldn't do that even if I wanted to. You and Mark will continue to find your powers increasing regardless of what you do. But the answer to that is physiological, not supernatural. Helen and I have discovered some very interesting things about the two of you from our blood tests. It looks as though we have finally found out what makes you two different from the rest of us."

"Mark and I are spiritual twins," Sylvia explained, "born of the same Satanic seed, from the same demon in another dimension. That is what makes us different."

"I don't know how you could prove anything like that," Jack said, "but tomorrow I'll prove what I'm talking about. I will show everyone here the physical evidence of what Helen and I have discovered about the two of you. I'm sure you'll find it interesting."

Sylvia shrugged her shoulders. "I can wait. Right now, I want to call the hospital and find out how Lilly and her grandmother are doing."

Sylvia appeared numb after speaking on the phone to the hospital. She set the receiver down slowly as the two of us sat on the edge of her bed in her room. "Lilly's in a coma," she said softly, her eyes staring sadly into mine.

I put my arm around her shoulders. Sylvia leaned her head against mine for support.

"I know how she feels. When I was in my coffin from 1766 to 1866 it was as if I were in a coma. But Lilly can't sleep for a hundred years as I did. Somehow, I've got to

144

be able to wake her up."

A knock sounded on the door to our bedroom. It was Susan. "I've just been to our ritual chamber. We need incense and candles for our ritual."

Sylvia sighed. "It looks like we'll have to take another trip downtown."

"Now?" I asked, incredulous. "You want to get back into another car right now and go back downtown?"

"Yes," Sylvia explained calmly. "We should perform our destruction ritual while we are the angriest—not that I'm about to feel any happier about it tomorrow, mind you."

Susan left our room to change, and Sylvia and I did the same. She put on a black knit dress, which hugged the curves on her body like a tight sweater. I wore black pants and a black turtleneck sweater because Sylvia explained that the color helped to put one in the mood for a destruction ritual. Sylvia put her arms around my neck and positioned the silver chain and the Baphomet so that they were worn outside the sweater.

"Why do you want that to show?" I asked.

"Don't worry," she assured me. "They're not allowed to burn Satanists at the stake anymore."

"No. Now they use car bombs," I said.

"I don't know if Callen's men were the ones behind that or not. Our ritual will seek out the guilty ones and punish them. Wearing the symbol of Satan on the outside will help you remember what you are."

"I hardly feel like a Satanist," I admitted. "I don't know how to do Satanic things."

Sylvia smiled. "Being a true Satanist is not so much a matter of what you do—it's what you are. Be what you are; what you do will follow. "

"Where's your Baphomet?" I asked.

"You're wearing it."

"I know that this Baphomet is yours. After all, you

gave it to me." I remembered how Sylvia had given it to me at her apartment next to mine in San Francisco. "But what I meant is if I'm wearing this one, what will you wear?"

"Oh, that's not important." Sylvia waved her hand. "As long as we're together, one symbol of Satan is enough for the two of us. After all, you and I are one. Remember?" When I nodded in agreement, Sylvia added, "But don't worry. I have several others here in my room." She admired the delicate lines of the pentagram with her fingers. "None have the sentimental value of this one, though."

Sylvia did not have to remind me why that was so. She had told me earlier how when the other vampires had rescued her from the coffin where she had lain for a century, they placed the same silver medallion around her neck as they brought her back to life by giving her their blood.

Downstairs, Joseph, Susan, and Yvette met us. They were similarly attired in black. For an audience of Jack, Helen, and Ronald, a lively debate took place. It had to be decided just how we were to get to Central London now that Joseph's car had been blown up. We had to list all the possible options: taking Sylvia's Aston Martin, Ronald and Yvette's Rolls Royce, or last, and definitely least, taking the Underground. Sylvia wanted to drive her Aston Martin, but it could accommodate four people as long as two of the passengers were small children, and Yvette wanted to come along for the ride. She suggested taking their Rolls Royce, but with Ronald along, that would increase our number to six, and his Rolls would fit only five comfortably.

"Why not take the Underground?" I asked. "At least we won't be blown up."

Yvette and Ronald both gave me a look that seemed to say that they weren't the type to ride the Underground.

146

"Why would we take the Underground when we own a Rolls Royce?" Yvette asked proudly.

"So that we can reach Central London in one piece?" I asked.

"No worries there," said Joseph. "You know we can't be killed at night. The worst thing that can happen is that we lose another car. But if it's going to happen again, better to have it blow up at night than during the day."

"That's right," agreed Ronald. "So who's riding with Yvette and me? We'll take two cars."

Jack and Helen announced they had no desire to visit an occult supply shop.

"Come with us," Yvette said to Joseph and Susan. "Our back seat is much larger than Sylvia's. We'll let the new couple have some privacy."

"Wouldn't that be a nice change?" Sylvia asked me with a smile.

The six of us, all clad in black, made our way outside to the massive garage that housed the cars. Each car had its own electrically operated garage door.

Sylvia's Aston Martin was a bright cherry red, the hand-rubbed paint job incredibly smooth and shiny. I stood on the right side of the car waiting to get in, then realized that the passenger side was on the left in England with everything being reversed here in this strange world I found myself in.

We settled into the plush Connolly leather seats and I admired the beauty of the interior, especially the walnut dashboard. The engine fired up with a deep, low growl. It gave the impression of vast power just waiting to be called upon.

"It feels strange not to have the steering wheel or the gas pedal in front of me," I remarked.

"You won't miss them when you drive with me," Sylvia said with a devilish grin.

"Why is that?"

"You'll be much too worried about where the brake is to worry about the steering wheel or the accelerator pedal."

As the Aston Martin roared out of the garage and zoomed down the driveway towards the gate, I could see that Sylvia had spoken the truth. Behind us, Ronald in his Rolls Royce sought to catch up to us. The electric doors to the garage closed, then the gate to the mansion, and the two cars drove into the night, through the narrow roads of the village of Highgate.

As we approached corners at faster than sensible speeds, my position in the car on the left side made me feel like a driver with no control over where it was going. Sylvia was correct; my foot instinctively reached for the brake, but of course it wasn't there. Everything had been reversed again.

I decided to relax and enjoy the view of Highgate as we drove at more moderate speeds on the main roads such as Highgate High Street. One feature that particularly arrested my attention was a similarity that most houses shared in common: in all houses where the drapes were open, I could see large bookcases filled with many books. House after house, it was the same picture. It brought back the memory of a novel I had read, *Fahrenheit 451*, by Ray Bradbury. In this nightmarish vision of the future, all books are banned, firemen work by burning books, and people get all of their information by television. In the movie made from the novel, it begins with the camera zooming in on one house after another showing how all houses had the same television antennas—but of course, no books. Here, then, in Highgate, was the very antithesis of *Fahrenheit 451*. I was living in a world of books—a world made up of the printed word.

I told this to Sylvia and she found it disturbing.

"I don't like the sound of that one bit," she said with

concern. "If we do live in a world made up of the printed word, someone is liable to come along with an eraser and edit us right out of existence. No doubt you've heard the joke about the solipsist who wondered whether he really existed?"

I told her that I hadn't.

"Of course not," she said, "because once his nonexistence came into his mind, he ceased to exist. He created himself and erased himself all with his mind."

"I see," I said. "At least I think I do."

"It's supposed to be a joke," Sylvia explained.

"Oh," I said.

"Only it's really not very funny," she pointed out. "Not funny at all. It's quite serious."

"Then I suppose it doesn't make a very good joke," I observed.

I admitted there were some philosophical questions I didn't quite know the answers to.

Sylvia shrugged her shoulders. "I don't have all the answers either. But I have some of them. An active mind is more dependent on the questions you have—not the answers."

"I have many questions about Satanism," I told her.

"In that case," Sylvia remarked, "let me give you the answers first. That will save us both a great deal of time."

I sensed that I was about to receive a lecture or a lesson, but I never tired of hearing Sylvia speak. Looking at her beautiful face with her eyes staring back at me, always staring back at me linking us together, listening to her mellifluous voice, a voice both soft and hypnotic— these I would never tire of.

"People assume that God and Satan are on opposite poles, but such is not the case," Sylvia began. "They exist on a hierarchical continuum. The hierarchy, from top to bottom, goes like this: God, Satan, Jesus, and finally, humans. God is so vast a power, is everywhere at all times, is everything, and includes all good and all bad. People refer to God as 'He,' but there is no 'He;' God is the force of nature and has no consciousness as humans understand consciousness, only a broad knowledge of everything that happens. God's only purpose is the existence and continuation of the universe. Our planet is of minor concern—much too minor to care about people and such things as prayers. People who pray are really talking to themselves. No one's listening.

"Next, we have Satan. Unlike God, Satan is not infinite. He has a finite existence. Satan's intelligence is more focused than that of God, but still much broader than human consciousness. Yet, in a sense, Satan is human consciousness, but he is more. He is also the consciousness of any being, spiritual or physical. It is God which attempts unity or harmony of all things as a mass— the harmony which preserves the universe as a whole, not the individual elements within it such as human beings. Satan rejects surrender of the will to nature, and celebrates in an awareness of life and the will to do what one wants, not be part of a mass. Satan represents defiance, individualism, rebellion against God and nature. If people are dying of an act of nature such as a plague, it is Satan and the will to live that keeps some of the individuals alive. If one gives their will over to God, Satan is out of their life, for they have no will. However, a person cannot give their will over to Satan—they may only keep it for themselves. If they do, then Satan can be with them. Satan doesn't want servants or worshippers; he wants thinking beings with wills of their own. In this way, we mirror Satan and honor him by living up to our potential. If we have wills of our own, then we are like him. It is human will that keeps people alive after the weak are willing to give up life; it is human will that creates the desire for sex and enjoyment, for wealth and power, for hedonism and self-gratification, and above all—for knowledge of the unknown.

"When one gives their will over to God or Jesus, all that goes away. But no one can give their will totally to God or Jesus, so they are always partly in tune with Satan even though they don't know it.

"Only Jesus gave his will over totally to God. He was supernatural—between God and man—spiritual and physical—able to perform miracles.

"As vampires, we have supernatural powers which humans don't have, but we are far closer to being human than we are to being like Jesus.

"But that's all right. Because what we have is our will. As long as that is kept intact, we are free to grow as Satan intended—to blossom from mundane perceptions to the height of ecstasy, to crawl out of the pit of ignorance and seek the pinnacle of knowledge, and to be all that we are capable of becoming. For, as we evolve, we become more like Satan. And in the mirror, we see Satan and Satan sees us."

There was a silence for a few seconds, then Sylvia asked me what I thought about what she said.

"It seems as though I still have much to learn," I told her.

"Deep inside, you already know all this," Sylvia said. "It's just a matter of remembering it."

"How can I remember something I never heard or experienced?"

"The subconscious mind has many thoughts inside it," Sylvia said. "More than you can imagine. It's just a matter of bringing these thoughts to the surface."

Even though these thoughts did not seem quite as familiar as Sylvia made them out to be, I soon had a feeling of both familiarity and recognition. Looking through the car window, I saw we were in the same area as before, in Bloomsbury, where Sylvia owned a flat, and where the original British Library stood. I glanced behind us and saw that Ronald's Rolls Royce had kept up with us. We drove further on into an area between Soho and Covent Garden, close to Pierre's Doll Shop. Our cars slowed considerably as we entered Monmouth Street, extremely narrow and lined with interesting small shops and restaurants. Sylvia pulled up in front of a shop with the name, Mysteries, and we parked directly across from it.

Ronald's Rolls Royce parked right behind Sylvia's Aston Martin. The six of us walked into the bookstore, all of us dressed in black, all of us wearing pentagrams around our necks—except Sylvia, whose pentagram was around my neck.

As we entered the shop, I noticed incense, oils, candles, and books. Some of the other patrons noticed us—our black clothes and pentagrams. They only glanced for an instant, though, as if allowing their eyes to linger would have been rude. Yet, while they quickly looked away, I realized that their eyes would occasionally stray back to us. Our presence not only aroused their curiosity, it also seemed to validate the store as being an authentic occult supply shop. For a few seconds, I amused myself imagining the six of us on a television commercial for the store, with Sylvia smiling into the camera, and saying, "When we need to perform a Satanic destruction ritual to kill our enemies, we buy our occult supplies at Mysteries. Shouldn't you?"

As I chuckled to myself over this thought, Sylvia asked what I was thinking about. When I told her, she laughed and said such a commercial wouldn't help the vampires to keep a low profile, but would probably be quite a boost for the shop's popularity.

"The Satanic aspect would make the store seem forbidden," Sylvia said. "Whatever is forbidden becomes irresistible."

"Mark Twain would agree with you," I said. "He

thought that prohibiting any behavior was the surest way to create a desire for it."

Sylvia nodded, smiling. "People are funny creatures, aren't they?"

I looked around the store at all the many books dealing with magic and the supernatural. "Think of all the esoteric knowledge in these books," I marveled aloud.

"Think of all the nonsense!" Sylvia exclaimed.

"Nonsense?" I asked. "But isn't this what you study to learn magic?"

Sylvia shook her head, and her long silky black hair brushed against her shoulders. "To truly understand magic is similar to truly understanding life: it often has less to do with finding the truth as it has with eliminating all the illusions. Most of these books were written to obscure the truth, not to reveal it. Those with the knowledge of magic wished to hide it, so they made elaborate and complicated rituals and initiations to discourage others from following them in their quest for power. Magical power does not come from books or wands or candles or accoutrements; it comes from within." And here, Sylvia pointed at her head.

"But what of your books and candles for rituals?" I asked.

"They're only props," Sylvia explained. "The power doesn't come from them; it comes from me—and from you." She pointed at me, tapping the tip of her finger on my chest for emphasis.

"You mean we came here for nothing?" I asked.

Sylvia spoke more softly. "Not at all. If Susan feels that the incense and candles helps her to perform a better ritual, who am I to disagree? Personally, I enjoy the ritualistic side of magic. I love the smell of incense, reciting chants in a candlelit room. It fulfills a certain emotional need. Just realize that all these magical trappings are only a means to an end—not ends in themselves."

Susan and Joseph busied themselves looking through the books on the shelves, while Yvette sniffed one package of incense after another, as Ronald stood around appearing bored, glancing at his watch and sighing.

The door opened, and another group of Satanists walked in, three couples. Like us, they were all dressed in black and had the same silver chains around their necks with the same symbol of Baphomet. Though none of them looked at all like the six of us, their clothes and medallions were alike enough so that they were a sort of mirror image of us. It may not have been an accurate mirror, but I could almost read Sylvia's mind as I saw the amusement in her eyes.

They stopped directly in front of the six of us, as if we were gazing into a funhouse mirror.

"We worship Satan, too," proclaimed one of the men to us.

"Worship?" Sylvia asked. "I don't worship Satan. I don't worship anyone. Satanists never worship anyone."

"Not worship Satan?" asked one of the young women, somewhat confused by Sylvia's remark.

"Worship is done by those from Without; the Elect do not worship, Sylvia explained. "If you've been worshipping Satan, stop at once! Get off your knees, for Christ's sake! Catholics and Muslims kneel before God in worship; Satanists stand before Satan in friendship."

"Then what do you think we should do as Satanists?" the man asked in surprise, apparently too stunned or too curious to be annoyed by Sylvia's remarks.

Sylvia was only too pleased to tell them what to do. "Set a symbol of Baphomet on the wall at eye level. Look the symbol of Satan directly in the eyes. You should see your reflection in those eyes. Say what you want, what is your will, and it shall be yours. Don't beg for anything.

Satan isn't looking for worshippers or followers."

"What is he looking for?" asked the young woman.

"Leaders!" Sylvia declared.

"But who will the leaders lead if there are no followers?" asked the man, confused by the apparent paradox.

"Lead yourselves and follow no one," Sylvia told them. "That's my advice, but don't follow me either. I only lead myself."

"What about him?" asked the young woman as she pointed at me.

"We walk side-by-side, hand-in-hand," Sylvia said. "No one's leading."

The six of them considered Sylvia's words with some interest for a moment, but then the man who had spoken with her suddenly saw something that arrested his attention.

"Wait a minute here," he said, pointing at Sylvia. "You're telling us what a real Satanist is, but I see you're not even wearing the symbol of Satan like the rest of us."

"I don't have to wear a symbol of Satan," Sylvia proclaimed. "I *am* a symbol of Satan!"

"She's not wearing the Baphomet," the man announced to his friends, "so she's not really one of us."

"Not one of you?" Sylvia asked, incredulous. "You're damn right, I'm not one of you! And you're certainly not one of us!"

Yvette smiled proudly at this revelation, obviously happy to be included in the elite group of Satanic vampires, as if we were some sort of an exclusive club that was difficult to join. Yet, as amusing as I found this idea, I realized it was basically true—we were exclusive and difficult to join.

"They aren't real Satanists," the man told his friends.

"Not real?" Sylvia repeated in annoyance. "Here I reveal the truth to the ignorant and you say I'm not real. I may be a Satanist, but Jesus was right about one thing: 'Do not throw your pearls before swine lest they trample them under foot and turn to attack you.'"

"Aha!" cried the man. "She cannot be a Satanist if she's quoting Jesus. A Satanist must be anti-Christian."

"A Satanist is more than just someone who is not a Christian," Sylvia pointed out. "I may not be a Christian, but there are a million other things I am not. I do not choose to define myself by what I am not; my identity is formed by what I am."

"I don't think you or your group could perform a magical ritual if your life depended on it," the man challenged.

"Your life may depend upon it if you don't stop pestering us," said Ronald.

"Are you threatening me?" the man taunted.

Ronald's face tightened and his fist clenched. I hoped there would not be a fight in the store. If Ronald were able to hit him as hard as I could—and I believed he could—then he might kill him on the spot. We had certainly had enough trouble for the night already.

Apparently, Yvette felt the same way. She stood between the two of them and shook her head at Ronald, then giggled as she whispered into Sylvia's ear. At first, I could not believe what she was proposing, but then I realized that with Sylvia's tremendous suggestive powers, it would be a shame not to make use of them. Evidently, Sylvia agreed. Her expression, which revealed surprise for just a moment, immediately changed to one of amusement. She suppressed a laugh, and turning towards the man and the rest of his group, spoke with a straight face.

"*After we leave the store, you will follow us outside,*" she commanded, making certain that her eyes had contact with everyone in the group. Sylvia focused her eyes intently upon the man who had been annoying her. "*And you will remove your pants and run down Shaftesbury Avenue until you either reach Piccadilly Circus or are stopped by the police — whichever comes first."*

We watched the man run towards Shaftesbury Avenue, where thousands of people would be out dining in elegant restaurants or going to the theater for an evening of culture. His friends ran behind him, but Sylvia had given them an additional command to run just fast enough to trail behind him a few feet, but not fast enough to catch him.

Yvette was doubled over laughing in the street. For the briefest of moments, I almost thought I saw the beginning of a smile on Ronald's face.

"Do you think he'll make it to Piccadilly Circus?" Susan asked.

Joseph shook his head. "Not a chance. It's about eight to ten blocks. I think the police will stop him before he reaches it. But then, I could be wrong. He seems to be a very strong runner."

"I noticed he was very well endowed," remarked Yvette, then she began to laugh uncontrollably again, as Ronald glared at her.

As Yvette's laughter died down, Susan went back into the store for a minute, returned to us with the incense and candles we originally came for, and the six of us drove back to Highgate in the two cars.

Once back at the mansion, we were welcomed by Jack and Helen. "While you were out wasting your time buying useless candles and incense," Jack began, "Helen and I made some important discoveries."

"You already told us that before we left," Sylvia pointed out.

"Yes," Helen admitted, "but now we know even more than before. We have the results of the blood tests we did of you and Mark. We'll explain it all tomorrow. I think we may have discovered the secret of your power."

"The secret of our power is Satan," Sylvia said, "and we're going to exercise that power right now with a Satanic ritual—to kill the people who bombed Joseph's car, and to heal poor Lilly."

Jack shook his head. "We won't be part of it. It's a waste of time."

"Fine," said Susan with ice in her voice. "We don't need you anyway. Your negative attitude would only be a drain on our power."

"You certainly missed some excitement by not coming with us," Yvette told them. She then proceeded to summarize, in great detail, the events at the Mysteries occult shop.

They were totally bored until Yvette got to the part where Sylvia commanded all of the Satanists to leave the shop and follow them out into the street. Jack's eyes lit up when he heard this. He looked at Sylvia. "You mean that with one glance, you were able to make all six of them obey you at the same time?"

Sylvia nodded. At once, I could see what she was thinking. She and I had the same thought at the same time. Her abilities had evolved. In the past, she had only been able to make one person at a time obey her commands, and that had taken constant eye contact. In just a matter of a few days, her abilities had changed so that now, only a glance was required—and that glance could affect not only an individual, but a group.

Right after Sylvia and I shared this thought and looked at each other knowingly, Jack and Helen verbalized what we had just discovered.

"Do you realize the significance of this?" Jack asked.

"Yes," Sylvia answered. "Mark and I will be able to control more than one person at a time. That's very nice."

Though Sylvia tried to sound bored, I knew that inside, she was very excited—just as I was.

"That could be useful," Ronald agreed. "Imagine the

business deals we could work to our favor."

"Stop thinking about money for a minute," Helen scolded. "Think of what this means to science." She turned to Sylvia and me. "Don't you realize what this means? If your abilities are constantly evolving, do you realize what the next stage in your evolutionary process will be?"

Ronald suddenly showed great interest. "What would the next stage be?"

Sylvia interrupted Helen before she had a chance to say. "Never mind about that now. I don't want to hear another word of this tonight. Not another word. We'll talk about it tomorrow. Right now, we're going to perform our ritual."

As Sylvia ended the discussion with Jack and Helen, I realized that she did not do so out of an impatience to start the ritual—she did so to stop them from revealing the next stage. Without them saying a word, I also realized what the next stage would likely be. A glance to Sylvia told me that Sylvia knew as well.

The six of us climbed the stairs to the second floor, where the ritual chamber was. Just before we were about to enter, Sylvia said she had to get a pentagram. The two of us went to her room for a moment. As she had told me earlier, she had several extra. This one was also silver, but rather than the size of a quarter, such as the one Sylvia had given me, this one was about the size of a silver dollar. She explained that it was not as old or as sentimental as the one she had given me, and that she only used the large one for rituals.

The six of us entered the ritual chamber. I looked around. The walls and ceilings were black. The room was also smaller than any other in the mansion I had seen. I estimated that it measured twelve feet by twelve feet because I knew the ceilings were twelve feet high, and the room seemed to be a perfect square. A thick black carpet covered the floor. On one side of the room was an altar that held black candles, a silver chalice, an incense holder, a bell, and a dagger. Above the altar, on the wall, was painted a symbol of Baphomet, its silver lines in sharp and vivid contrast to the flat black of the walls. Because of the darkness in the room and the non-reflectiveness of the black paint, the Baphomet was not only the focal point of the room; it seemed to almost float in space.

Yvette placed a piece of incense in the holder and lit it. A pleasant fragrance filled the air. Susan lit two black candles, one on each side of the altar. Sylvia picked up the bell, ringing it towards each point of the compass, as she turned counterclockwise.

Sylvia stood closest to the Baphomet, with me right next to her. "Hail Satan!" she professed, with her arms outstretched in front of her.

"Hail Satan!" the rest of us repeated, all in the same position, staring into the goat's eyes—Satan's eyes.

"In the name of Satan, I command the Forces of Darkness to act in accordance with my will," Sylvia declared, staring intently at the pentagram.

"Our will," Ronald corrected.

I saw Sylvia's expression tighten in anger as Ronald interrupted the flow of the ritual.

Sylvia picked up the dagger. To my relief, she pointed it not at Ronald, but at the Baphomet. She traced the lines of the pentagram in the air. "With this dagger, I cut through the natural order and open the Gates of Hell." She replaced the dagger on the altar. "To all the demons, come forth and greet us, your friends, as we perform this ritual."

Susan picked up the silver chalice, which was passed around to the group, and each of us took a sip of the water it contained.

Sylvia faced the pentagram and addressed it with her hands outstretched. "Satan, our friend, we have enemies—enemies who have tried to kill us. We command, with our combined power, that these enemies be destroyed. In your name, we curse them to die. Hail Satan!"

"Hail Satan!" the rest of us repeated.

"So it is done," Sylvia declared. She then picked up the dagger once more, traced the lines of the pentagram in the air and said, "I hereby close the Gates of Hell." With that, she rang the bell again, and blew out the candles.

As we left the room, I turned to Sylvia. "Is that it? Is it over? Was it an effective ritual?"

"It's over," Sylvia answered. "As to its effectiveness, it would have been much more effective had it not been for someone trying to interfere."

"Don't blame me if your ritual doesn't work," Ronald retorted. "Mark here is brand new to this. If your ritual doesn't work, maybe it's due to his inexperience."

"Mark did not interrupt in the middle of the ritual," Sylvia pointed out. "You were the one. You killed the entire mood. And this wasn't just my ritual. All of us are targets for the car bombs."

"That's right," I agreed with Sylvia. Then turning to Ronald, I added: "Perhaps you don't want this ritual to work."

"What are you saying?" Ronald asked angrily.

"That you may not care what happens to us," I said. "After all, you didn't seem too happy about me sharing part of the money you said Graystone's murder would create and I know you would be happier if I weren't here."

"As far as the money from Graystone's murder is concerned," Ronald said, "it may take two years before we realize any of that. There is no money immediately available just because Sylvia killed him. As to whether I would be happier if you weren't here, you're correct.

You've been here less than a week; Sylvia demands we split our profits with you, you expose us to a CIA agent by trying to be a hero on a plane, you expose us to Father Callen's men, and Yvette is almost killed by a car bomb from enemies you have led to our path."

"None of those things were my fault," I said.

"Perhaps you didn't want them to occur," he said, "but you were reckless enough to cause them to happen. So, yes, you are correct. I would be happier if you weren't here."

"That's fine with me," I replied. "I don't need these problems with you. Sylvia and I can live somewhere else."

"Indeed you can," Ronald agreed. "She has a nice flat in Bloomsbury and an even nicer one in Belgravia."

"Belgravia?" I asked.

"It's the most expensive section of London," Ronald explained. "Many of the residences are now embassies. Sylvia's flat is worth millions."

"Sounds great," I admitted. "When do we move?" I asked Sylvia.

"I don't want to move," Sylvia told me. "Could we discuss this later? Privately?"

"Certainly," I said, placing my arm around her. "Whenever you like."

The group split up at this point, and Sylvia and I went to her room. Sylvia sat on the edge of the bed. Her large, melancholy eyes stared at me.

"Please don't ask me to move out of here now," she pleaded.

"I would never try to force you to do that," I assured her. "I care too much for you to make you move if you don't want to."

Sylvia smiled. "And I care too much for you to force you to live here against your will. If you truly want to leave, I'll follow you, no matter where you want to go."

I sat on the bed next to Sylvia and put my arm

around her. She embraced me, holding me tight.

"I wouldn't want you to move if you would be unhappy, but it seems like you have nothing but trouble from the others anyway."

"Oh, but that's not true! Susan and Joseph are great friends. I love them like brothers and sisters. And Yvette and I do lots of things together. We're good friends, too."

"Yvette? You must be kidding! You two argue all the time."

"Yes, but it's usually just in fun. We really do like each other. Our conflicts only escalated recently because you moved in."

"What did I do?"

"You didn't have to do anything. Your attention to me has made Yvette jealous. She's jealous of my attention to you and also of our relationship. It reminds her of how badly things are going between her and Ronald. She sleeps with other men because he sleeps with other women. Jack and Helen don't like her. She has nothing in common with Susan and Joseph. Ronald ignores her. I'm her only friend. Naturally, she would be jealous."

"I didn't realize that."

"How could you? You don't know her. Anyway, I hope that you can learn to like the others. We can't move into either one of my flats. They're both on long leases. One has thirty years left. The other has over fifty. So we can't move into one of them now."

"All right. I'll try to get along with Ronald. Helen and Jack are tolerable, even though annoying, and the others don't bother me."

Sylvia kissed me. "I'm glad to hear that. Things will get better. You'll see. We'll all get along better. Besides, this is the safest place for us. We're totally secure here."

I tried to keep this thought in mind as Sylvia and I undressed, got into bed and cuddled up with each other. Her smooth skin and voluptuous body made me quickly forget the troubles of the day.

We were blasted awake the next morning by the mansion's burglar alarm. Sylvia jumped out of bed and onto her feet, pulling me along with her.

"Quick!" she urged me. "We must get up! Someone's broken in!"

Chapter Thirteen

As the wailing siren of the burglar alarm woke everyone in the house, Sylvia and I slipped on our clothes as quickly as possible. We rushed out the door at the same time that Susan and Joseph came running down the hall, followed by Jack and Helen, with Yvette trailing not far behind. All of us ran towards the front of the house, then stopped at the stairway.

We could see that the front door stood wide open. Looking down, we found Ronald standing over a body that was sprawled out at the landing below the large staircase. The body lay face down and did not move.

Ronald waved up at the rest of us. "I got one of them," he announced.

The wolves came loping happily into the mansion from outside, viewing the scene with curiosity and sniffing the inert body on the floor.

Ronald turned towards them and pointed his finger accusingly. "Useless bastards! Good for nothing but eating and shitting on the grounds. That's all they do."

The two wolves stared at Ronald and growled, raising their fur.

"I can't believe they would let someone in," Sylvia said, defending them.

"Well, believe it," Ronald retorted. "Here's the proof." He pointed at the body.

As we came down the stairs, Jack asked, "Who is it?"

"I have no idea," Ronald answered. "I've never seen him before."

Sylvia and I drew closer for a better look as Ronald turned the man over on his back. His lifeless eyes stared up at the ceiling and a small trickle of blood dripped from his mouth, as if from an internal injury.

"Father Clifford!" Sylvia exclaimed.

Ronald shot an icy stare to Sylvia and me. "I should have known you'd lead them right to our mansion."

"But isn't this wonderful?" cried Yvette. "You've killed him. You're a hero. Now we're safe."

"I'm not a hero," sighed Ronald in exasperation, "and we're certainly not safe. He wasn't alone."

I asked Ronald if he could identify the other man, and he said he could if he could see him again. Quickly, I ran upstairs and got the pictures I had taken when Sylvia and I were in Highgate Cemetery.

"Is this the man who was with him?" I asked Ronald as I showed him the photo.

"That was him, all right," Ronald confirmed.

"Brother Phillips," Sylvia told the group.

"He had a camera around his neck," Ronald told us. "He was faster than this one. I couldn't stop them both.

He seemed to be carrying some glass vials filled with liquid."

"The lab!" Jack yelled, as he and Helen rushed down the hall. They came back in just a minute and he gave us his agitated report. "They broke into the lab. Stole some of our chemicals. And apparently, they photographed many of our research papers—particularly the ones about you." He pointed at Sylvia and me.

"Why would they do that?" I asked.

"They must want to know about your powers," Helen said.

"No, I mean why would they photograph the papers?" I asked. "Why didn't they just steal them?"

"Perhaps they planned to get these secrets from Jack and Helen and then leave without being discovered," Ronald offered. "Perhaps they thought they would have the time to put the papers back before leaving and I put an end to their plans by catching them in the act."

"Perhaps," I said, somewhat suspiciously. "Not very likely, though. How would they even know about the existence of the laboratory? How to get into it? And especially, what Jack and Helen were researching about Sylvia and me? Perhaps you'll forgive me if I don't believe that theory."

"So what is your explanation?" Ronald glared at me.

"I don't have an explanation yet," I admitted, "but when I get one, it will make a lot more sense than yours."

Ronald stood up and tried to stare me down unsuccessfully.

"This is not the best time for the two of you to argue," Helen told us. "We have to stick together now more than ever."

"What are we going to do about the burglary of our lab?" Jack asked, almost rhetorically.

Sylvia pointed at Father Clifford's body on the floor. "One thing we're definitely not going to do is call the police."

"You should have stopped him and questioned him," I told Ronald. "He certainly can't tell us anything now. Why did you have to kill him?"

"I didn't intend to kill him," Ronald snarled. "He fell off the damn railing when I chased him."

"When you chased him where?" I asked.

"Upstairs!" Ronald yelled, as he pointed up at the railing by the end of the upstairs hallway. "I chased him down the hallway and he fell over the railing."

I glanced down at Father Clifford and noticed for the first time that he had a large crack on the side of his head and that his hair was matted with blood.

"It must have been a very nasty fall," I observed, "cracking his head open on a carpet."

"Oh my!" Yvette said at this news. "The blood stain might not wash out of our expensive Persian carpet."

"Then we'll destroy the carpet," Ronald said.

"No. Wait!" Yvette said, suddenly excited. "I saw this advertisement on the television. I believe it was an

167

American product," she went on to the group as she faced me in particular since the product was American. "Anyway, it was for a cleaning detergent that cleans both blood and chocolate stains. Think of that! The greatest pleasures—blood and chocolate—oh, and sex, of course—leave stains which must be cleaned away. Just think what kind of moral Jack and Helen could make of that!"

"Who cares about your idiotic advertisements?" snapped Helen.

"We're not going to clean the carpet," explained Ronald. "We're going to destroy it, get rid of it, just like the body. If his partner should come back with the police, there should be no trace. After all, if there's no body, there's no murder, is there?"

"We can dispose of the body in the lab," Jack offered. "In the incinerator."

"What are we going to do?" Helen wailed. "If this Brother Phillips has photographed our papers, all our secrets will be out. And these chemicals he stole. I hope it's not what I think it was."

Everyone looked at Helen.

"And what was that?" Sylvia inquired.

Jack sighed. "I think we should all go down to the lab together. We'll find out which chemicals were stolen and which documents were photographed."

Ronald and I rolled Father Clifford's body up in the Persian carpet, then we followed the rest of the group downstairs to the lab. Helen opened the door to the incinerator and we pushed the carpet roll into it. Jack closed the heavy metal door to the incinerator.

Helen looked through her papers, which had been spread out, sheet by sheet, on top of two dissecting tables.

"Whoever did this," Helen explained, "probably wanted to photograph these papers, then put them back so it would not be noticed that they had been tampered

168

with."

"Then why didn't they do that?" Joseph asked.

"Ronald probably put a stop to their plans," Jack offered. "I imagine he surprised them. Most likely, one of them, Brother Phillips, was down here photographing documents and stealing chemicals. The other was upstairs. The burglar alarm went off late for some reason. Ronald came out, caught Father Clifford, but was unable to stop Brother Phillips. That's my scientific opinion based upon the evidence."

Ronald nodded. "That's exactly what happened."

"That's an interesting theory," I remarked. "Tell me, Jack. In this chronology you're constructing, when did Ronald go to the lab?"

"Ronald?" Jack asked. "Who said anything about Ronald going to the lab?"

"Ronald said as much himself just a few minutes ago," I pointed out. "Ronald said perhaps they thought they had enough time to put the papers back before leaving. Now, how would he know that the papers were out in the first place unless he was already down there?"

"If you will bother to remember," Ronald addressed me in a condescending tone, "I said that after Jack and Helen ran down to the lab and after they told us that their papers had been photographed. It doesn't take a genius to realize that if Jack and Helen believed certain documents were photographed, then they must have been out. If all the documents were in their file together and not spread out, then how would Jack and Helen have concluded that only certain documents were photographed?"

I had to concede a certain logic to Ronald's explanation. "That makes sense," I admitted, "but it doesn't explain why the alarm went off after they had been here for awhile rather than when they first broke in."

"I don't have the answer to everything," Ronald said.

"I only got on the scene slightly earlier than you did. Why do you expect me to have all the answers? Just be happy that I caught one of them."

"I don't think we have much to be happy about with this burglary," Helen said. "Let me tell you what Brother Phillips knows now—what I told you Jack and I had discovered about Mark and Sylvia."

All of us listened to Helen with great interest.

"You may remember," she began, as she looked at Sylvia and me, "that I said you two were more vampire-like than the rest of us. Your abilities are greater than ours, but then, so is your need for blood. To make a simple analogy, if we were cars instead of vampires, the rest of us here would be ordinary cars using a moderate amount of fuel, while the two of you would be racing cars—capable of greater performance but with the drawback of requiring more fuel."

"No problem there," Sylvia said. "I enjoy drinking blood."

"It is a problem," Helen disagreed with annoyance in her voice. "It's quite a problem for your victims. But now, Jack and I may have solved the problem. By isolating the difference between human and vampire blood, and then between vampire blood and that of your own, we have been able to come up with an antidote to vampirism."

"Since vampirism is not a disease," Sylvia pointed out, "and since none of us here would care to be human again, it would seem there won't be much demand for your antidote. You would have been better off trying to find the cure for a human disease."

"Ah, but there is a link," Joseph explained. "By isolating the good aspects of vampirism, it would be possible to allow humans to be immune from disease and aging—as we are—but without the terrible need for blood."

"You don't mean that you've found a cure for all

disease and aging, do you?" I asked.

Joseph shook his head sadly. "I'm afraid not. But we may have found the first step—the antidote to vampirism."

"Did you find the antidote or not?" Susan asked. "You just said a minute ago that you found it. Now you say you may have found it. Which is it?"

"We're certain it works," Helen said. "We just haven't tested it."

"I can tell you one thing," Sylvia declared. "You're not testing it on us!" She put her arm around me.

"We would never do that against your will," Jack said. "However, that doesn't mean that Brother Phillips won't."

"Brother Phillips?" Yvette asked.

"He's got part of the antidote, unfortunately," Jack admitted. "That means he can make any of us become human whenever he wants to. Then it would be quite simple to kill us."

"But how could he force us to take the antidote in the first place?" Sylvia wondered.

"Oh, that part is simple enough," Jack said. "It just has to get into the bloodstream. It could be done with a dart gun like they use to sedate animals. Or it could even be mixed with other liquids, which would allow it to penetrate the surface of the skin. In that case, we could get shot with a squirt gun. Or it could be sprayed onto our skin in some other way. Or it could be placed in water that we drink. There are any number of ways."

"One more thing we have to worry about," I said.

"Oh, you and Sylvia have much more to worry about," Helen said. "Since Brother Phillips not only took the antidote, but also photographed the research papers dealing specifically with you and Sylvia, it would seem only logical that he would go after you and her first. After all, from his point of view, the two of you would be the

171

most dangerous.

I looked at Sylvia. "Now do you think we should move?"

Ronald interrupted before Sylvia had a chance to respond. "Forget what I said last night in anger. I certainly wouldn't expect the two of you to move out with this kind of threat against you. I may have lost my temper, but I don't want to be responsible for you moving out to your deaths."

"Why the change of heart?" I asked.

"It's not a change of heart," Ronald said. "I still find you irritating, but I'm not going to try to make the two of you move when it would mean that you would be killed."

I shrugged my shoulders. "I don't see how it could be any more dangerous on the outside than here. They already broke in."

"True," Ronald admitted, "but since Brother Phillips saw Father Clifford fall to his death in here, he knows how alert we are. I doubt he'd try it again. It would be suicide for him to try."

I agreed with Ronald, much to Sylvia's relief. Perhaps it would be safer to stay at the mansion than try to find a more secure place.

"What were these new powers you said Mark and Sylvia were getting?" Yvette asked Helen, changing the subject.

"It appears that the changes in their blood are also changing their abilities," Helen explained. "Particularly those abilities involved in influencing other people's minds. It may become easier for them to put someone into a trance. They may be able to hypnotize several people simultaneously under the right circumstances, such as Sylvia did last night. They may find it easier to hypnotize people during the daytime, something we find more difficult to do. But I think it will go beyond this. I think they will be able to not only control a person's will, but also their perceptions."

"What do you mean?" Yvette asked.

"Sylvia and Mark may be able to cause hallucinations in humans—both visual and auditory. If this is true, they could make someone see and hear something that doesn't exist or fail to see and hear something which does exist." Helen looked at Sylvia and me to gauge our reaction.

"That's a very interesting idea," I said, as Sylvia stood silently. She obviously did not want to talk about it, so I said nothing more.

An awkward silence arose for several seconds, then Sylvia broke it. "Well, I think we have many things to do today. We need to try to track down Brother Phillips. I'm also going to have the license plate traced of the man on our plane—the one who may be a CIA agent. I don't know whether all of the events in the past two days have to do with Callen's men alone. I think there's more to this than meets the eye."

As Helen and Jack started organizing the laboratory, the rest of us went back upstairs to the living room. Sylvia called a private investigator and asked to have the license plate traced. While she waited for the investigator to discover the identity of the owner of the car, she made another call, this one to the hospital. She asked to speak to the doctor of Lilly and her grandmother. Her face brightened somewhat as she had some good news to tell.

"Lilly's grandmother has regained consciousness and will be okay. They think Lilly will make it, too," she said, as if trying to sound happy.

"Then what's wrong?" I asked.

"Lilly's still in a coma." Sylvia's large melancholy eyes stared at me. "They don't know when she'll wake up."

"Maybe we could visit them," I suggested.

"Yes," Sylvia said, suddenly excited. "You're right. We'll see them tonight."

A little while later, the investigator called back to tell us that he had indeed found the owner of the Jaguar at the airport. It was owned by a car rental company. The investigator would try to find out the real name of the man who rented the car, if he could, and he would get back to us.

Yvette entered the living room to speak with us, followed by the rest of the household.

"So what will you do with your new abilities?" Yvette asked us.

"What do you mean, what will we do?" Sylvia asked.

"I think what Yvette means," Ronald explained, "is that since there is so much potential here to increase our income, we should take advantage of it."

"Take advantage of it?" Sylvia chuckled. "What you mean is take advantage of *us*."

"That's no way to talk," said Ronald. "Remember, the eight of us here are a team."

"Funny how it didn't seem that way just a few days ago when you spoke of the money from Graystone's murder," I remarked.

"These new abilities will be too important to squabble over," Jack cautioned us. "They must be used in the pursuit of scientific knowledge—for the betterment of mankind, of course."

"You could use them to make more money," Yvette said, obviously casting her vote with Ronald. She looked over at Jack and Helen. "Mind, now, I'm not saying there's anything wrong with science. I'm sure your experiments are very nice, but—" and here she turned back to Sylvia. "Wouldn't it be just grand to use this on some of the people Ronald does business with? It certainly would turn things to our advantage. He would get the best deal every time. We all would come out ahead. I think you'll agree, we are a fun-loving group, but it's so very hard to have fun without money. Isn't that the awful truth?"

"Don't worry," Sylvia assured them. "I have no intention of wasting any new talents. Perhaps my new abilities will allow me to play the harpsichord better than before, or maybe my paintings will improve. Or I could write a book dealing with Satanic philosophy. Yes, those are the important things: to reach the peak in music, art, and philosophy. What could be better than that?"

Ronald, Yvette, Jack, and Helen all looked at Sylvia with an expression of disgust.

"Yes, Sylvia's right," Susan said. "Besides, it's up to her and Mark what they want to do. I'm sure they'd help us if we needed it."

"But of course," Sylvia agreed. "It's just that if Mark and I are to progress and evolve magically, then we must aim higher than just the mundane things which most humans seek. After all, we are elite! We are the Elect!"

"God damn this elitist snobbery of yours!" Helen told Sylvia. "You can take your Nietzsche and your Machiavelli and your Satanism and stuff them up your ass! I'm sure there's plenty of room."

Sylvia glanced back at her shapely rear end as if trying to evaluate Helen's judgment.

I gave Sylvia a slight caress there with my hand and reassured her. "Don't worry about what Helen says. I think it's perfectly shaped."

Sylvia smiled and leaned her head against my shoulder and sighed.

This only angered Helen more. "Sylvia can be such a snob," she told me. "With all this talk about humans being less than vampires and all. That's why she feels no guilt about killing them. She considers them nothing more than animals."

"That's not true," I said. "What about the little girl at the doll shop? I think Sylvia loves Lilly like a daughter."

"You must be kidding, Mark," Helen said. "That little

girl is just like one of Sylvia's cute little dolls. Just another one out of her collection."

"I don't believe that," I said. "Sylvia really cares for her. And what about me? I was human when Sylvia met me and she fell in love anyway."

"You weren't quite human—and it was the demonic side of you that attracted Sylvia. Your demonic side and the power you gave Sylvia. That's what she really loves—the supernatural power you gave her," Helen said accusingly.

"That's a cruel thing to say about me. I love Mark for himself, not the power. The power wouldn't even exist without our love."

"That's right," I agreed, as I put my arm around Sylvia's shoulder. "She's very loving."

Sylvia nodded. "Yes. Actually, I love people."

Yvette laughed. "Right. Like wolves love sheep."

"Really," Sylvia protested in earnestness. "I need people."

Yvette shrugged. "All of us here need people. Not because we love them. It's because we need their blood."

Sylvia disagreed. "Mark was human when I fell in love with him. I didn't need his blood—just his love."

The two of us waved good-bye as we left the living room.

The others asked us where we were going.

"We're going upstairs," Sylvia answered. "As long as there's no objection."

The others were silent at this, so we made our way to Sylvia's bedroom.

"I don't see how you can tolerate them," I said. "Jack and Helen just look at you as if you were a specimen under their microscope. Ronald and Yvette just care about how much money you can bring them, not to mention that Ronald uses you for his own dirty work."

"Dirty work?" Sylvia asked.

"Killing his enemies," I answered.

"Oh, as far as that's concerned, Ronald's not totally to blame. Nor am I, for that matter. As Jack and Helen already explained, I need more blood than the rest of them do. My metabolism is different. So, if killing someone like Graystone brings our household millions and all I have to do is drink the blood I would need anyway, well..."

"What if you didn't need the blood?" I asked. "What if you weren't a vampire?"

"If I didn't need the blood, then I wouldn't be a vampire, and if I weren't a vampire, I wouldn't need the blood. But I do need the blood because I am a vampire. Or am I a vampire because I need the blood? Well, no matter. It's the same either way, isn't it?"

"But what if Jack and Helen's antidote works?" I asked. "What if they could make us human again?"

Sylvia mounted her life-size carousal horse at the corner of the room. She gave a light tug on the reins, and the pole, which ran from the floor to the twelve-foot ceiling, bobbed up and down for several seconds. It was as if Sylvia's room had been turned into a child's amusement park.

"Make us human again?" questioned Sylvia as she regarded me suspiciously out of the corners of her eyes. "So we can lose all our abilities and grow old? Grow old and die? Were you hoping to do this to both of us or just to yourself?"

"When you put it that way—" I began.

"How else can one put it?" Sylvia asked. She swung her leg over the carousal horse and dismounted. "Taking the antidote would be slow suicide at best, because we would eventually age and die. At worst, though, it would likely mean our enemies would kill us off soon. I don't want to die and I can't live without you. So, where do you stand on this?"

"I suppose you're right," I admitted.

Sylvia walked over to me and placed her arm around my shoulder. "I'm just like Peter Pan," she said. "I don't want to grow old." She became thoughtful for a moment. "We've got to get the antidote away from Callen's men. They'll use it on us if they get the chance."

I nodded in agreement. "How can we find them? And how do we even know it's Callen's men and not someone else? I don't trust Ronald's story about the burglary."

Sylvia thought about this, then said "I don't know if I do either. We've got to protect ourselves without him."

She went to her writing table and opened one of the drawers, then reached up inside a hidden compartment. She pulled out a .380 automatic, complete with silencer, similar to the one the CIA agent had on the plane.

"Another Walther .380? Like the one on the plane."

"His was the Walther PPK."

"Like James Bond's gun," I observed.

"Yes, but this is the PK 380. A much newer model. I'm a modern girl. Let's carry it with us at all times, in case enemies attack during the day. Any more worries I can dispel for you?"

My first worry was whether Sylvia was a good shot. She assured me that she was. To prove it, she opened her window and pointed at some of the trees on the grounds. High in the branches, hidden from view, were tiny metal targets that rotated in the wind. Sylvia could point at any of them and shoot them at will. The pistol shot quietly, just a hushed zipping sound as the bullet went through the barrel and an almost inaudible plink as it hit the target.

"Here, you give it a go." She handed the pistol to me.

I gave it a few tries, but hitting a target about the size of a human heart at a distance of fifty to one hundred feet was not as easy for me. Yet after several shots, I got one of them.

"All it takes is practice," Sylvia encouraged.

"Do the others know about this?"

"We still have some secrets from each other," Sylvia revealed with a smile.

"Speaking of secrets," I began, "there's something I wanted to ask you about."

Sylvia's eyes widened as she stood facing me. Her hands were clasped in front of her and the slender fingers played nervously with each other. Her expression of guilt reminded me of a little girl caught with her hand in the cookie jar.

"You may recall," I said, "that when we were at Pierre's Doll Shop, he mentioned what a good likeness it was. At first, I thought he meant the painting you did of me before we met, but then he said that he meant the likeness he created. So, of course, I assumed he meant the doll he made of you, but then he started to say that he was referring to something else. I never did find out what the 'something else' was. You were giving him some kind of gesture to stop explaining. There aren't any secrets between us, are there?"

"I suppose there are always some secrets," Sylvia admitted. "But this one won't be a secret anymore. Let me show you what he was referring to."

Sylvia went into her closet and pulled out a box about a foot across and three feet long. She stood it up on the floor next to the doll that Pierre made of her, then she opened the box.

Inside was another doll, a perfect half-size version of me.

Chapter Fourteen

I stood there for quite awhile staring at Sylvia and myself in miniature. The doll of me was accurate in every detail except for one—the eyes. To be more precise, since it was apparently made before Sylvia and I ever met, the eyes should have looked human. Instead, they had the black pupils and irises together just as Sylvia had when I met her—and just as I had after she turned me into a vampire.

As I stared at the dolls, Sylvia stared at me, watching my eyes for my reaction to the doll.

"Well?" Sylvia asked. Her hands were still clasped in front of her body in a nervous gesture.

"Well, what?"

"Well, what do you think?" She pointed at the doll, waiting for my response.

"I think Pierre was right. It's a wonderful likeness."

"That's it?" Sylvia said. "You're not angry with me?"

"Angry? Why should I be angry with you?"

Sylvia sighed with relief. All the tension seemed to flow out of her, like a balloon whose air had been let out. She put her arms around me and leaned her whole weight against me, as if she were swooning under a heavy burden. "I was afraid you would be upset with me for having the doll made of you before we met. Since I didn't want Ronald to have a doll made of me, I thought you would be angry with me for having one made of you— that you would think me a hypocrite."

"You may be a hypocrite," I admitted, "but I still love you and I'm not mad at you."

Sylvia winced when I said the word "hypocrite," so I added, "Perhaps I shouldn't say you were hypocritical. Maybe you were just...inconsistent in your judgments on the two dolls."

"Yes, perhaps I was," Sylvia conceded, nodding her head. "But they were made for different reasons. I had

180

yours made because I had already painted a portrait of you from a vision I had long before we met. The vision occurred during a Satanic ritual I performed by myself. Once I painted the portrait, it wasn't enough; I needed more of you. So I took the portrait to Pierre and had him make the doll. A doll is much more like a real person than a painting can be. But that still wasn't enough. So I used the doll in Satanic rituals to lead me to you."

"You cast a spell on me with the doll?"

"No!" Sylvia protested. "Absolutely not! I told you before. I've never cast any spell on you and I never would—even if I could—and I can't. We're both vampires, so I can't do it. Both of our wills are too strong."

"But I wasn't a vampire when you first got the doll and performed the ritual. You could have cast a spell on me then."

"I could have, but I didn't. I wouldn't do such a thing. I wouldn't want you to love me because of a spell. I want you to love me for myself."

"I do love you for yourself."

"Well, then. There you are. We love each other for ourselves. You love my doll. I love your doll."

"And I think the dolls love each other," I added. "They seem to be a very well-matched couple. Don't you think so?"

"Yes, I agree. It's funny. I never imagined there would be dolls of both of us together as there are now. I had the doll made of you as a means to an end—not an end in itself."

"As you suggested yourself, art often becomes an end in itself. You said it takes on a life of its own."

"Yes," Sylvia admitted. "But the reason I had the doll made was so that I could perform a ritual on you—so that I could find you. It worked. The ritual allowed me to find you."

"If only I had owned the doll of you earlier," I said. "Then perhaps I could have found you first."

"That wouldn't have been possible. I'm sure Ronald had Pierre make it very recently—probably after I met you in San Francisco. It was probably made within the past two weeks."

"It's a good thing he had it made. Now if you're ever lost, I can perform a Satanic ritual and find you through the doll."

Sylvia shook her head. "That's one thing you needn't worry about. I'll never be lost. You'll always know where to find me."

"I certainly hope you're right," I said. "I couldn't imagine what life would be like without you."

"I'm sure you could imagine it," Sylvia answered. "Just remember what life was like before we met. That's what it would be like without me."

"No, it would be different," I explained. "Before we met, I didn't know what I was missing all those years. If you were gone now, I would experience a profound loss."

Sylvia gave me an affectionate hug. "Don't worry. I'm not going anywhere without you. Not for a moment. I'm not taking any chances."

This brought to mind what Sylvia had said to Yvette and me when she first received the doll as a gift—that she didn't want to be away from me ever. At first, I thought perhaps she had only spoken figuratively, to emphasize our closeness. Now, I could see that she meant it literally.

I stood admiring the incredible craftsmanship that went into making the two dolls. They were perfect representations of Sylvia and me, except that they were exactly half our size. The Sylvia doll was exactly half an inch taller than the Mark doll since Sylvia was an inch taller than me. Despite her original denial to Yvette regarding this minor difference in our height, Sylvia must have known our correct height all along—even before we met. How else could one explain the way the dolls had been crafted exactly to scale?

When I mentioned this to Sylvia, she admitted that it was true. "Oh yes. When I had my vision of you, it became clearer and more vivid as time went on. How do you think I knew I had to go to San Francisco to find you? Or what you would look like? All these things came to me in magical rituals. That's one reason the others here have wanted me to stay here with them all these years. I'm more useful to them than they care to admit. But enough about me. Since you seem to have acquired my interest in dolls, how would you like to see the world's greatest doll house?"

"Is it in one of the other rooms here?" I asked, expecting perhaps an entire room devoted to Sylvia's hobby.

"No, not here," Sylvia laughed. "I'm referring to Queen Mary's Dolls' House."

"Is it all right for us to go see it?"

"Certainly. It's at Windsor Castle. We can go there right now. It will be a nice drive for us. Let's go."

As we passed the others gathered in the living room, we told them of our plans: to see Queen Mary's Dolls' House and Windsor Castle through the early afternoon or later, and to visit Lilly at the hospital afterward.

We drove out of Highgate, taking North Circular Road in a somewhat irregular half circle on the map till we reached the large M4 Motorway. We immediately accelerated to the legal limit, seventy miles per hour.

"This car can break the speed limit by a hundred miles per hour," Sylvia informed me. "Would you like to see?"

I glanced around at the many other cars on the freeway. "Perhaps a bit later, if it's not so crowded."

Windsor Castle stood about twenty miles west of Central London. We arrived soon, and found ourselves in the countryside. After parking the car, Sylvia and I walked along the River Thames, where swans sailed by in tranquility. We reached the castle after a pleasant fifteen-minute stroll along the riverbank. A tour group was just about to enter the castle, so we followed right behind them. The castle was much larger than I had imagined. I had thought it might be one large building. Instead, it was made of three main sections: the Upper, Middle, and Lower Wards. In the Lower Ward was St. George's Chapel, a beautiful work of Gothic architecture, as well as King Henry VIII Gate. Sylvia informed me that the arch for the gate had holes for pouring molten metal or boiling oil on those attempting an assault; however, since Sylvia and I had purchased our tour tickets, she assured me we were safe. The Middle Ward contained the massive Round Tower, the most prominent of the buildings not only for its size, but also for its shape. The lack of a flat surface also made the walls more difficult to penetrate during an attack. In everything we saw, form and function of design worked together, combining beauty and strength.

The Upper Ward of the castle was the largest. This was where the State Apartments stood. Inside, we saw the paintings of Van Dyck and Rubens, elaborate woodcarvings by Grinling Gibbons, as well as drawings by Leonardo da Vinci.

Perhaps the most magnificent of these rooms was the Queen's Presence Chamber, one of only three rooms to completely retain its Baroque style. The woodcarvings of Gibbons could be found all around the room. Enormous tapestries and paintings of religious scenes and portraits of royalty covered the walls, and there were several busts. The tour guide informed us that one of these was the composer, Handel, who often performed in this very room.

"That's right," Sylvia whispered in my ear. "I've

heard him play right in this room several times. King
George III was very fond of him. I learned to play all his
music while he was alive, just by listening to him play.
Once I hear any music, I can play it. I'm so lucky not to
have to bother with reading the notes. After all, the notes
aren't really music, are they? They're just symbols on a
page."

Sylvia and I departed from the tour group a little
later, and went for a stroll along the East Terrace next to
the neatly manicured grounds, which included shrubbery
that had been pruned and shaped into perfect geometrical
forms. Continuing on to the North Terrace, we reentered
the main door to the State Apartments to see Queen
Mary's Dolls' House.

The Dolls' House was designed to be a grand
mansion in the classical tradition of Ancient Rome and
Renaissance Italy, but with some modern updating.

"Everything here is one-twelfth scale," Sylvia
explained, "one inch to the foot — much smaller than my
dolls at home. The dolls who would live in a house like
this would probably be about five and a half inches tall."

The exterior of the house was a hollow shell, which
could be raised or lowered over the rooms of the interior.

Naturally, it was in the raised position, above the
interior, so that observers could see the inside of the
house. This made it possible to view the mansion from
any direction and see into all of the rooms, regardless of
which side they were on.

Sylvia expounded at length on the Dolls' House to
me. As there was no tour group at the moment in the
room with us, several tourists eavesdropped on Sylvia's
lecture. She described how the Dolls' House had first
been exhibited at the British Empire Exhibitions at
Wembley in 1924. She pointed out the fine details. Tiny
books in the library with leather bindings inscribed with
real gold engraved with the use of a microscope held

works of writers such as Rudyard Kipling, Joseph Conrad, and Conan Doyle. Miniature paintings hung on the walls of most rooms—paintings so intricately done that the viewer would swear that only a five and a half inch tall artist could have rendered them with such accuracy. Miniscule locks opened and closed on the little doors to the rooms with the turn of tiny keys almost too small for a normal human hand to grasp. Hot and cold water ran inside the faucets of the bathtubs and sinks. The floor of the scaled-down kitchen contained 2,500 wood blocks. The bottles in the wine cellar, only an inch tall, contained the best wines of the day. The grandest room of all, the Saloon, contained the thrones for the King and Queen, miniature portraits of King George V and Queen Mary in their Coronation robes, a harpsichord, and walls covered with a cloth woven to the scale of 120 silken threads to an inch.

"I'll bet you would like to have a doll house like this at home," I said to Sylvia.

"There isn't more than one," Sylvia laughed, "and it's quite unlikely one will ever be built again like this."

"What would it cost, I wonder?"

"Far more than our mansion in Highgate," Sylvia answered.

"You mean a real mansion like this would cost more than the one in Highgate?" I asked.

"Yes, a life-size mansion like this would cost far more than our mansion in Highgate," Sylva said. "But this, the Dolls' House, would cost more than a real one."

"More than the real one," I gasped. "How can that be?"

"Simple," said Sylvia. "It takes more work and care to make things this small and yet perfect at the same time."

"So the representation is worth more than that which is represented?" I asked.

"It can happen that way," Sylvia agreed. "I told you that art can take on a life of its own. One must be careful."

"Careful of what?" I asked.

"That art does not take precedence over life."

"I don't think we need to worry about that," I said.

"I worry about it all the time," Sylvia admitted. "If I am turned into an art object, I might cease to exist as a person. That's why I'm fascinated by dolls. I love them and fear them both at once. There is something about a doll—which, of course, is three-dimensional—that a painting or photograph cannot convey. A doll is more real. It's closer to one's real essence."

"Yes," I agreed. "They're like us. We're like them. Someone must have worked very hard to create that world for them," I commented, as I pointed at the Dolls' House. "What if our own world were the same? What if we were created by someone just for their own amusement?"

"What a dreadful idea!" Sylvia declared. "I would hate to be just a creation from someone's mind."

"Why?"

Sylvia pointed her finger at me accusingly. "Because if that someone stopped thinking about me, I would cease to exist."

I put my arm around Sylvia's shoulder and drew her towards me. "How could anyone stop thinking of you? I know I never could. You'll always be in my thoughts."

Sylvia smiled. "Then I will always exist."

"But if we were just dolls, and not real people," I wondered aloud, "wouldn't you like it if we lived in Queen Mary's Dolls' House?"

"What?" cried Sylvia. "And have giant tourists, twelve times our size, peering into our bedroom and pointing at us? Certainly not! How awful that would be. I'd much rather be real."

Thus, with our existential dilemma solved — at least for the moment — we left Queen Mary's Dolls' House.

We began our drive towards Central London with the sun behind us. Within the next two hours, the sun would set, making us perfectly safe again. But during the daylight hours, we had to be more cautious. As Sylvia had explained to me earlier, we probably could survive a gunshot wound, even inflicted during the day. Our bodies would heal as soon as night came, and even if we "died" from a bullet in the heart during the day, we would still revive that evening. However, as reassuring as this all was, it did not provide a safety net for those unusual circumstances — such as a car bomb. Such an incident would have left us with no bodies left to revive.

Sylvia turned on the radar detector and accelerated to 85 miles per hour, 15 miles per hour above the legal limit. I glanced at the tachometer and noticed the engine was barely working above an idle.

Looking around us, I observed the green of the countryside, the trees, the flowers, the Mercedes that was following us.

"Do the police here drive Mercedes?" I asked.

"No, they drive Rovers," Sylvia answered. "Why do you ask?"

"Oh, just curious. Not to mention the fact that a Mercedes is following us now."

Sylvia glanced into the mirror. "Well, let's see if they're really following us after all." Sylvia pressed the pedal to the floor, the acceleration pressed us into our seats like two astronauts blasting off, and when I looked down at the speedometer again, it read 120 miles per hour as it continued to climb upwards.

The Mercedes behind us was apparently trying to decide whether to keep a low profile or catch up to us. In trying to do both, they could do neither.

They suddenly decided that we knew they were

following us, so they threw discretion to the wind and seriously tried to intercept us.

Sylvia motioned to the back seat at her purse. "If you'll open my purse, you'll find something that may slow them down."

I reached back and opened it. Inside was Sylvia's automatic, complete with silencer.

Sylvia pressed down a bit more on the accelerator pedal and we were now going 140 miles per hour. Though the traffic was not heavy, those cars which were in front of us quickly got out of our path.

"By the way," Sylvia remarked. "How do you like the way my car drives at this speed? I think it's remarkably smooth and quiet, considering how fast we're going. Wouldn't you agree?"

"Yes, I suppose it is," I mumbled, as I noticed the Mercedes pull into the lane next to ours. Although it still had difficulty in trying to catch us, it had made progress since Sylvia had stopped accelerating. The men in the car clearly intended to drive up alongside us.

"I really hate to ask you this," I began, "but do you think you could drive a little faster? Not enough to kill us, you understand. Just fast enough to pull further away from this car."

Sylvia kept her eyes on the road ahead as I glanced back at the Mercedes and noticed that one of the two men had a gun in his hand.

"I would love to accommodate you, Mark, and believe me, this car is more than happy to go up another thirty miles per hour, but I'm afraid there's a bit of a traffic jam up ahead."

"Oh shit!" I yelled, as I looked forward to see traffic piled up which we could never get out of.

Our speed slowed down to 110 miles per hour in anticipation of the traffic ahead. The Mercedes was narrowing the gap, pulling up behind us, then about to pass.

I racked the slide, chambering the first round, and switched off the safety.

"I don't think I'm a very good shot," I confessed.

"Oh don't worry about that," Sylvia said. "You won't need to be. They're quite close."

Indeed they were. Very close. The man in the passenger seat pointed his pistol at us as he pulled next to us on Sylvia's side. Sylvia pressed a button and her window rolled down. A blast of air hit us making a loud rippling sound. I looked past Sylvia and her long hair streaming into my face from the wind and aimed at the car next to us. I fired three times in rapid succession. Their side window and their windshield exploded with bits of flying glass, the Mercedes swerved and struck the guardrail. The side of the car was smashed.

"I got the car," I said. "I don't think I hit anyone inside."

"Would you like me to turn around and go back so you can try again?" Sylvia asked. "Or shall we continue on to Central London to visit Lilly at the hospital?"

I replaced Sylvia's pistol inside her purse, then picked up the three cartridges that had been ejected into the back seat, making sure not to get any fingerprints on them as I threw them out of the window.

Sylvia decided against driving directly to the hospital. Instead, we went on a leisurely tour for about an hour. She wanted to be absolutely certain no one was following us.

When we finally got to the hospital, the sun was just getting ready to set as we pulled into the underground parking lot.

We locked the car, then walked hand in hand for just a few steps when we heard a voice addressing us.

"Don't move at all or I shoot," I heard a man say.

It was a familiar voice with a foreign accent, in fact,

the same voice and the same two men who told Joseph what a nice car he had just before it exploded.

Sylvia and I turned around. Two men stood facing us, both with guns pointed at us, both apparently angry. Behind them a Mercedes was parked, with one side terribly dented, and a shattered windshield with bullet holes.

"If it's money you want, I have some in my purse," Sylvia said as she started to reach for her gun inside there.

"Do not move or I shoot you both," one of the men told us. "I do not care about your money."

"You will come with us," the other man demanded.

Sylvia shook her head and smiled in haughty defiance. "I would never be seen in such a banged-up car. It lacks class."

I started to consider our options. We had perhaps half an hour till sunset. I could feel myself growing stronger already. Yet, we were still vulnerable at that very moment and the two men stood about fifteen feet away. They were too far for me to hit them without getting shot or having them shoot Sylvia while I hit them. If Sylvia could have gotten them both to look into her eyes at the same time, she had a chance of stopping them by hypnotizing them, yet I had never seen her do that during the daylight. Despite what Jack and Helen said about our abilities growing, this seemed like a dangerous way of testing them out to see if they worked as well during sunset as during darkness.

"What do you want from us?" Sylvia asked.

"You are to come with us," said one of them.

But even as he spoke, I heard a car in the parking lot accelerate sharply, then suddenly turn in our direction.

I looked to my right and saw a Jaguar F-Type racing straight for the four of us.

The two men turned for an instant towards the

oncoming car as Sylvia and I started to move out of the way.

For a moment, they couldn't seem to decide whether to aim their guns at us or at the car heading towards them.

Everything happened within one or two seconds— from the time I heard the car's engine till I heard the Jaguar strike them both. One flew over the top of the car and landed in a heap, inert. The other limped to his feet, picked up his gun and pointed it at the driver.

The driver got off the first and only shot—one bullet fired from a silenced automatic. The man's head jerked back, then he fell at our feet, blood oozing from his temple, his eyes staring vacantly at the ceiling.

The door of the Jaguar opened quickly and the driver jumped out.

Sylvia and I recognized him right away from his blond hair and moustache.

It was the same stranger from the plane.

Chapter Fifteen

The blond stranger rushed towards the man he had just shot, who lay motionless on the pavement of the underground parking lot.

Sylvia looked down at the man who lay at our feet, saw the blood dripping from his temple and his glassy vacant stare. "You've killed him," she told the stranger.

"Damn!" he exclaimed, then ran several steps to the other man on the pavement, the one he had struck with his Jaguar F-Type. The man's gun lay about ten feet away from him, and though he had not been shot, he was apparently in no shape to get up and reach for it. The man on the pavement looked groggy. Though no external injuries were visible, he breathed with some difficulty, with quick, short, gasping breaths.

The stranger stood over the man and pointed his silenced .380 automatic at his head. "Who sent you?"

The man looked up at the stranger. "You wouldn't shoot me," he said, with a foreign accent.

It was a voice that Sylvia and I recognized. He and the other man were definitely the same two men who stood next to Joseph and Helen's Bentley right before it was blown up by a bomb—a bomb certainly meant for Sylvia and me.

"Who sent you?" the stranger repeated.

"You need me alive," the man managed to gasp weakly. "You can't shoot me."

The stranger shot the man in the thigh. The man let out a scream and clutched his leg in pain. Still, he would not reveal the information.

The stranger from the plane turned to Sylvia and me. "I'm certain these were the men who tried to kill you and your friends. Can you do anything to help me?"

Sylvia and I looked at each other. We knew what kind of help he wanted. What we did not know was exactly he much he knew about us. However, we could find that out afterwards. The first priority was to find out who gave the orders to the two men who tried to bomb the car.

I looked at my watch to see what time it was and realized it would soon be dark. I felt certain that it was sundown and rapidly falling into darkness. My strength had increased in just the past few minutes, and I knew that Sylvia felt the same way. She and I looked at each other and nodded.

Sylvia stood over the man and gazed directly into his eyes. Involuntarily, his eyes remained fixed in place, unable to break the stare once begun. *"Who sent you?"* she asked.

The man spoke in a flat, emotionless voice, mesmerized by the eye contact with Sylvia. "Robert Brandon," he said.

"Robert Brandon?" the stranger asked, obviously puzzled. He looked at us and shrugged his shoulders. "Who the Hell is Robert Brandon?"

The man on the pavement did not respond to the stranger's question. He could hear only Sylvia's voice.

She continued eye contact. *"Who is Robert Brandon?"* she asked him.

"He is the man who hired us," the man said, his voice lacking in the normal human tones, but still betraying the difficulty in speaking due to his injuries.

"What organization is he with?" the stranger asked.

The man on the ground didn't respond to the question. The trance had rendered all sounds inaudible — except for Sylvia's voice.

"What organization is he with?" Sylvia asked, repeating the question.

"I am not aware," the man answered.

"Why did he want you to kill us?" Sylvia asked.

"We were told not to kill you."

"*Then why did you plant a bomb in the car?*" Sylvia asked, with some frustration.

"To kill you."

"But you just said you were told not to kill us," Sylvia pointed out. "*So why did you plant the bomb?*"

"We were told to kill you then. Not now." The man's voice wavered, despite the trance Sylvia had placed him under.

He began to cough violently. A trickle of blood spilled from his mouth, then his head flopped to the side, limp.

"He's dead," Sylvia said.

"Are you sure?" the stranger asked. He felt for the man's pulse. "Perhaps his heart is still beating."

"No," Sylvia said. "His heart stopped as he coughed."

The stranger froze, suddenly realizing that Sylvia and I heard the man's heart stop beating. "How did you know that?" he asked. The question seemed designed to merely confirm his correct suspicions about us.

"Suppose we ask you some questions?" Sylvia proposed. "For example, what were you doing down here in the car park?"

The stranger smiled. "Actually, I was waiting for you. I called the hospital and found out that you planned to visit the little girl who was injured in the bombing. So I thought I'd wait here to talk to both of you. I didn't expect those two men. They were a complete surprise to me."

"To us, too," I remarked, then turned to Sylvia and added, "How did they know to come here for us? We hadn't seen them for an hour. We had lost them, yet they were here first, waiting for us."

"The hospital staff knew you were coming to visit the girl," the stranger offered. "Perhaps they found out from one of them."

A security guard suddenly stumbled onto the scene,

his mouth and eyes opening wide in shock at seeing the two dead bodies and the stranger holding a gun with a silencer.

"Don't worry," the stranger explained to him in a calm, soothing voice. "Everything's under control here." He pulled his wallet from his pocket and flashed it open and closed rather quickly, too fast to possibly read it. "I'm with the Secret Service."

"Should I be calling the police for you, sir?" asked the security guard.

"No need," the stranger answered. "I've already called them. They're on their way. Why don't you wait out front for them and direct them here as soon as they arrive."

"Yes, sir," the man said, in a snappy military fashion.

After he left, I remarked, "You're not with the Secret Service." I didn't tell him how Sylvia and I knew this — that we could listen to his heartbeat just as we did with the man who just died, but in this case, use the slight fluctuations in his heartbeat as a lie detector.

He shrugged his shoulders. "Close enough. A mere technicality. We're all on the same side, anyway."

"We are?" asked Sylvia. "What side is that?"

"The side against these people who tried to kill you. The side against the terrorists who hijacked the plane."

"And who are you with?" Sylvia asked.

"Like I said, I'm with you two. We're all on the same side." He pulled his wallet out again, but this time held it open so that we could see his identification. "I'm with the CIA. The name is Henry — Matthew Henry."

He reached out to shake hands with me. As we did so, I glanced at Sylvia and knew that she was thinking the same thing as I was. She and I had both listened carefully to his voice and his heartbeat for the slightest waver as he spoke to us. We both concluded that he was telling us the truth.

"Just how much do you know about us?" Sylvia asked.

"How much does who know about you? Me? Or the CIA?"

"Both," Sylvia answered.

"Myself, I don't know all that much about you. I know what they think I need to know. Of course, I have no idea what they know. I assume they know more than I do, but then there is no way for me to be sure. I'm given a few pieces of the puzzle. Maybe someone else has the whole picture somewhere. Maybe not. Maybe they only have a few pieces of the puzzle. What I do know is that you're responsible for killing one of the terrorists on the plane. That saved hundreds of lives. I know that you have some kind of strange power to make people do what you want them to. The CIA thinks that kind of ability could be very useful."

"Useful to whom?" Sylvia asked.

"To us," Matthew replied.

"Do they understand how I killed the hijacker on the plane?" Sylvia asked, "Or where these abilities come from?"

Matthew looked down at the ground. "There are a lot of things we don't understand."

"When someone looks away, I always feel it's a sign of dishonesty," Sylvia remarked. "You're not afraid to look us directly in the eyes, are you?"

He looked up nervously, his eyes moving around, not settling on either one of us. "No, of course not. Why should I be afraid of that?"

"Yes, why indeed?" I said. "After all, you mentioned that we're on the same side. Aren't we?"

"Listen," he pleaded, looking at both of us directly at last. "If I were your enemy, I wouldn't have come here to stop these men. You can hypnotize me if you want. I realize that I can't stop you. But you'll find it won't be necessary. I can tell you what I know because I really don't know everything anyway, and what I do know I'm allowed to share with you. They wouldn't have told me anything about you that they didn't want you to get out of me because they knew that you could hypnotize me and get the information anyway."

"So what do you know?" Sylvia asked.

"I know how you killed the hijacker. I know that both of you practice Satanism, that you have some sort of unusual psychic powers, and that you are vampires." He paused here, as if this revelation came out with a great deal of effort.

"Does the CIA know this?" Sylvia asked.

He nodded. "Yes, they knew before I did. Of course, when I say 'they,' I'm not talking about the whole agency. Probably only a tiny handful of people know. We want to keep it a secret. "

"So they approve of our activities?" questioned Sylvia.

"I wouldn't say that they are about to hand you the Mother Theresa award for humanitarianism," Matthew remarked, "but they are very understanding in regards to your situation."

"Understanding?" Sylvia queried with a sly smile. "You mean that you and the CIA don't mind that we kill people?"

"I'm not a policeman," he said. "And we're not concerned with a few random murders that you commit. We're interested in the big picture. We take a larger view of life. The little details you're referring to don't concern us. We're concerned with threats against our whole country—and your country," he added, addressing Sylvia specifically. "We believe you can help millions of people with your abilities. If a few individuals need to die to accomplish that, it still works towards the greater good, doesn't it?"

Sylvia looked at me and chuckled. "It would be fun to introduce him to Jack and Helen, wouldn't it?"

"Yes," I agreed. "They could sit around and discuss ethics together."

"Speaking of discussing things, I've got some things I'd like to discuss with both of you." Matthew glanced around nervously to see if anyone was watching, but we were quite alone. "I really do have to call the British Secret Service so that we can try to identify these bodies. I must get them over here and get these bodies removed before the police or the press find out about this."

"I don't think we'll wait around for them," Sylvia said.

"No, of course not," he agreed. "But I still need to talk to you two later."

"About what?" I asked.

"About helping us."

"Helping with what?" I asked.

"Helping us to track down the leader of this group would be a nice start. After all, they are trying to kill you."

"Suppose we helped you to find their leader," I said. "Then what?"

"You could help us get all the information we need on this terrorist group—the ones who hijacked the plane. All you would have to do is put them in a trance like you did before."

"You make it sound so simple," Sylvia said. "Do you realize how a vampire is able to put someone in a trance?"

"I'm not exactly sure," he admitted.

"More importantly," Sylvia said, "do you know when a vampire is able to put someone in a trance?"

The CIA agent thought for a moment. "Not really."

"Usually right before drinking the subject's blood," Sylvia explained. "That is when the vampire has that power—just as the thirst comes on."

Matthew glanced uneasily at the body of the man Sylvia had hypnotized. "What if..." he began, as he swallowed nervously, "what if you used your energy to hypnotize someone and then you were unable to satisfy your... your thirst?"

"Oh that would never happen," Sylvia reassured him. "I always satisfy my thirst."

Unconsciously, his hand went to his neck, as if checking to make sure it was still there.

Sylvia laughed. "Don't take things quite so seriously. It's bad for the heart, you know. We're not going to attack you. After all, you helped us out twice."

He breathed a relieved sigh. "Then you don't have to satisfy this thirst right now?"

"Hmm, that's an interesting question," Sylvia remarked. "I didn't feel I needed to before you mentioned it, but now..."

Matthew's eyes widened and his heartbeat quickened.

Sylvia laughed again. "Where's your sense of humor?"

He attempted a weak smile. "I'm happy to hear that things are under control."

"Oh, they're under control, all right," Sylvia agreed. "Our control."

"Will you help us then?" he asked.

"I hate to get involved with politics," Sylvia said. "I'm much more interested in the arts."

"But these people are our common enemies," he said.

"This year perhaps," Sylvia answered. "In the future, though, these terrorist countries may be our allies. I remember when the Germans, the Japanese and the Russians were all considered enemies of England. Times change. If you go back far enough in history to the American Revolution, you'd find that we were your enemies. I try not to look at countries as being enemies;

only individuals are enemies. After all, countries are just names of places. The places would exist without the names. The people would still be individuals even if they didn't identify themselves with others who live in the same area. I'm not interested in fighting abstract enemies."

"These aren't abstract at all," Matthew protested. "These are individuals who tried to kill both of you."

"He's right," I told Sylvia. "I think we should try to help him. Together, we could be a lot more effective in getting rid of our enemies, and at the same time, we'd be helping both of our countries." I pointed at the bodies of the two men. "Don't forget, they not only tried to kill us, they're responsible for what happened to Lilly."

Sylvia nodded. "All right. I agree."

Matthew stepped forward and handed a card to us with an office phone number and his cell phone number. "If you'll call me tomorrow, I'll be able to tell you everything we've found out about these two men—who they are and who they work for."

"One of them already told us who he worked for," I pointed out. "Robert Brandon."

"Whoever he is," Matthew said.

Sylvia and I turned to walk away after saying good-bye, but right before leaving, she looked him directly in the eyes, locked her gaze onto his, and said, *"Do not repeat to anyone what we have said about us. Do you understand?"*

He nodded his head mechanically as we walked away.

After taking the elevator upstairs, we went to visit Lilly and her grandmother. The grandmother lay in a separate room. Apparently, she was not as close to the bomb blast as Lilly. The hospital told her that she would be able to leave within the week, while Lilly would have to stay there until she came out of the coma—if she ever did.

We pushed the grandmother down the hallway in her wheelchair The three of us entered a room where a nurse sat inside. She glanced up from reading a book as we entered, then stood. Lilly lay upon the bed, her eyes closed as if she were merely sleeping.

"Lilly, you have some visitors," her grandmother said. "Sylvia and Mark have come to see you."

Lilly lay perfectly still. Only the slight movement of her chest from breathing told the casual observer that the little girl was not really dead.

"Lilly, we're so sorry this happened to you," Sylvia began, as she stood closer to the little girl's bed and leaned over towards her. "I know how you feel, Lilly. I fell asleep for a very long time once. I thought I would never wake. No one else thought I would, either. But they were wrong. Eventually, I did wake up. So will you."

"She can't hear you, Miss," the nurse said. "She's in a coma, she is."

Sylvia turned and glared at the nurse with hate in her eyes. *"Silence!"* she commanded. The nurse froze.

I held Sylvia's hand as she turned back towards Lilly.

"Listen to me, Lilly," She placed her other hand on Lilly's face and stroked her hair. "You're too young to stay here in this bed. You should be out playing and having fun. You must get better. Your grandmother is here. So is Mark. We're all waiting for you to get well."

As Sylvia said this, one of the doctors came into the room with us. He stood silently, trying not to allow his feelings of futility to show. While he did not echo the thoughtless remarks of the nurse, I could tell that his feelings were not much different. While his education and his experience had not increased his hope or faith, it had developed his sense of tact.

Sylvia looked down at Lilly in melancholy adoration. She still held Lilly's hand and mine. Her eyes welled up with tears. She did not let go of Lilly's hand or mine, so the tears brimmed over the lower eyelids and rolled down her cheeks and fell on Lilly's face. Sylvia's grasp on my hand tightened somewhat as her emotions increased.

"I want you to open your eyes and look at me," Sylvia told her. *"Open your eyes and look into mine."*

As she said those words, I felt something pass between Sylvia's hand and mine, like an electrical current joining our two bodies. For several seconds, I felt as if my energy were drained, then restored. We stood between the hospital bed and the nurse and doctor and grandmother, so they did not see what I saw. As Sylvia told Lilly to open her eyes and look into hers, Lilly's eyes opened with the suddenness of a doll coming to life by magic.

"You will wake up now," Sylvia told her. *"You will be perfectly well."*

"Sylvia!" Lilly cried, reaching out for her as she sat up.

The nurse gasped and dropped her tray. As it hit the floor, a glass shattered. The doctor gaped in shock at Lilly and Sylvia.

"It's a miracle!" Lilly's grandmother declared. "A miracle from God!"

"Not quite," remarked Sylvia, as she cast me a devilish grin. She gave Lilly an affectionate hug.

"Where are we?" Lilly asked, looking around confused.

"We're in a hospital," Sylvia answered, "but you're all better now, so you'll be going home."

"Just wait a minute here," the doctor protested. "You can't tell her that."

"You're too late," Sylvia said. "I already told her."

At this point, another doctor walked into the room. Chaos broke out as both doctors, the nurse, and Lilly's grandmother all began shouting at each other simultaneously.

Lilly turned left and right like a mechanical doll, watching the action with amusement. She turned to Sylvia, then said, "I'm so glad you're here. You're always such fun. "

"And I'm so glad my little girl is well," Sylvia answered.

Despite the fact that Sylvia wanted to spend time with Lilly, she suggested that we both leave. The doctors had called in other doctors; they began to ask questions Sylvia did not want to answer. Sylvia preferred the grandmother's explanation: a miracle. She told Lilly she would call on her soon at her home, then we walked out of the room.

As we left the pandemonium behind us, I turned to Sylvia and said, "So the power of Satan can be used to heal as well as to hurt."

"But of course," Sylvia replied. "Magical power is neither good nor evil, black nor white. It can be used for any purpose. It is only the minds of people that label something as good or evil. There is no such thing as black magic or white magic. Those are only names—value judgments. The magic exists without the labels and names, so there is no such thing as good or evil magical power. Whether an action is good or evil depends not only on how it's done and what the result is, but also how it is perceived. Good and evil are not inherent in deeds— they exist within the minds of those who interpret them."

"Well, I interpret it as a wonderful thing you did back there."

"What we did," Sylvia corrected. "You and I did it together."

"I didn't do anything."

"No?" Sylvia asked. "Didn't you feel something pass between us right before Lilly woke up?"

I admitted that I had, as I recalled the strange feeling of an electrical current joining us.

"Don't you understand yet? It's not just me. It's the two of us. Part of my power comes from you. You watched me hypnotize the terrorists and heal Lilly, and I know these things seem incredible to you, but I couldn't do them nearly so well before we met. Don't put me on a pedestal; there isn't room for both of us to stand on one. Better to put me at your side."

"All right," I said, as I put my arm around her and we made our way to the Aston Martin in the parking lot underground.

The bodies and the CIA agent had both disappeared.

We drove back to Highgate and summarized the events of the day to all the others—all except for Helen and Jack, who had gone out.

"Here's one of the strangest parts," I said. "These men said they were sent to kill us yesterday, but that they were told not to kill us today. Why would they change their mind from murder to kidnapping in one day?"

"Perhaps they felt you would be worth more alive than dead," Joseph offered.

"Maybe they were going to hold you for ransom," Yvette said. "Make the rest of us pay to get you back."

"Perhaps they wanted to force you to reveal everything about the rest of us," Ronald suggested. "After all, we are worth more as a group than as individuals. We're worth more money that way, and I suppose we're also more formidable enemies. They might have felt that they would be better off trying to kill all of us than just the two of you."

"Then why didn't they try to kidnap us yesterday?" I asked.

"Yesterday, they had the opportunity to kill five of us at once," Susan said. "They may have believed it better to kidnap just the two of you now, then kill all of us later."

"Doesn't it seem odd that a murder attempt was made on us last night and a kidnapping today by the same two people and that we were burglarized this morning?" I asked.

"If you're looking for oddities," Ronald said, "don't you think it is odd that all this trouble started when you came here?"

"I didn't bring the terrorists or Father Clifford here," I protested.

"We've had more trouble in one week with you here than in all the many years without you," Ronald told me. "And now you're even making friends with the CIA. I can't believe that you two just let him leave like that without finding out everything he knew. That was the time to use your hypnosis."

"We talked to him," Sylvia said. "We could tell when he was telling the truth. He may have left something out, but the things he told us were basically true. Besides, we'll be able to talk to him again."

"That will be another mistake," Ronald said. "If you were both smart, you would have hypnotized him, found out what he knew, then killed him."

"But he saved our lives twice," I responded. "He killed one of the terrorists on the plane, and he killed the two men who were after us today—the same men who almost killed your wife yesterday."

"Yeah, what about that?" Yvette yelled at him.

"Next time you see him, give him my appreciation," he said to me with a sneer. "Anyway, you can all stand here and argue among yourselves. I have to go out."

"Did you want me to come?" Yvette asked halfheartedly.

"It's business," Ronald stated, shaking his head slightly.

"Hmm, business," remarked Yvette. "Yes, I suppose I have my own business to attend to."

"I suppose you do," Ronald said crisply as he strode out the door without looking back.

Yvette stamped her foot angrily. "Damn him! He's out seeing some girlfriend or mistress, isn't he?"

Joseph and Susan shrugged their shoulders.

"I hope you won't take this the wrong way," I told her, "but you and Ronald are the most mismatched couple I've ever seen in my life. How did you ever meet and stay together all these years?"

"That's really two questions, but I suppose I can answer them both. We met in 1856, just two years after Joseph and Susan met. We had an affair for about a year, then he turned me into a vampire."

"A year seems like a long time to have an affair with him a vampire and you still human," I said. "Why did he wait so long to change you?"

"He was already married to someone else—the woman who made him a vampire. He couldn't just leave her right away and marry me. If he had, he wouldn't have been able to keep her money without raising suspicions."

"So after a year, he divorced her and married you?"

"No, he married me a year after he killed her."

"Killed her! He killed his wife to marry you?"

"Of course," Yvette explained. "It was the only way. She had all the money. They met. She turned him into a vampire. We met. He killed her. We waited a year. He turned me into a vampire. We married. Quite simple."

"What could be simpler?" I asked sarcastically.

"Don't be so self-righteous," Yvette scolded.

"Aren't you worried that if he could kill someone he was romantically involved with before that he might do it again?" I asked.

Yvette smiled and raised her eyebrows. "Aren't you?"

"Why should I be afraid?" I asked. "You're the one who's involved with him, not me."

"And you're the one involved with Miss Femme Fatale here," Yvette said, pointing at Sylvia. "You've only been together for what, two weeks?"

"It will be three weeks tomorrow," Sylvia said.

"Well, Mark, if you and Sylvia stay together for just one more week and she doesn't kill you, she'll have set a new record—a one-month relationship! Think of that! A whole month! Most of her other relationships didn't last that long. Do you know why? Because she killed them all, that's why."

Sylvia looked at me and shook her head. "That's not true. They weren't relationships."

"What a nasty thing to say," Susan said to Yvette.

"It is a nasty thing to say," said Yvette, nodding her head in agreement, "but a far more nasty thing to do."

Sylvia turned away from Yvette and began to walk upstairs to her room. I put my arm around her shoulder.

"Will I never be rid of my past?" she asked.

"I don't even know all of your past," I admitted.

"But I told you about my life when we were in San Francisco," she said.

"Apparently, not quite all of it," I said, as I opened the door to her bedroom.

Sylvia sat on the side of the bed and tried to wipe her tears away as she looked at me. "How can I tell you all of it? It would take me three hundred and fifty years to tell you everything. That's how long I've lived. Then at the end of three hundred and fifty years, I would have to summarize our time together discussing the first three hundred and fifty years. We'd never catch up. We'd spend our lives talking about our lives instead of living them."

"Perhaps you could tell me the most important parts," I suggested. "What happened after you became a vampire and how you happened to kill previous lovers accidentally. I assume it was accidental, wasn't it?"

Sylvia nodded and dried her tears. "All right. I'll tell you what happened before we met. I can't guarantee that it will all be nice, but it will all be true."

Chapter Sixteen

"As I told you in San Francisco," Sylvia began, "my family was not large—I had only one brother and one sister, both older than me. We lived in a small village north of here. I was born in 1666—the same time as the Great Fire and the Great Plague. Together, those two events destroyed most of London, but later, the city was completely rebuilt. However, as a girl, I never visited London. We lived about thirty miles north. In those days, that was a much longer distance.

"I lived a particularly isolated life. My family practiced witchcraft. Not Satanism, just paganism, but even so, this did not endear us to the rest of the village. We used magic just to grow a better crop, to help banish sickness, things of that sort. We didn't use it against the villagers. Even so, I had no friends in the village. The parents did not want their children to play with me. I worked on my parents' farm, played with my brother and sister, but rarely saw people from outside. We were considered outcasts.

"Fortunately, there were fewer public witch trials in England during the 1680s, the time I was growing up. This was just a decade before the Salem witch trials in America. However, mob rule could still take over, and it did so against us. In 1685, a man tried to force my father to sell our land. Later, this man was killed by a vampire. Although the vampire had nothing to do with us, the villagers believed that if we practiced witchcraft, we must be vampires, too. They came one day while I was out in the field picking flowers. Dozens of them descended on our small house. I was too far for them to notice me, because I was just one person and they were so many. They pulled my mother and father and brother and sister out of our little house and murdered them, hanging them from a tree. I sat out in the field in shock, unable to do anything to help my family. After all, what could I do against dozens of crazy people? Although they couldn't see me, I was close enough to see everything clearly—clearly enough so that to this day, I can still remember it as if it just happened. When I screamed, some of them heard me and chased me into the forest. It felt as if I ran forever. I lost most of them, but one of them caught up to me, and as I turned, I twisted or broke my ankle. The villager was about to attack me with a pitchfork, when he was attacked by a stranger—not one of the other villagers. The stranger killed my attacker. But then I realized there was a price for me to pay. My savior was a vampire.

"The vampire they feared lived in the mausoleum there. After rescuing me from the villager, he raped me. This was my first sexual experience. I had made it all the way to nineteen years old without ever having sex because girls did not have sex until they were married, and of course, no one wanted to marry me. You may think that nineteen is still a young woman these days, but back then I was considered an old maid. Most girls were married by sixteen or seventeen. By nineteen, most had children. Yet, here I was, unwanted and untouched by any man all my life, and my first sexual experience was to get raped at the edge of a graveyard by a vampire. After he was done, he drank my blood, almost killing me. But at the last few seconds, he had a change of heart and decided to make me a vampire. He forced me to drink his blood, and I passed out.

"When I woke, it was three days later inside the mausoleum. He told me that his name was Alex, and that he decided to spare my life so that he would have a companion. He certainly picked the wrong woman and the wrong approach. I hated him more than anyone I had ever known, except maybe the villagers who killed my family.

"However, as he began to explain what vampires could do, I realized that perhaps becoming a vampire was not so bad. While I hated Alex and had no desire to be with him, he had unintentionally given me the one thing I wanted most of all: the ability to seek vengeance on the villagers who murdered my family.

"I planned to leave him as soon as I knew all I needed to know about my new condition. He must have suspected this, because he was always threatening to kill me if I left him, but we both realized this was an empty threat. I refused to have sex with him, and as a vampire, I was now strong enough to resist him. We didn't love each other, so although he was angry that things did not work out the way he wanted, I think he realized that there would really be no advantage for him to keep me around. I never found out, because just a few days after my first encounter with him, I left during the day while he slept. I never saw him again.

"With my new power, I was able to kill off several of the villagers responsible for my family's death. I killed one every night for several nights, then finally decided on a plan to kill all of them at once. I placed a number of posters up around the village in the middle of the night, saying for all the villagers who killed the Martin family to meet at the church. I promised that a vampire-hunter would meet with them to discuss killing the vampire. By preparing oil-soaked rags in the basement of the church the night before the meeting, I was able to trap them inside by using my new strength to board up the exits with heavy beams, then light the church on fire. No one escaped the blaze. As far as I knew at the time, I had avenged my family and brought their murderers to justice.

"The village was in chaos for days after this happened. I used the confusion to my advantage. The same evening that I killed the villagers, I broke into the houses of the wealthiest among them, stole their gold and fine jewelry, and a horse and small carriage to carry it all in. By the time the rest of the villagers realized that the wealthiest victims had some of their valuables missing, I was gone.

"I disappeared from that village and arrived in London. I had the most expensive ladies' clothing from the women I had stolen from who were my size, though most of the women weren't my size. In 1666, a girl five feet, five inches tall was taller than average. I know what you're thinking. How could I have been five feet five then, when I am five feet eight now? Simple. I grew three inches in the three and a half centuries. People are getting taller all the time. If a vampire were to stay the same height for centuries, after a long time everyone else would be taller than the vampire. A hundred years from now, you'll probably be an inch taller—but then so will I, so I'll always be one inch taller than you. But anyway, the point is that I was considered to be slightly tall then, just as I am now. I think that my height, combined with my fine clothes and substantial wealth, allowed me the respect and freedom I needed in London. I bought a magnificent house and opened several businesses. While women certainly did not have all the rights that a woman has today, money was a great equalizer. By passing myself off as a wealthy widow, I had many privileges that a young never-married woman with no money could never hope for. After all, I was a high-class lady.

"This all seemed like a funny game to me. Me—an unsophisticated farm girl, pretending to be a wealthy widow of position and breeding. But then a strange thing happened. I became what I pretended to be. Not a widow, of course. But I began to read all the classics, became curious about science, read all the literature and philosophy that I could find. I studied art and learned to paint. I studied music and learned to play the

212

harpsichord, something I had started while a teenager at home.

"What had started as a charade turned into a self-fulfilling prophecy.

"But even though I had the education, the culture, and the breeding of a fine lady, something still wasn't right. I felt that somehow I was still just acting and that one day everyone would discover that I was just a simple farm girl who was pretending to be someone else. This may sound strange. One would think that what I should have worried about was that they would learn that I had killed almost a hundred people from my village in vengeance, but I rarely thought about that. My main concern was that people would learn what the real me was like and that I would lose their respect. So I spent even more time reading and studying and painting and practicing my music.

"I even had a special harpsichord built for me. As you know, the notes of a harpsichord die away faster than those from a piano, thus the reason music can be played so quickly on them. I had one built so that the notes could be even shorter. Coupled with my speed on the keyboard, I could play music faster than any human in history, music more complex. Now, just as the instrument and the composition are more complex, so is my hearing as a vampire. Not only can I play faster, I can hear the fast notes distinctly in a way that humans cannot. They can't play this music nor can they hear it the way I intended it. In addition, I have played so long that my musical knowledge and talent exceeds that of Bach and Scarlatti, but there are no humans who can hear all the notes! You can hear them as a vampire, but still can't appreciate it fully yet, because you haven't learned enough about music—but you will, you will eventually. For now, though, in the entire world, there is only one individual who can hear this music the way it was composed—me. I play for an audience of one. This is the price of genius—an ever-dwindling audience for one's art until most people cannot understand or appreciate it. Is it worth it? Yes. The important thing is to reach the top of the mountain. Don't be surprised if no one is watching when you are at the peak. After all, there's very little room up there. It's only logical that when you climb to such lofty heights, you will look around and discover that you are alone.

"Anyway, I looked around and saw that I was alone. What could I do about it? As time went on, I had less and less in common with humans. In my attempts to become 'good' enough to be accepted by them, I became so much better that I became bored with them. I gave musical concerts. I sold some of my paintings. But regardless of how much approval I received for my art, I never felt that the approval was actually for me. I never felt loved.

"I didn't understand what love was. I didn't even understand sex. I had only had sex once, and that was when I was raped. The only real physical pleasure I received was when I drank blood. Usually, I didn't kill my victims. When the thirst became strong, the ability to hypnotize would occur—but only then, just as with other vampires. I could put victims into a trance when the thirst was strong, then drink their blood. I would stop before killing them. The saliva of the vampire causes the wound to close back up and heal right away, so they would wake up weak, but alive, with no marks to show what had happened and no memory of the feeding. This was the way it was for me. This is the way it is for other vampires.

"But I soon learned that there would be occasions when things would not work so smoothly. And wouldn't you know it, those occasions were sex.

"After several years of celibacy after my rape by Alex, I decided to give sex a try. Now, of course, you already know that becoming a vampire has made it possible for you to feel things physically that you never could when you were human. You know that pleasurable sensations are many times more enjoyable for a vampire. So you can imagine what it was like for me. All the pleasure and none of the pain. My pulse shot up, my sensations went wild, every feeling in my body increased—especially my thirst.

"Against my own intentions, I found that right in the middle of sex, my thirst increased beyond my control, my canine teeth grew from normal length to the temporarily longer length for feeding, and I could not control myself. I could not stop. I bit him on the neck and began to drink. The trance was automatic. He didn't struggle. It was just like a continuation of the sex act. In the passion of the moment, I felt wonderful. I had now found a new sensation to add to that of drinking blood. In the swirl of all these sensations, I thought how wonderful it would be to combine these two pleasures.

"But then as my pulse and breathing gradually slowed down to normal, I realized that my partner was more than just weak and tired. He was dead.

"At first, I couldn't believe it. I tried to wake him up. Then I began to cry and couldn't stop.

"The first time I had ever enjoyed sex, after years of celibacy, and then that happened to me. Even though I didn't actually love the man I had slept with and accidentally killed, the experience gave me a terrible message: I could not love or be loved.

"I tried to disprove this message, over and over, but each time, the result was the same. Finally, I learned that if I drank a great deal of blood from one or two victims before I had sex, then it would be possible to limit the amount of blood I drank from my sex partner. By the way, that's the reason why I wouldn't sleep with you when we first met in San Francisco. That's why I waited for over a week of seeing you every day. I needed to be sure that you were serious enough about me to not just have sex, but to survive the blood drinking, the transformation, and still stay with me afterwards."

"As I recall," I said, "you didn't ask me whether I wanted to be a vampire. It was forced on me."

Sylvia frowned. "Well, yes. I suppose it was." She nodded. "But then, what choice did I have? If I had told you the truth about me on the first day that we met, what would you have done?"

"I don't know. I probably wouldn't have believed you. If you told me that you were a vampire and wanted to turn me into one, I would have just assumed that you were crazy."

Sylvia nodded knowingly. "Then I was right in not telling you the truth."

"Let's hope that the days of surprises are over," I remarked. "No secrets between us from now on."

"Right. No secrets," Sylvia agreed. "That's why I'm telling you all the terrible things about me now."

"You don't seem terrible to me."

"Wait, there's more," Sylvia promised. "Despite the wealth I had, and all the wonderful talents and abilities I was able to cultivate, everything was still not perfect. I had lost my family. I had no real friends because I couldn't share my secret with anyone. Last, but not least, I had no love.

"I tried to share my secret a couple of times to see if a man could still love me after realizing that I was a vampire. One tried to kill me. The other tried to escape to tell others about me. I had to stop them. What else could I do? In both cases, I had to drink all their blood. I realized that it would be impossible to tell my secret to anyone, which meant that I could never really be loved. And, if I could never be loved, how could I love someone else knowing that the feeling could not be returned?

"My life started to feel more and more empty. One

day, in 1766, eighty-one years after I had become a vampire, I decided to return to my village for a visit. Even though my face had not changed in all those years, I looked different. I was a wealthy lady from London, not a poor farm girl. The people from the village had changed even more. Most of the ones I had known had died in the fire I set, which I felt was justice for their murder of my family. The few who might have known my family or me had died, it seemed. After all, it had been eighty-one years. I was nineteen when I left, so anyone who had been the same age there when I was young would have been one hundred years old when I returned. Let me tell you, in the middle of the eighteenth century, no one lived to be one hundred years old.

"So it seemed reasonable that there probably weren't any inhabitants left at the village who would still be alive and who would recognize me after my absence of eighty-one years.

"I was wrong about that. The village had changed. The people had changed. My clothes and mannerisms had changed. But even after all that time, one thing had stayed the same—my face. In all those years, I had aged maybe five years, and that happened in the first five years of being a vampire. So I may have aged just a few years into my mid-twenties and then I stayed the same ever since. Always in my twenties.

"My face that had not changed—the eternal youth that is perhaps the nicest thing about being a vampire— that was to be my undoing. That and my own foolishness, for I did the stupidest thing in my entire life. I made the worst mistake, and then paid dearly for it.

"Just on a silly whim, I decided to visit the mausoleum where I had been turned into a vampire. This was after I had walked around the village. I hadn't seen anyone there I recognized, so I thought I was safe. Though I did not recognize them, that did not mean that they did not recognize me. They had heard about me. Ancestors had described me to them. There were even people who had drawn pictures of me in case someone should see me in the future. They had been waiting for my return all of those years! I had become a legend. I don't know what I was thinking. Perhaps I was being self-destructive by going back there. I was so lonely and unhappy, I often thought of killing myself, but lacked the courage. Perhaps going back to my village was some sort of subconscious death wish. I don't know. But if it was, it was about to be fulfilled.

"I decided to spend one day's rest inside the mausoleum where I had become a vampire. I woke to a stake being driven into my chest. A crowd had gathered around me and I found that the stake had paralyzed me. As they gaped at me, debating what to do with my body, I found myself unable to do anything. It was like the coma Lilly found herself in, except this was worse, far worse. Although I couldn't move my eyes, I could see anyone who happened to pass in front of me. The man who had driven the stake into me was William Callen's great-grandson—both related to Father Callen. William Callen died in 1685 in the fire I set inside the church. I had been particularly satisfied by his death because I had seen him murder my mother. And now, years later, his great-grandson—an old man, had driven a stake into my chest, had paralyzed me, and was telling the rest of the villagers that the final solution was to chop off my head.

"No matter how miserable life is, there is nothing like the threat of death to inspire the will to live.

"Some of the other villagers weren't sure about whether decapitation was the best answer; some believed that burning my body would be more desirable. Because of my cataleptic state, they were not aware of my terror. They discussed my decapitation and burning as if they were mulling over the fine points of farming.

"Fortunately for me, one elderly man, apparently a leader of some sort, told them that it would be sacrilege to destroy my body because the stake through my heart had already killed me and sent my soul to God. Little did he know! Anyway, he left the stake in my chest, but stuffed a piece of garlic in my mouth, then placed a cross around my neck. Despite Callen's protests, the old man won the approval of the crowd.

"They hammered the lid of the coffin shut and left me in the darkness. Eventually, I must have lost consciousness. I don't really know. As I said to you before, I lay inside the coffin for exactly one century."

"Can you remember what it was like?" I asked. "Do you remember the entire one hundred years or was it all a blank?"

"That's the strange thing," Sylvia explained. "It wasn't either one. I cannot remember the entire time. I remember almost nothing of being inside the coffin, yet it was not a blank. "

"But wouldn't it have to be one or the other?" I asked.

"No, it was something different," Sylvia said. "My body may have stayed inside the coffin, but my mind did not. My mind or spirit or soul—whatever you want to call it—did not stay inside the coffin. It went somewhere else for that century."

"Where did it go?"

"You may remember," Sylvia said, "that I explained how the first three dimensions occupy space, the fourth dimension is time, and the fifth dimension is mental activity. I was in this fifth dimension. It exists right alongside us all the time."

"But if it's only a mental activity, is it real?" I asked.

Sylvia laughed. "Only a mental activity? What do you think reality is? Without our mental activity, what would reality be?"

"I don't know," I admitted, "but it seems that reality exists without it being perceived by us."

Sylvia smiled. "Our perceptions create our own reality. How is this? A snake sees infrared light; humans can't. A dog hears a high-pitched sound; humans can't. The light and sound both exist, don't they? Yet human perception says they do not. To the human eye and ear, that infrared light and high-pitched sound do not exist. Such is human reality. In perception of abstract ideas, some humans can grasp the most intricate concepts; others cannot, and for them, the intricate concepts cannot exist. What is real? That depends upon what is inside of us just as much as what is outside of us. We perceive both the inner and outer worlds with our minds."

"But isn't our perception of the inner world dependent upon our perception of the outer world? By outer world, I mean external reality."

"Certainly," Sylvia agreed. "Our inner thoughts and perceptions are influenced by the outer world. But realize that the reverse is also true. Our perception of external reality depends upon our sensory perceptions. A human hears only those sounds within a narrow range. So who hears reality—a human or a dog? A human only sees a certain spectrum of light and misses those infrared rays that the snake can see. So who sees reality—a human or a snake? One can come up with examples for every sense. If we have knowledge of reality only through our senses, then it must be very limited, certainly limited to the limits of our senses.

"But that's not all. Our perceptions of external reality are influenced by our mind. Our attitudes and expectations allow us to experience things others cannot. A mother searching for her lost baby in a crowd can see it more clearly than someone else. A soldier in the jungle sees the slightest movement that could be the enemy. We notice and remember that which we look for and concentrate on.

"Finally, there is an internal world, the fifth dimension, apart from space and time. It coexists alongside reality, yet is separate. One can exist within it and perceive things beyond the five senses. Such was my existence for one hundred years."

"I can't imagine what that would be like," I admitted.

"I suppose not, because you haven't experienced it yet. However, the funny thing is—you were there with me."

"How can that be?" I asked.

"Don't you remember what I said?" Sylvia asked. "You and I are one."

"I remember, but I thought you were speaking figuratively."

"No, I'm not," Sylvia answered, shaking her head. "As I said before, you and I are twins, born of the same Satanic seed. The same demon has existed in both of us for hundreds of years."

"But I didn't even exist back then."

"Not in this form," Sylvia explained. "But you did exist. We were together during the entire one hundred years that I slept."

"But I can't remember," I protested.

"Don't worry," Sylvia said. "Eventually it will come back. Some of it, anyway. I can't remember everything from my century-long sleep, either. Much of it was a blank—like sleep itself. When I woke, I could not remember everything that had happened during the entire one hundred years, just parts of it. Even in normal sleep, one cannot remember everything that is dreamed at night, but every part of every dream is stored in the brain and in the mind, just as every external experience is in the memory.

"What finally woke me was the sound of the mausoleum being entered. Someone broke down the door. I heard voices. Then the lid of my coffin was ripped off its hinges, as if it were merely cardboard. A candle burned so brightly after a century of darkness that I couldn't see clearly. Later, I realized that the change in my vision was not just due to being accustomed to the darkness—it was a change in my eyes. During the century that I slept, my pupils grew larger until they reached the size of the pupil and iris together. My eyes, which had been brown, both as a human and as a vampire, had changed to black because of my isolation in darkness."

"But why did my eyes become like that immediately after becoming a vampire?" I asked.

"Because you were made from me," Sylvia explained. "You are part of me. And I am a part of you.

"So I looked at whatever crossed my field of vision. I still could not move my eyes. All I could see were silhouettes. These silhouettes called my name—Sylvia Martin, and asked each other what they should do with me. I was so terrified, feeling that the villagers had come back to finish me off. Instead, they passed the candle around so that I could see their faces. Four men and four women dressed in an unfamiliar manner. One of the men pulled the stake out of my chest. One of the girls approached me with a dagger, but instead of plunging it into me, she slit her own wrist, as if it were the most natural thing to do, and allowed her blood to drip into a silver bowl. One by one, the others followed her example. When the bowl was filled, the girl parted my lips and began to slowly pour the blood into my mouth. As it started to go down my throat, I was able to actively drink it, then raised the bowl with my own hands. The others helped me to sit up in the coffin. The wound in my chest healed right away. After a few seconds of stunned silence, I asked them who they were, and whether they realized that I was a vampire.

"They all thought this was very funny and began to laugh. Not only did they know that I was a vampire—they knew my name, that my family had practiced magic when I was a girl, and that I had been staked in 1766.

"When they said all that, I knew that something was not right. I was correct. They told me I had slept for one hundred years! My first reaction was to cry. I had lost a hundred years of my life. Everyone I knew in the eighteenth century would be dead, my house would have been taken over by someone else, my bank account empty. Most of what I had gained during my eighty-one years in London as a vampire before 1766 was now gone, except for some jewelry and gold I had buried in case of an emergency.

"They tried to comfort me by explaining that they were also vampires, and that I could come live with them. This sounded fine, but I wondered what they expected of me in return since I had nothing to give.

"They told me that they practiced magic and they knew that my family was executed by a mob for witchcraft. They expected me to have some sort of magical power, but I explained to them that I knew almost nothing of the magic my family practiced. Besides, my family practiced a form of witchcraft closer to the celebration and worship of nature. These vampires were Satanists. I didn't know anything about Satanism or about them, but that didn't stop them. They apparently knew all about me—or at least they thought they did. It seemed that a legend had grown around me. My family's execution, my murder of all the villagers who had killed my family, my transformation into a vampire, my return to the village eighty-one years later looking the same, and my presumed execution by the stake—all these events created a legend that these Satanic vampires had heard. They believed I had powers that they did not.

"This struck me as somewhat amusing at first, but I

soon discovered that they were right. I did have powers that they did not. My century of sleep created a change. At first, the most obvious was the color of my eyes, but then I noticed other things. My power to put someone into a trance was much stronger than theirs. I could do so whenever it was dark. They could hypnotize only immediately before they drank someone's blood, and then only to stop their struggles. They couldn't make them do something against their wills. Something happened to me during that long century which increased my powers, just as something happened again when I drank your blood a few weeks ago. Those two incidents created a change within me. Of the two, let me assure you, it was far more pleasant to drink your blood than to sleep inside a coffin for a hundred years.

"The point is that I became what they expected me to be. Just as in the eighteenth century, I pretended to be a lady of class and sophistication and then became one; now, in the nineteenth century, I was to assume the role of a Satanic vampire with great powers. This also came to pass. Just one more self-fulfilling prophecy. Action leads to thought; thought leads to becoming. One can become what one pretends to be if action and thought are strong enough.

"I was very happy to go back with them to the mansion in Highgate. Before we left the mausoleum, Susan gave me a Satanic medallion. I have worn it ever since, until only three weeks ago—when I gave it to you."

I looked down at the silver symbol of Baphomet around my neck, on a silver chain. "Do you miss it? Do you want it back?"

"Oh no!" Sylvia protested, placing her palm on it pressing it and her hand against my chest. "You must wear it always—as a symbol of my love. I don't need to wear it. Remember what I told the pseudo-Satanists in the Mysteries bookshop? 'I don't have to wear a symbol of Satan; I am a symbol of Satan.'

"Anyway, as I said, Susan gave me the medallion and we all left together in two coaches to the train station. I was so shocked to see the train and hear all the noise it made. Its speed frightened me. I had never gone that fast on a horse before. As Joseph and Susan told you, the Underground had already started back then, though it certainly wasn't that extensive. But you cannot imagine my bewilderment at all the changes that had occurred over the century while I slept.

"It was now 1866. The standard of living had gone up for most people, but many were still poor. A cholera epidemic that year killed thousands of people. That same year, my favorite book was published: *Alice's Adventures in Wonderland*. Bookstores sold many books. I could read as much as I wanted. In 1766, it had been much more difficult to find things to read. But the Victorian age was one of incredible progress: industrial, artistic, and literary. In 1766, St. Paul's Cathedral dominated the London skyline, but by 1866 there were many new buildings. The designs, which may seem quaint to you, appeared modern to me. I spent time reading in the British Library. I even went to a women's college in the 1870s, which was quite a progressive thing for one to do at the time. A few years later, I got my own bicycle, something that gave women a new sense of freedom.

"My life in the nineteenth century was far happier than the previous century. I had new abilities. I had new friends. I had money as I did before. But once again, I lacked love.

"This was accentuated all the more because I was the odd person out. Four couples—but only one of me. Susan and Joseph were my best friends. She knew more about magic than any in the group. As Joseph told you in the car, he actually paid a female vampire to transform him so that he and Susan could have eternal life together. Some of the other 'love stories' aren't quite so nice.

"Ronald had been turned into a vampire just over ten years before my reawakening in 1866. Yvette was a prostitute and began having an affair with him, even though he was married to a vampire. If this sounds not too good regarding Yvette or Ronald, both were actually quite common."

"Ronald and Yvette?" I asked.

Sylvia laughed. "No. Their two situations—his philandering and her prostitution. Prostitutes were a much larger percentage of the population in Victorian times. There were few occupations open to the unmarried woman in 1866. Oh, she might work as a governess if she had the education. Or she might work as a dressmaker if she didn't mind a sixteen-hour day. Or she might be a servant. But none of these occupations suited a beautiful girl like Yvette. Because of all the prudery of the Victorian times, prostitutes were in demand. It was often the only way a man could enjoy sex. Women were told they were not supposed to enjoy sex. It was a duty to be endured with the lights out and for having babies. There was a terrible double standard, a schizophrenic standard. A man would marry a virgin who was pure and try to keep her pure, so he often had his good times with a prostitute whose purity he wasn't concerned with. However, some prostitutes were not streetwalkers, they were just 'kept' women—mistresses. This is what Yvette became for Ronald. Divorce was almost unheard of, so these dalliances were to be endured. However, Ronald's first wife was not an ordinary woman—she was a vampire—and a rich one at that. Ronald saw no way out of the problem except to kill his wife. He waited a year for mourning purposes, naturally. After all, he had to keep up appearances. Then he married Yvette."

"Not exactly a storybook romance," I remarked.

"Nor was Helen and Jack's," Sylvia said. "They also

met around the same time as Ronald and Yvette. Helen was married to a man who was a vampire. Helen and Jack killed him, then married later. Of course, they now say that it worked out for the greater benefit of humanity. You know, all the scientific knowledge that they will contribute together. They rationalize everything."

"Can't someone become a vampire without someone else being killed?" I asked.

"Yes, but who is going to transform someone into a vampire?" Sylvia asked. "Only someone who is already a vampire can do that, and they were probably transformed by someone else. Starting a new relationship usually means breaking off the old one."

"Yes," I agreed, "but it doesn't require murder."

"Back then it was easier to get away with murder than to get a divorce," Sylvia explained.

"And what happened with you?" I asked.

"I never intentionally killed anyone I was involved with," Sylvia said. "As I explained before, I had trouble having sex because sex aroused my thirst. Many times, I tried to have a normal relationship, but as I told you, when I explained the truth to men, they either tried to kill me or tell everyone else. There were a few times when I actually found someone willing to become a vampire. I drank only part of their blood, then allowed them to drink mine—the usual method for the transformation. But for some reason, they didn't change into vampires. They just died. My blood killed them. Helen and Jack already explained that my blood is different. The vampire nature is more present in it, thus the reasons for my extra powers. At least, that's the way they explain it."

"Then why didn't your blood kill me?" I asked.

"As I said before," Sylvia explained, "you and I are one."

"But didn't you make someone else into a vampire?"

"Yes," Sylvia said. "About thirty years ago. He went

through the entire change. But then, whilst we both slept, I accidentally drank his blood. When I woke up, he was already dead. That's whom Yvette referred to. This was what I was so afraid could happen to you."

I remembered back just a couple of weeks in San Francisco when Sylvia and I woke to discover that she had drunk some of my blood while she slept. She cried and cried, afraid that she might accidentally kill me, but she didn't go into all the details at the time.

"How long were you together with this man?" I asked.

"Less than a month," Sylvia replied. "About the same amount of time I've been with you."

"Happy anniversary," I said, somewhat sarcastically.

"This is serious," Sylvia pleaded. "Don't make light of it."

"I'm trying to keep my sense of humor," I said. "Believe me, it isn't easy. It's not a pleasant thing to think about."

"You're absolutely right," Sylvia agreed. "Let's not allow ourselves to think about it. Let's think happy thoughts."

We did so. Before we knew it, one happy thought led to another. We found ourselves gazing into each other's eyes, which led to caressing each other, which led to making love.

This we did with extreme passion, as if it might be our last opportunity.

Chapter Seventeen

Sylvia and I woke together the next day, seemingly both simultaneously, our eyes opening at the exact same moment.

After gazing at each other for a long time in silence, Sylvia said, "I like it when you stare at me without turning away. It makes me feel close to you."

"Thank you," I answered. "I like it, too."

"However, to truly see my mind and how I think, don't try to only look into my eyes; rather, look through them—as if you were me. See the world as I see it—and you know me."

"That's exactly why I wanted to hear more about your life—to understand and know you better. To learn all about your past."

Sylvia sighed. "We British are always looking back at our past, our history, our background. Vampires have a much longer past than humans because we've lived so much longer and have more memories. So, it stands to reason that since I am both British and a vampire, I live in the past more than almost anyone. It makes me sad and nostalgic. Before I met you, I would become depressed thinking about the past all the time. The span of my life overwhelms me sometime."

"Don't let it depress you. If where we have been were more important than where we are now or where we are going, then we would all walk around backwards, wouldn't we?"

"You're right," agreed Sylvia, suddenly cheerful.

"And speaking of where we're going, it's Saturday. Should we do something special?"

Sylvia smiled. "All days are the same to me. The names don't matter. The days don't even realize that they have names. But to answer your question, we should always do something special, no matter what day it is. We should go to Central London this evening. See a play at the West End or maybe see a show at the Hippodrome. Or go dancing, something I wouldn't normally do unless Yvette dragged me along with her. But now that you and I are together, perhaps dancing would be fun."

"We should also call the CIA agent and find out if he knows who those two men were and who this Robert Brandon is."

Later, as the two of us were walking downstairs quietly, we heard part of a conversation between Yvette and Susan.

"He thinks he's the only one who can play that game," Yvette told her quietly, "but the truth is, I'm seeing someone else myself now."

"Oh, I don't believe that he thinks he's the only one who can play that game," Susan answered. "I don't think that at all. I think he knows that you're seeing someone else. Maybe that's why Ronald is seeing another woman."

Yvette shook her head. "No, that can't be. He started this first. He's been having weird schedules for months now. I just started seeing this man, so Ronald started it first this time." Yvette suddenly turned around upon hearing Sylvia and me coming down the long circular stairway. "Eavesdropping?" Yvette asked us.

"If I wanted to be nosy," Sylvia replied, "I would barge into your bedroom unannounced while you and Ronald were in your underwear. That's how nosy you are."

"Well, if you're going to listen in," Yvette said, "you may be interested to know that we're going to do some very serious shopping today."

"Mark and I could do that," Sylvia said. "He should see all the great places to go."

"We'll be spending more money," Yvette retorted. "We're both buying new cars."

"Susan and I are going to replace the Bentley,"

Joseph told us.

"What are you getting?" I asked.

"Another Bentley," Joseph said, and then with a gleam in his eye, added, "but this time, the turbo version. It will be practical in case we should be chased as you were."

"Joseph is so practical," joked Susan.

"It costs more than Ronald's Rolls Royce!" Yvette exclaimed.

"I certainly hope our superior car won't upset him," Joseph said.

Yvette shook her head. "That won't bother him at all. I'll tell you what will really upset him..."

Everyone looked at Yvette as she paused for effect.

"What will really upset him is when he gets the bill for my new car." Yvette beamed with satisfaction.

"You haven't told him?" Susan asked.

Yvette shrugged her shoulders and grinned. "As you know, we don't tell each other everything. I want this to be a surprise."

"What's this about a surprise?" asked Ronald, as he entered the room.

"Joseph and Susan are getting a new Bentley," Yvette said. "Isn't that a surprise?"

Ronald stared at Yvette as if she were crazy. "What's so surprising about that? They had one before."

Yvette turned away from Ronald to change the subject and addressed Sylvia. "I'm sorry about what I said to you and Mark last night. I'm sure you wouldn't kill Mark — at least not deliberately."

Sylvia glared at Yvette.

"Wait," Yvette said. "That came out wrong. I don't think you'll kill him accidentally either. After all, it happened a long time ago."

I noticed that Helen and Jack had just entered the room and listened to this exchange with their ever-present scientific curiosity.

"Yes," Sylvia agreed. "It was a long time ago. Over thirty years ago."

"Thirty-three, I believe," said Helen.

Suddenly, Sylvia and Susan looked at Helen and then at me, and finally at each other.

"Mark," Susan began, "didn't you say that you were thirty-three years old?"

I nodded, and while I could not see the significance of this fact other than Sylvia's last significant lover had died in the same year that I was born, I noticed that for Susan and Sylvia, this seemed to be a revelation of sorts. I also knew that as powerful as Sylvia's magic was, she still relied on Susan for her magical theories.

"I think I know why your last lover died," Susan said to Sylvia. "You remember what you've said about the same demon from another dimension splitting into two halves and uniting you and Mark? I believe that this demon did not want you to unite with any other man, especially as a vampire. So it made your blood unacceptable to the systems of most of them and killed them. When you were finally able to create a vampire, you did so at the same time of Mark's birth—thirty-three years ago. But after you turned that man into a vampire, Mark was born. The demon now had two physical bodies in this dimension: yours and Mark's. It caused you to kill the other vampire while you both slept to cut off any bond between you and any man but Mark. The act of killing him was unintentional by you, but deliberate on the part of the demon. The demon was actually jealous of you and the other man. After all, your union with the other man could have prevented you and Mark from joining, which would have prevented the demon from uniting its two halves."

Everyone looked at Sylvia.

"Do you remember the date that you killed him?"

232

Susan asked.

Sylvia said the date aloud.

It was the exact date of my birth.

"Then that's it." Susan nodded her head. "During the demon's transitional state, right before Mark was born, you were able to create a vampire for the first time because the demon was in a state between that of the fifth dimension and ours. Once Mark was born, the demon came into its full existence in this dimension since there were now the two halves. Once Mark was born, it immediately killed the other lover. You have nothing to fear as far as Mark's safety is concerned. It would not allow you to kill Mark. That would be spiritual suicide."

"That all makes sense," Sylvia admitted, "but why did I drink Mark's blood while we slept just a couple of weeks ago? "

"That was just to exchange the blood," Susan said. "It was to mix and unite the two halves of your magical selves—not to kill Mark. I don't see any danger to Mark at all."

"I agree," said Helen. "Even though I don't believe in all of Susan's magical theories, I think she is basically correct. The blood drinking between Mark and Sylvia was instinctual and done for the purpose of the evolutionary process. As a scientist, I can't call it magical, but I have to agree with most of what Susan said. I just don't have the proper name for what I want to describe."

"That's one of the reasons for practicing magic. To fill the gap that science can't always fill." Sylvia turned to me. "And that's just one more reason why the names don't matter. Two people might be trying to say the same thing, but use the wrong names and don't understand each other. Meaning is inherent in reality—not in the labels used to describe it."

"With all this talk of demons and dimensions, I guess Sylvia could just say that the devil made her do it." Yvette laughed. "That's always a good excuse."

"Don't be stupid," Sylvia told her.

Yvette looked at me. "As stupid as Sylvia makes me out to be, even I have read some literature during my century and a half on this earth, and I certainly know that light symbolizes good, and dark symbolizes evil. Since I have hair and eyes that are light, and Sylvia has hair and eyes that are dark, I must be the good vampire, and Sylvia is the bad vampire."

Syliva shook her head. The shiny black bangs of her hair swept back and forth above her exotic dark eyes. "On the contrary, I'm much better at being a vampire because I rarely even think about good and evil."

Helen sneered at Sylvia's comment and turned to me. "How can you love Sylvia, knowing how evil she is? All the people she's killed needlessly and her total disregard for morality?"

"I'm not sure if I know what you mean by needlessly," I replied. "I know that she needs more blood than you do because of her metabolism. I know that she killed the people who murdered her family. I know that she accidentally killed several men she tried to become romantic with. Is that as bad as killing your husband or your wife?" I first looked at Helen, then at Ronald. They had no answer immediately, so I continued: "I'm not God passing judgment on her morality. I'm just a man who is returning the love she gives to me. Maybe she hasn't been nice to the whole world, but she's been nicer to me than anyone else ever has; she's loved me as no one else ever has, and I love her as I've never loved anyone else before."

Sylvia gazed into my eyes and smiled. Her large eyes, misting over in a combination of joy and sadness, reminded me of one of Margaret Keane's paintings of wide-eyed children.

"What a nice thing to say," remarked Yvette. She

clapped her hands as if she were applauding a play or a speech, then turned to Ronald. "Why don't you ever say anything like that?"

"Because I'm not in love with Sylvia," Ronald said.

Sylvia grimaced. "I certainly count myself as fortunate in that regard, but let's not think of such unpleasant things. How about some music?"

With that, she crossed the room to her other harpsichord—in the living room. Unlike the one in her bedroom, this one was ornately painted and decorated with real gold leaf. It had a double keyboard, with black naturals and white sharps, the reverse of the black-white combination on a piano. She began to play, then reminded me that it was a piece she had played for me in San Francisco, *Partita Number 2 in C minor*, by Bach. Her fingers flew across the keyboard playing the complicated tune with perfection.

Helen, Jack, and Ronald appeared bored by this. However, Susan, Joseph, Yvette, and I enjoyed it. Her music enchanted me, just as did her voice; it was a delight for me to listen to either one.

"Isn't that wonderful?" asked Susan as Sylvia finished.

"Don't encourage her," Helen said. "She already has a superiority complex."

"It's not a complex," Sylvia retorted. "I am superior."

"We don't care about your superiority in music," Jack said. "But we're very interested in what you were able to do with your hypnotic powers yesterday. Making someone answer questions is something that is probably not that unusual for you, but how did you hypnotize that little girl to get well?"

"Yes, tell us the secret behind that," Helen urged.

Sylvia regarded them warily. "Do you really want to hear my explanation?"

"Yes," Jack said. "You must have transferred your

energy to her somehow. The way I see it, in a healing of this type, healing energy goes from the healer to the sick, renewing and healing the sick, but leaving the healer drained of energy. Psychic vampires reverse the process, taking energy from the victim, leaving the victim sapped of energy while the psychic vampire is renewed. A real vampire transfers so much energy—not just blood—that the victim sometimes dies from lack of energy and sometimes also from lack of blood, while the vampire receives so much energy that he or she is renewed to the point of having superior longevity and other powers."

"That's an interesting scientific explanation," Sylvia said. "However, according to someone religious, a Christian or a Satanist might say that the healer or the vampire is not the source nor the end recipient of the energy, but rather, a conduit or transformer."

Jack considered this, then rejected it. "Well, a Christian might say that it's a three-stage process, with energy flowing from God to healer to the sick person, but that theory breaks down and falls apart if you reverse it. The energy starts with the victim, flows to the vampire and stops there; it does not go on to Satan."

"That depends whether you see it as a two-stage or three-stage process," Sylvia elucidated. "If the healer and God are united as one, then you still have three entities in the process, but two of the three are united. If I am at one with Satan, then the power flows through both of us simultaneously."

Jack appeared confused. "If you and Satan are one?"

"Yes," Sylvia replied with a smile. "Satan and I are one." As Jack and Helen looked at each other trying to make scientific sense out of Sylvia's magical explanation, Sylvia suggested that we all play a game of croquet. It worked out the same as before: Jack, Helen, and Ronald thought the idea a waste of time, but Joseph, Susan, and Yvette were happy to play with us.

We strolled onto the grounds with our mallets. The sun shone brightly almost directly above us, since it was around one o'clock. Though it was sunny for a winter day, clouds gathered menacingly above. With the dark gray clouds came a breeze that chilled us. Despite the sunny picture of a pleasant day, we could feel a change in the air. We ignored the impending dark clouds with their threatening chill.

Instead, we concentrated on the serenity of the present.

Sylvia spotted the wolves about a hundred yards away and called out to them: "Here Tweedledee! Here Tweedledum!"

On hearing this, their ears pricked up and they bounded towards us.

"Oh no." Yvette frowned. "Not them again."

"With their similar names, how do you tell them apart?" I asked. "How do they tell themselves apart?"

"The names aren't important," Sylvia explained. "If I call either one of them, they both come, so it doesn't matter which name I use; the result is the same."

"But each of them has an individual name—an individual identity," I said.

"Yes, but the names are almost the same—as are their identities. They are so alike, they wouldn't think of answering separately. They do everything together."

"Like us?" I asked.

Sylvia smiled and nodded.

"Then why don't you and I have just one name for the two of us?"

"We do."

"We do?" I asked. "What is it?"

"It begins with an "S" and ends with an "N.""

"Of course!" I said. "My last name: Sheridan."

"That's not the name I was thinking of, but as I said—names aren't important."

Just then, two red Ferraris pulled up in front of the large main gate to the mansion. Yvette waved her arms at them.

"Do you know who they are?" Joseph asked.

"My new car!" Yvette replied. "The salesmen are to bring it here to the house." With that, Yvette walked to the gate and had them drive up the large circular driveway and park in front of the house. There were two red Ferraris in the driveway.

One of the men approached Yvette. He held papers in one hand and keys in the other. "Are you the lucky lady?"

"That's me, Mrs. Lucky," replied Yvette.

As Yvette signed some papers, the front door opened. Ronald came out, followed by Jack and Helen.

"What's going on here?" Ronald demanded.

One of the two men explained that they were just delivering a car.

"Delivering it to whom?" Ronald asked.

The man looked down at his papers and read aloud: "To Mrs. Yvette Benedict. One new Ferrari 488 Spider, red. Paid in full."

"Paid in full!" Ronald exclaimed. "Where did—"

But here, Ronald's sentence was cut short as the two men congratulated Yvette and Ronald on their fine taste in cars right before they entered the other Ferrari and sped off.

"I can't believe you did this without even consulting me," he said bitterly. "How did you pay for this?"

"I just took something out of our savings account," Yvette said. "With all the time you've been spending away from me lately—on 'business,' of course—I thought it might be a good idea for me to have my own transportation. I know you can appreciate my independence; you certainly appreciate yours."

"And you just had to buy a Ferrari?" he said

accusingly.

"With all the trouble we've been having lately, there's no telling when I might have to drive away from someone in a hurry. This car will hurry."

Ronald put his palm to his forehead and winced, then shook his head in exasperation. "Is it insured?" he inquired.

"Of course it's insured," Yvette said. "Do you think I'm stupid?"

Ronald looked at her, then the car, then back at her. "Yes," he said, then turned and stormed off into the mansion.

Yvette watched him go in, then turned to the rest of us as she pointed at the car. "What do you think? Isn't it nice?"

We all agreed that it was nice.

Yvette jumped into the driver's seat and called to Sylvia. "Get in. Come for a ride."

Sylvia shook her head. "No. There isn't enough room for three of us in there."

"So what?" Yvette asked. "You don't need to have Mark by your side every second. I'm not driving across Europe. We'll just go for a short drive to try it out." Yvette looked at me. "You can let Sylvia go for ten minutes, can't you?"

"It's up to Sylvia," I said. "She can go if she wants to."

"I don't like being apart from you," Sylvia said.

"I don't suppose we would be apart for long," I answered. "The main thing that worries me is the chance that someone could come after you—especially when we're apart."

"You worry too much," Yvette said. "Both of the hijackers are dead. Father Callen is dead. Father Clifford is dead. The two attackers from yesterday are dead. We're running low on enemies at the moment." She turned to Sylvia and opened the passenger door. "Come on! We'll be back in ten minutes. I don't want to go alone."

Sylvia paused at the door and wavered, then slid into the passenger seat uneasily.

"You're not worried about someone following you?" I asked.

Sylvia pointed her finger at Yvette. "Ten minutes. No more. I mean it." Sylvia turned back to me. "We'll be back in a few minutes. I'll try to leave all the worrying to you until we get back."

"What good will that do?" I asked.

"I have faith in you. I know you love me too much to let me be killed."

"Of course I love you. But I don't have the power to save you from everything."

"Ah, but you do!" Sylvia said. "You are the only one with that power. My fate rests in your hands."

Yvette revved the engine for effect, then zoomed out the gate to the road.

I watched as Sylvia turned around in her seat looking back at me waving sadly until we could no longer see each other

The gate shut with a solid click, and I turned to Joseph and Susan. "Did I make a mistake?" I asked. "Should I have insisted that she stay?"

"No," said Joseph. "You have to let go of her sometime. After all, you're not Siamese twins."

A feeling of emptiness came over me, a sense of being alone that I had never experienced before. I let go of my mallet. I had lost all desire to finish playing the croquet game. The change in weather that I expected came earlier than I anticipated. The wind blew harder and colder, and the gray clouds grew darker and thicker.

Joseph looked up at the menacing sky. "We better go in," he said. "It's about to rain."

"You go on," I said. "I'm going to wait here for Sylvia. She should be back in just a couple of minutes."

The two of them went inside and I waited as the first drops of rain began to fall. I stared at my watch, then on the road beyond the gate. The wind grew stronger, and I could feel my clothes against my skin, wet and cold. I kept looking beyond the closed gate for Sylvia, and as I did, time stood still for me, just as it must have stood still for Sylvia when she was sealed in her tomb.

"Mark, come in!" shouted Susan through the rain.

I looked at the gate, but it still stood closed.

The rain ran down my face. My hair and clothes were drenched. The wind chilled my cold body.

"Mark, you've been standing out here for an hour," Joseph yelled. "Come inside and wait."

Off in the distance, beyond the sheet of pouring rain, a pair of headlights pointed at us beyond the gate. As I began to walk towards the headlights, Joseph and Susan opened the gates from the electric switch inside the mansion, and they came out, along with Jack, Helen, and Ronald.

The lights came towards us as the gates closed behind.

As it came up the driveway towards us, we all noticed that it was not the Ferrari. It was a police car.

Two policemen got out and addressed all of us as we stood in the rain. "Someone from here owns a red Ferrari?"

Ronald nodded. "Yes. My wife."

The policeman looked down at the ground. "I'm afraid I have some bad news for you, sir. There's been an accident."

The other policeman looked at us directly and shook his head. "It weren't no accident. Someone was murdered with a car bomb."

Chapter Eighteen

All of us stood in shock at the words of the two policemen.

Finally, sensing that Ronald and I could not quite articulate our thoughts, Joseph broke the awful silence.

"Excuse me," said Joseph, "but you said that someone was murdered with a car bomb. Who?"

"I thought you could tell us," the policeman said. "After all, the registration for the car gave this as the address, and Yvette Benedict as the owner. There was only one person in the car."

"But the two of them went out together," Susan said.

A growing sense of dread engulfed me. My body felt numb, as if my brain subconsciously shut off all feeling so that I could not feel the pain. Had I lost Sylvia? I didn't know whether to scream aloud in anger, throw myself to the ground and cry, or stand frozen to the spot in numbed horror.

"There were two women in the car when they left," Susan told the police. "Can you tell us who was in the car?"

"We don't know. You'll have to come identify the body—if you can," he said.

"Which seat was the person in?" asked Helen. "The driver or passenger side?"

"It's hard to tell," the policeman answered. "The woman was actually between the two seats."

My mind recoiled in horror at the thought of going to the morgue to identify the body—especially after the words of the policeman: "You'll have to come identify the body—if you can." I kept trying to reassure myself that somehow Sylvia escaped, that the body in the car was Yvette. Even though I never wished Yvette any harm, I could not help but hope that she was the one who had been killed because if that were so, then Sylvia would

242

probably still be alive. Or would she? If it were Yvette who was killed, then where was Sylvia now? Or if Sylvia had been killed, where was Yvette? The only way to find out would be to follow the police to the morgue. On the one hand, I wanted to rush down there to confirm that it was not Sylvia and that she was still alive. On the other hand, I could not bring myself to face the awful truth if it turned out that Sylvia was the one who had died.

"What color hair did the woman have?" Jack asked.

"We're really not certain," one of the policemen admitted. "The car exploded into flames. If it hadn't been for the rain, it would be even more difficult to be certain. The rain kept the car from burning as much as it might, but the interior of the car was badly burned—as well as the woman inside."

Ronald and I both winced at this disclosure, so the other policeman added, "This may be little comfort, but whoever was in the car probably died instantly from the blast. The car burned afterwards."

If this news was supposed to comfort me, it did not. Every word they said just helped to confirm the finality of death, the certainty that either Sylvia or Yvette had been killed. With each passing second, I found it more difficult to deny that we were standing in the driveway discussing someone's death, maybe Sylvia's. I felt the original numbness and shock starting to slowly wear off, being replaced by a growing feeling of horror and loss, alternating with denial. It couldn't be Sylvia. It couldn't be. I loved her too much. She loved me too much. Therefore, it had to be Yvette. In a world that was fair, Sylvia could not be taken from me. But the world seemed a very cruel and unfair one.

There was no way to speculate further. We had to face the inevitable and go to the morgue. We followed the police in two cars. Jack and Helen rode with Ronald in his Rolls Royce. Joseph and Susan rode with me in

Sylvia's Aston Martin.

I found it difficult to see the road to follow the two cars. Between the rain pouring down and my eyes filling with tears, the entire world seemed submerged, drowning in my depression.

"I never should have let Sylvia go with Yvette," I said. "I should have insisted that it was too dangerous."

"Don't blame yourself," Joseph told me. "It's not your fault. The two of you would have been apart sometime, even if it hadn't been today."

"Yes," I agreed, "but today was the day the car was bombed. If I had insisted Sylvia stay, she'd be alive and with me now."

"She may still be alive," Susan said, trying to sound encouraging. "You must hope for the best."

"I can't bring myself to find out the truth," I admitted. "I couldn't bear to see Sylvia the way the police described the bombing."

"You don't have to," Susan said. "When we get to the morgue, Joseph and I will go in with Helen and Jack to make the identification. There's no reason why you and Ronald have to go in if you don't want to."

We reached the morgue, and Susan and Joseph explained to the police that I didn't want to go in. With four people who knew Sylvia and Yvette for years, the police were willing to have them make the identification. They understood that Ronald and I would not want to see the grisly results of a bomb blast and fire.

Ronald and I stood in the hallway alone waiting for the rest of them to come out of the room. Both of us stared at the door to the room. Neither of us spoke.

After only a minute, everyone came out.

Jack put his hand on Ronald's shoulder. "I'm sorry, Ronald, but we think it must have been Yvette."

Susan and Joseph came over to me, walking me a little further away from Ronald, who stood staring at the floor.

"The body was badly burned," Susan said quietly. "Even all the clothes were burned off. The face isn't even recognizable."

"Then how do you know that it was Yvette, and not Sylvia?" I asked.

"The height," Susan said. "Sylvia's five feet eight. Yvette is five feet four without her high heels. Even with the damage from the burns, there's no mistaking the four-inch difference in their height. It definitely was not Sylvia."

A wave of relief washed over my entire body. There still existed hope. "Then where is Sylvia now?" I asked Susan and Joseph.

The police and Ronald heard my question. "That's a question we would like the answer to," said one of the policemen. "It would seem that she might have left the scene of the crime."

"If she left, she was probably kidnapped," I said. "We've got to find her or she could be next."

"She must have left," the policeman said. "Both women were in a pub called The White Knight right before the bomb went off. The bartender saw them leave together. The next thing he knew, there was an explosion outside. He went out and saw the Ferrari on fire. There were no other cars or people seen leaving the area of the crime. At this point, the other lady looks more like a suspect than a kidnap victim."

"A suspect!" I yelled. "Sylvia has been kidnapped or killed and you idiots want to make her a suspect?"

"Watch your tongue, laddie," warned one of the police, "or you'll be sitting in a jail cell."

Susan and Joseph pulled me away from the police and Ronald.

"Be careful what you say," Susan cautioned. "We need to stick together. The three of us need to find Sylvia if we can."

"Is there anyone who would have wanted to kill your wife?" the policeman asked Ronald.

"As a matter of fact, Sylvia threatened to kill her twice in the week that she and Mark have been here in London," Ronald replied.

The policemen both looked at me, gave each other a knowing nod of the head, then one of them said, "This certainly puts things in a clearer light."

"Now why would she threaten this woman if they were friends?" one of them asked.

"Sylvia thought Yvette might try to sleep with Mark here," Ronald said, pointing his accusing finger at me.

"You stupid son of a bitch!" I shouted.

"Shut up!" one of the policeman yelled at me.

"Wait a minute," the other policeman said to Ronald. "If it's true that your wife was trying to sleep with this bloke, then it seems to me that you may be the most likely suspect we have."

"I wouldn't kill my own wife," Ronald protested.

"It's been known to happen," one of the police pointed out.

"Yes," I said quietly to Joseph and Susan. "But the police would never believe that Ronald killed his previous wife in 1856, would they?"

"It certainly wouldn't be in any of our interests to try to prove that," Susan said.

"If I may make a comment," Jack offered to the police. "Both Mark and Ronald are extremely upset. Ronald's wife has been murdered. Mark's fiancée is missing. Naturally, they may say some things to each other that they may later regret. Please believe me when I say that Sylvia and Ronald are not responsible for what happened today. You must concentrate on finding the real person or people responsible. To spend time trying to persecute Ronald will only waste your valuable time. The time must be spent finding the real killers. Let's not let them escape while we all fight among ourselves."

"I think we all need to go down to the police station and talk about this some more," said one of the policemen. "We'll have to call Scotland Yard on this one, too. A bombing will be of interest to them."

A phone rang at the end of the hall. One of the clerks picked it up and called for the police. The one who seemed to be the boss answered it and looked at us from down the hall as he listened to whoever was on the other end.

He put the receiver down and returned to us. "I think we won't be needing you to come down to the police station after all."

"Why is that?" asked Ronald. "Did they find the killer already? Did you get some kind of a clue over the phone? Don't leave us in the dark on this. Tell us what you know."

"All I can tell you is you're all free to leave," the policeman told us. "Rest assured that every effort will be made to find the killer, not only by the police, but also Scotland Yard and the Secret Service."

"The Secret Service?" Ronald asked. "Surely this is more of a police matter than something they would get involved with."

"On the contrary," the policeman interrupted. "They're already involved. They just told me to let you go. I would think you would be pleased, Mr. Benedict. If they thought you were guilty, they would not have asked me to let you all go free now. This must mean they have some kind of lead." He placed his hand reassuringly on Ronald's shoulder. "I realize this has been stressful. Why don't you all go home? We'll ring you up the moment we learn anything new."

Jack and Helen left with Ronald in the Rolls Royce, while Joseph and Susan left with me in the Aston Martin.

"This is just like what happened in the hospital," I said to Joseph and Susan.

"You mean the way they let us go after a phone call?" Joseph asked.

"Yes," I said. "That CIA agent. But how did he know of the bombing of your car? And how did he find out about Yvette's car being bombed? How did he know so soon?"

"Those would be very good questions to ask him," Susan suggested.

"I fully intend to," I said, "but first, I'd like to talk to the bartender at The White Knight."

Joseph and Susan directed me to the pub, which was at the border between the northern part of London and the southern part of Highgate. It stood on a hill overlooking part of London. Built mostly of stone in the eighteenth century, it had the look of a small castle or fortress. The name seemed appropriate. Along the side of the street next to the pub was a stone wall, similar in construction to that of the building itself. Part of the wall and the grass next to it as well as part of the street were all scorched from the bomb blast and fire.

The three of us entered the pub, which was mostly empty. A few people sat at tables and a couple at the bar, but it was too late for the lunch crowd, too early for the patrons who would come after work, so we were in between the two—just as we were in between the day and the night, caught in the murky gray of twilight. The clock on the wall said three-thirty, so it was almost dark. There was almost no sunlight left, especially on such a dark winter day.

"What'll it be?" the burly bartender asked us as we approached.

"Are you the one the police talked to a couple of hours ago about the bombing?" I asked.

"Are you police?" he asked me warily.

"No, we're not," I said.

"Then I don't have to tell you nothing."

I wanted to wipe the smug look from his face with my fist, and take along some of his teeth for good measure.

"This is the fiancée of one of the two women," Joseph told him.

"Now, you listen here. I already told the police what I know. You want to know something, go ask them. I been here for twenty years and I ain't getting involved with no terrorists or crazy people. I plan to stay here another twenty years."

"Then you better tell us everything you know," I told him, as I moved closer to the bar.

He leaned his massive weight on the counter. His two large hands clenched into fists as we stood close enough so that either of us could strike the other. "I ain't telling you nothing." He stared me directly in the eyes to let me know he meant what he said.

I stared back directly into his eyes locking our gaze. *"You will tell me everything you know."* I was about to strike him in the face, when I suddenly realized it was unnecessary.

He stared at me vacantly. "I will tell you everything I know," he repeated mechanically.

What he told me differed from the police version. According to the bartender, he saw the two women come in for a few minutes, saw the blonde make a phone call at the end of the bar. The brunette constantly looked at her watch as if trying to make the other one hurry up. Just a minute after they had entered, two men and one woman entered and were staring at the first two women. They ordered nothing from the bar, and when the first two women left, the three immediately got up and followed them out. The bartender heard some yelling and screaming like an argument outside less than a minute later. Soon after, there was an explosion. By the time he got outside, the Ferrari was on fire, the woman inside was dead, and no one else was around. He called the police at that time. The bartender did not want to get involved with terrorists, so he did not mention the three people who he had seen come in to follow the first two women. I asked him if he had seen any of these people before. The two men were strangers, but the woman who was with them, an attractive woman with red hair—she had been in the pub a number of times, always to meet the same man—a man the bartender did not know, but who always appeared well-dressed, as if he had a lot of money. He remembered that of the two women, the one with the dark hair had never been in the pub before, but the other one, the blonde, had been in twice during that week. Both times she had been with the same man. He had blond hair and a moustache. He remembered that the man drove a Jaguar F-Type sports car.

I now had everything the bartender knew. Before releasing him from his trance, I told him that he would forget his conversation with us, that it would be as if we had never been in. Then I punched him in the face hard, breaking his nose. He fell back, blood streaming down his face. His head hit the bottles stacked behind him. These shattered and fell on top of him. He collapsed forward in a heap on the bar.

The other patrons in the bar stared at us in shock as we walked out, but none of them followed.

As we drove away quickly, Susan asked, "Why did you do that? You already had him in a trance."

"That was the only reason he told me anything," I explained. "If it hadn't been for that, he would have been just as happy to let Yvette and Sylvia be killed and forget about it. He deserved worse, but that's all I had time for. We've got to find Matthew Henry. He's going to have a lot of explaining to do."

I pulled out the card he had given to Sylvia and me, and showed it to Joseph and Susan.

"Hmm, he has good taste in hotels," remarked Susan. "Grosvenor House Hotel on Park Lane. It's only a few blocks from the American Embassy."

"That doesn't help me very much," I said. "I don't know where the American Embassy is."

"It's practically right across the street from Hyde Park," Joseph said matter-of-factly. "Next to Grosvenor Square."

They gave me directions, and soon we were driving down Park Lane, next to Hyde Park. Susan informed me that Sylvia owned a flat in Belgravia, on the other side of the park, but the travel commentary was of little interest to me. I didn't care where we were; I only cared about finding Sylvia.

As we entered the magnificent lobby of the hotel, Joseph informed me that the desk clerk would want to ring the CIA agent on the phone before giving the room number. I told him I would take care of that just as I had the uncooperative bartender at the pub.

"This would not be a good place for a row," Joseph cautioned.

His reaction amused me. "I don't plan to punch out the desk clerk in the lobby. I'll just put him into a mild trance if I need to in order to get the room number."

We approached the desk. I found that merely by looking the clerk directly in the eyes and keeping contact, I could easily tell him what to do. He gave us the room number and informed us that Mr. Matthew Henry was out.

We took the elevator upstairs to his floor and found one of the maids making her rounds.

"Excuse me," I said, making eye contact with her and holding it. "*Would you open this door for us?*"

She opened the door like a robot following directions.

"Thank you," I said. *"You have never seen us."*

She walked away and the three of us slipped inside.

"It's really too bad Sylvia isn't here to see me use hypnosis the very first day," I told them. "She would enjoy seeing it. I guess I had the power to do it all along, only I never had to do it alone when Sylvia and I were together."

As we searched the room, Susan suddenly said, "Take a look at this."

Inside the drawer in the desk next to the bed were several photos of Yvette. They appeared to have been taken without her knowledge, all candid shots.

"He must have taken these from quite a distance with a telephoto lens," I said.

"How can you tell?" Susan asked.

"The face is very sharp, but everything in the immediate foreground and background is completely blurred. The shallow depth of field means he used a very long lens. And these small rings that make up the colors in the out-of-focus portion mean that it was a mirror lens—probably five hundred millimeters or longer."

"But what does all that mean?" Joseph asked.

"It means that he took these photos without Yvette's knowledge, that he was probably fifty to one hundred feet away from her outside, that he did not want anyone to know that he was photographing her."

I carefully replaced the photographs, making sure I held them by the edges so that my fingerprints would not get on them, then placed them in the exact position we had found them so it would not look as though they had been moved.

"Could he be the killer?" Susan asked. "He has these pictures of her in the room. He knew about the bombing of our car right away. He knew about the men who were after you and Sylvia at the hospital parking lot. He knew about Yvette's car being bombed before we even got to the morgue."

"It doesn't look very good, does it?" Joseph asked.

"There must be a reason he knows all these things," I said, "and I intend to find out what that reason is."

On the way out of the hotel, we stopped by the front desk. By using the same technique as before, I found out that the hotel clerk would be there until nine o'clock that evening and that he expected Mr. Henry would be back before then but he wasn't certain.

While still maintaining eye contact, I told him "*In the next few hours, I will be calling you on the telephone. As soon as you hear my voice, you will answer any question I ask and do anything I tell you. You will not let anyone know that we have spoken to you or that you have seen us. Do you understand?*"

"Yes," he agreed, with a nod of his head, as if he were a marionette whose strings I was pulling.

Susan, Joseph, and I began driving back to Highgate in the darkness of the early evening. The clouds overhead slowly moved across the sky. The rain had stopped and the blackness above and around us began to get clearer with each minute with the sharpness of the stars that had appeared. Each star added a little more light to the darkness of the sky.

"Won't Ronald be angry when he learns that the CIA agent and Yvette were at the pub together earlier this week?" Susan asked rhetorically.

"Not to mention the pictures of her in the agent's room," Joseph added.

"Yes indeed," I said. "Do not mention it. Definitely do not mention any of it to Ronald or Jack or Helen."

"What?" said Susan in surprise. "You want to keep that a secret from the others?"

"Yes, I certainly do. At least for right now. I had enough trouble with Ronald at the morgue. That idiot ranting to the police that Sylvia threatened to kill Yvette. Telling him anything will only allow him to make things worse. And Jack and Helen can't be trusted to keep any secrets from Ronald, so it would be best not to tell them anything, either."

Joseph nodded. "I'm afraid Mark is right," he said to Susan.

"Then what do you plan to do?" Susan asked me.

"I'm going to go back to the Grosvenor House Hotel in a couple of hours and have an interview with the CIA agent—one where I ask the questions."

"Then what will you do?" Susan asked.

"That depends upon what his answers to my questions are," I said.

After we pulled into the driveway and entered the mansion at Highgate, I expected everyone else to come to the hallway to greet us with questions about where we had been and what we had found out, if anything. Jack and Helen came to the door, but told us that Ronald was in his study, making phone calls in private.

"I think he's ringing up some of his contacts trying to find out who was behind this," Jack said. "He has friends on the other side of the law—friends who will do anything for a price. Perhaps one of them will know something about this."

"Perhaps they will," I said. "I wish only to get Sylvia back safe and have revenge on whoever did this. I don't care what has to be done to achieve that."

"What will you do now?" Helen asked.

"I'm going up to our room." With that, I left them all in the hallway as I climbed the stairs. Halfway up, I glanced back over my shoulder at Susan and Joseph for an instant, just to let them know how serious I was about not telling Jack and Helen what had happened at the pub and the hotel.

As I entered the bedroom, the first thing to catch my eye was the Sylvia doll against the wall. It was as if Sylvia hadn't left at all—she had merely grown smaller.

I walked over to it and picked it up, looked into its beautiful life-like eyes and held it tenderly in my arms as if it were real.

Then Sylvia's words to me from yesterday morning came back, when we discussed why she had a doll made of me: "But the reason I had the doll made was so that I could perform a ritual on you—so that I could find you. It worked. The ritual allowed me to find you." I remembered telling Sylvia that if only I had owned the Sylvia doll earlier, I could have found Sylvia first, but she said that would have been impossible because Ronald must have had Pierre make it after Sylvia and I got married—within the past two weeks. But while it seemed at the time that the doll was only recently bought by Ronald, I remembered telling Sylvia: "It was a good thing he had it made. Now if you're ever lost, I can perform a Satanic ritual and find you through the doll."

If there was ever a time to use the doll for a Satanic ritual to find Sylvia, this was it.

I immediately located Joseph and Susan and asked them about performing a ritual with me in the special room. They thought it an excellent idea. Jack and Helen had already gone back to their bedroom, Ronald was still in his study, so we would be able to take advantage of our combined magical power without having any of our energy drained off by the negativity of the others.

Once inside, we donned our black robes. Susan lit the incense, the two black candles, then picked up the bell and rang it towards each point of the compass as she turned counterclockwise. All the things she did were the same ones that Sylvia did during our ritual.

But when Joseph and Susan held their arms out and looked into the eyes of the Baphomet and said, "Hail Satan!" the result was slightly different when I followed their example.

My hands had been holding the Sylvia doll the entire

time of the ritual, and when I held my arms out like Joseph and Susan, I still held the doll, and instead of looking into the eyes of Satan in the symbol of the Baphomet as I said, "Hail Satan!" I was looking into the eyes of Sylvia before me in the form of the doll.

As the doll and I looked into each other's eyes during the ritual, I felt a new connection between Sylvia and myself being forged at that very moment. As the ritual went on, and Susan verbalized our wishes—to save Sylvia and seek vengeance on the ones who attacked her and Yvette—I realized the truth of what Sylvia had told me so many times: the words didn't really matter. The doll in front of me and my feelings about Sylvia meant more than any words I could speak during a ritual. I allowed the words to disappear until what was left was Sylvia's image before me in the form of the doll and my love for her as well as my hate for those who attacked her. The image and the feeling consumed and overtook me. I felt a power rising inside.

As I held the doll and looked into its eyes, I felt the connection Sylvia had alluded to before regarding the demon from another dimension. I had always considered it as a separate and abstract entity, but now felt it was something else—an energy that bound Sylvia and me together.

It was the one hope I had for getting Sylvia back.

The ritual was soon over. I found myself looking into the eyes of the doll, feeling the connection with Sylvia through it, and knowing that it could lead me to her.

"Where are you going?" Susan asked me as I left the ritual chamber in a sort of daze.

"To the hotel," I said.

"Aren't you going to find out if the CIA agent returned?" Joseph asked.

"I'm certain he has," I found myself saying, though I couldn't say how I knew this.

"Why don't you call?" Susan suggested.

I did so. The clerk answered. When I spoke to him, he immediately recognized my voice as well as my instructions from the trance. He told me what I wanted to hear: the CIA agent had returned.

I placed the Sylvia doll inside its box, then tucked it under my arm as I quickly descended the stairs.

"Wait for us!" Susan said, as she and Joseph trailed behind in my wake.

"No, I'm going alone," I said.

"Are you crazy?" Susan asked. "What good does it do to have us sit here?"

"If I need to come back or if I need to contact the police, I can call you if you're here. I don't trust leaving that responsibility to Jack or Helen or Ronald. Or the police might call here. It would be best if you were here. That way we have two bases covered instead of just one."

They reluctantly agreed and made me promise to call them if I found out anything important.

I drove like a maniac to the Grosvenor House Hotel and went straight to the front desk. It was eight o'clock. The same clerk still had an hour left on his shift.

Looking him in the eyes, I asked, *"Is Matthew Henry in?"*

He nodded.

I opened the box and asked him to look at the doll and tell me if he had ever seen anyone who looked like that.

He told me he hadn't.

While he was still in his trance, I had him give me the key to Mr. Henry's room.

For a few seconds, I stood outside Matthew Henry's door in the hallway. I heard the door to his bathroom close, then I heard him walk across the floor and sit on the bed. Through the door, I could hear the slightest creak of the springs as he rested his weight on it.

The key went into the lock and my hand turned the knob in one smooth motion.

His reactions were almost as fast. On hearing the door open, his hand reached across his chest to his shoulder holster, but he stopped as soon as he saw who I was. He sighed with relief. "I'm glad it's you and not someone else."

"Don't be too happy yet," I said. "I have some questions to ask. If I don't like your answers, I'm going to kill you."

He held his hand up in a defensive gesture. "Wait a minute. We're on the same side. Remember?"

"Yeah, I remember," I said. "I remember that you knew about both car bombings right after they happened. I remember that the bartender at The White Knight pub said he saw you with Yvette twice this week. I remember seeing her pictures in your desk this afternoon. And I remember Susan and Joseph saying that after the bomb blast, the body was burned beyond recognition."

Matthew nodded in agreement. "All true. Every word."

"Then you admit that you killed Yvette?" I asked.

"Me kill Yvette?" he asked, incredulous. "You can't be serious."

"Serious?" I repeated. "Yvette has been murdered. Sylvia has been either kidnapped or murdered. You bet I'm serious. You won't find anyone more serious than me right now. Just to show you how serious I am, I'm going to put you into a hypnotic trance to get the truth out of you. When I'm finished, if I don't like what I hear, then you will become the first victim of my thirst in London. It's been exactly a week since my last victim—the weekend before we took the plane over here together."

"You don't need to go to all that trouble to get the truth."

"It's no trouble," I reassured him. "No trouble at all."

Just then, I heard a sound from inside the bathroom.
"What's that?" I asked.

"Proof that things are not as they appear," said the CIA agent.

The door opened and I stood face to face with Yvette.

Chapter Nineteen

"Yvette!" I yelled in shock, as she walked into the room. "I thought you were killed by the car bomb."

"Not me," said Yvette. "Fortunately, I got out right before it exploded."

My mind whirled as I tried to comprehend that Yvette stood before me after I had thought she died. The next thing I said, I asked slowly, cautiously, afraid to hear what the answer might be. "Then if the body the police found in the Ferrari wasn't you..."

"It wasn't Sylvia," Yvette quickly interrupted, much to my relief.

I sat down on the edge of the bed. A tremendous weight had been lifted from my shoulders. "Is she still alive, then?"

"I'm certain she is," Yvette said. "They went to a lot of trouble to kidnap her. They could have just killed the two of us with the car bomb if they had wanted to."

"Wait a minute. If they planted a car bomb, then they must have wanted to kill you."

Matthew shook his head. "They planted a car bomb to make you think it was a murder instead of a kidnapping. A murder would be harder to pin down because of all the enemies you have. But the kidnapping—that makes the possible suspects a smaller group."

"Then if you and Sylvia were not in the car when it blew up, who was?" I asked.

"Let me tell you what happened after Sylvia and I left in my new car. I only intended to be gone for a short time. We drove to The White Knight, a pub I've been to a couple of times with Matthew here."

I pointed at him. "You're the boyfriend Yvette is having an affair with?"

"I wouldn't call it an affair," Mathew explained. "I

260

was told by my boss in the CIA to keep an eye on you and Sylvia, to make certain that you were safe, and to eventually persuade the two of you to help us track down and hypnotize the terrorists we're dealing with. They never told me that the others living in your house were vampires. Their eyes aren't like yours or Sylvia's. I thought they were people who you kept your vampirism a secret from. Following you from the airport, I happened to see Yvette at the mansion. With a telephoto lens on my camera, I took the pictures that you found in my desk. I haven't been able to stop looking at them. I guess you could call it love at first sight. She's the most beautiful woman I've ever seen. Perhaps it was unprofessional of me to see her the way I did, but the CIA can't really complain. I did my job. I followed you and Sylvia, kept you from getting killed twice, asked you to help us. I've also tried to track down your enemies for you. I did my job, but after all, I'm only human. I may work for the CIA, but I didn't take a vow of celibacy for this position."

"Thank God for that," Yvette said with a sexy smile.

"Did you know that he was a CIA agent?" I asked Yvette.

"Not right away," she answered. "Remember, it was you and Sylvia who saw him on the plane, and then Susan and Joseph saw him in his Jaguar at the airport. Then you and Sylvia saw him at the hospital parking lot. But I was never with you then. So when you talked about him, I had no idea what he looked like or who you were talking about. I didn't realize that you were talking about someone I was sleeping with."

"You certainly didn't waste any time," I said to both of them.

"I've wasted years with Ronald after he stopped loving me. Why should I waste any more time?"

"And I've been travelling for my job for years, never settling in one place," said Matthew. "When I met Yvette,

I realized she was the one I had always waited for."

"But you didn't know that she was a vampire and she didn't know that you worked for the CIA?"

"Not until today. We just found out the truth about each other a few hours ago. Remember, we've known each other less than a week."

"I was afraid that if I told Matthew that I was a vampire, he might not like it," Yvette explained.

I nodded knowingly. "Sylvia didn't tell me the truth about herself until the very last moment—the point of no return."

"I was afraid to tell Yvette the truth," Matthew admitted.

"I thought that if I told her I was following you and Sylvia for the CIA, she might stop seeing me and also reveal my plans. I didn't want to lose her or my job."

"Now that you've both found out the truth, perhaps you'll clue me in." I turned to Yvette. "What happened with you and Sylvia?"

"As I said, we drove to The White Knight pub. We were only there a few minutes. I made a phone call to Matthew and wanted to show him my new Ferrari, but Sylvia kept looking at her watch and insisting that we go back so that you wouldn't be kept waiting. I guess I didn't notice that two men and a woman had followed us into the pub. I had gotten into the car before Sylvia and started it up. Just as she was about to get in, these two men sprayed her in the face with something, then grabbed her and held a cloth over her nose. I think it was chloroform. Since I had already started the car, I pulled forward and ran into one of the men who were grabbing her. I'm sure I broke one of his legs. But the other man was able to get Sylvia into the Mercedes he had there. The chloroform must have made Sylvia very drowsy. She could barely stand, once it had been held to her face, though I must admit, she put up a good fight until then.

The woman who was with them jumped in my car on the passenger side and tried to put one of those chloroform cloths on me, but she didn't have the element of surprise like they had with Sylvia. I hit her in the face and grabbed the cloth and held it over her nose. She started to fall over, between the two seats, so I jumped out of the car and tried to help get Sylvia out of the men's car, but one of the men knocked me down. When I got up, they locked the doors and drove off. I ran after them, but of course, I couldn't catch them. But it's a good thing I did run after them, even if I didn't run that far. Just a few seconds later, my Ferrari blew up with that woman in it."

I looked at Matthew. "You said they planted the car bomb to make it look like a murder instead of a kidnapping, but it sounds to me like they wanted to kidnap Sylvia and murder Yvette. When the bomb went off in Joseph and Susan's car, the killers were trying to get all of us. When the two men in the hospital parking lot stopped Sylvia and me, they wanted to kidnap us. In only one day, they changed their plans from murder to kidnapping. Now we need to ask: what happened in the space of that one day to make them change their plans?"

"Our house was broken into," Yvette said.

"Right," I agreed. "And information was stolen specifically about Sylvia and me, along with an experimental antidote for vampirism."

"An antidote for vampirism?" Matthew asked.

"One which could make us human again," I explained, "and which is somehow linked to separating the vampire's need for blood from the positive elements of vampirism such as longevity."

"If such a thing could keep people young, there would be quite a market for it," Matthew suggested.

"Yes, there certainly would," I said. "But the question is, who knew about it? The terrorists from the plane? I don't think they knew about the experiments

Jack and Helen were conducting. You would be one of the prime suspects," I added, pointing at Matthew, "because you may know more about us than you let on. But let us just look at what we are certain of. We know that Father Clifford was found in our apartment seconds after the burglary, and that Ronald saw Brother Phillips leaving with a camera and vials of chemicals from the lab. It would seem, then, that Brother Phillips would know something of great importance. He would know what was in the notes in the lab, and he would also know whom he passed the information to. Whoever tried to kidnap Sylvia and me the first time and whoever succeeded in kidnapping her this time most likely knows of Jack and Helen's experiments."

"If only we could find Brother Phillips," Yvette said.

I pulled a card from my wallet. "He's as close as the telephone."

I dialed the number, but got his answering service. This time, however, I told the woman on the other end that I wanted to speak directly to Brother Phillips — that leaving a message just wouldn't do. When she hesitated, I told her that it was regarding Father Clifford. She had me hold on for a minute, then transferred the call.

"Brother Phillips here," said the voice on the other end.

"Brother Phillips, I met you the other day at Highgate Cemetery. My friend and I wanted to write a story about you and Father Clifford and how you've been hunting down vampires."

"Yes, I remember," he said. "You were supposed to call me back the next afternoon. I waited for you but you called late, after I had already left."

"I'd still like that interview."

"Things have gotten much worse since then," he explained. "Father Clifford left yesterday morning. I haven't seen him since. I'm beginning to get worried. This is how Father Callen disappeared."

"You didn't go with him?" I asked, as I listened carefully to his voice to detect any waver that could indicate a lie.

"No, he left without me."

"Do you know where he went?" I held the receiver so that Matthew and Yvette could hear. "Did he go to find the vampire?"

"No, on the contrary. He went to see someone to help him fight the vampire. I don't know where the person lives."

"Do you know who he is?"

"His name is Robert Brandon."

"Robert Brandon!" Matthew said. "The same man the two killers in the parking lot worked for."

"Why was he going to see this Robert Brandon?" I asked Brother Phillips.

"Father Clifford hoped he could help us to locate the vampire we were looking for—just as he did last year."

"Last year," I found myself repeating, as I remembered what Sylvia had told me about how the other vampire couple who had been with the group for many years had been murdered a year ago by Father Callen's vampire-hunting cult. "Did you ever meet this Robert Brandon?"

"Yes, I met him last year when he gave the information to Father Callen about how to find the two vampires. He even gave us some money to help us with our cause. This Robert Brandon has a lot of money, he does. Even drives a Rolls Royce with his own initials on it—R.B."

"Thank you very much for this information," I said. "I may be getting back to you soon."

Yvette tried to wipe the tears from her face, but could not stop crying. "Our Rolls Royce with our license plate. Robert Brandon. Ronald Benedict."

265

"So Ronald actually helped to kill your friends?" I asked. "Then he must have also been the one who told Father Callen how to find Sylvia and me in the hotel room at the Atlantis Casino last weekend. He must have been the one to have hired those men to—"

"Hired the men to bomb the car I was in," Yvette interjected, finishing my sentence for me. She sobbed uncontrollably.

"Then Brother Phillips never even burglarized the house," I said. "Ronald must have invited Father Clifford over to murder him and frame him and Brother Phillips for the burglary of the lab—a burglary actually committed by Ronald himself. Maybe Ronald actually killed Father Clifford first and brought his body to the mansion. It all makes sense now. No wonder the wolves didn't make any noise during the burglary. There was no burglary by Father Clifford. Ronald killed him, stole the antidote and photographed the papers in the lab himself, then turned on the burglar alarm to make it look like he had walked in on the middle of it. He opened the front door and said Brother Phillips had just run out, but he had never even been there."

"And it was after he stole these chemicals that he decided to kidnap you and Sylvia rather than kill you," Matthew pointed out. "He must have decided you two were worth more to him alive than dead."

"But he didn't feel that way about me," Yvette sobbed. "Over a century together, but he tried to kill, me, not once, but twice this month. How could he do that to me? What would I have had to do to be worthy of his love?"

"Worthy of his love?" asked Matthew. "Anyone who would do what he did isn't capable of love. Don't concern yourself with someone who can't love you—especially when there is someone else who can."

Yvette looked at him through her tears, and then

hugged him tightly.

I watched them for a few seconds, then interrupted them. "I'm happy the two of you have found each other, but now we've got to locate Sylvia."

Yvette looked at me and nodded, then noticed the box I had laid on the bed. "What's in there?"

I opened the box, revealing the Sylvia doll inside.

"Why did you bring that?" Yvette asked.

"It could help us if we question anyone about Sylvia since I don't have any pictures of her," I explained. "Susan and Joseph and I used it to perform a ritual at the house so that I could locate Sylvia. She told me before that she used a doll of me for a ritual and that it had helped her to find me. I told her that if she were ever lost, I would use the doll to find her."

"Good thinking," Yvette said. "A doll is the best way to focus your energy on someone for a ritual, and this doll looks exactly like Sylvia. I'll bet when Ronald had the doll made a couple of months ago, he never realized it would be used for this."

"A couple of months ago?" I asked. "Sylvia and I met less than one month ago. Ronald said this was going to be an engagement present."

"He did give it to the two of you as an engagement present," Yvette replied, "but that couldn't have been the original reason he had it made."

"A destruction ritual!" I said. "He must have had it made to perform a destruction ritual against her. That's why Father Callen was able to almost kill Sylvia in our hotel room a week ago."

"Sure, that doll in the ritual and actually sending Father Callen there to kill her," Yvette said.

"Yes, but the ritual made it possible for Father Callen to get into our room without waking us up. I always wondered why we didn't wake up when he entered the room. Now I see. The destruction ritual Ronald did enabled him to almost kill Sylvia. It's a good thing I have the doll now."

"Yes, it is a good thing," Yvette agreed. "Too bad you didn't bring the doll of yourself as well. If you left it at the house, Ronald can use it in a destruction ritual against you."

"We've got to find Sylvia," I said. "I'll go back to the house and get the information out of Ronald."

"I don't think he'll give that information willingly," Yvette said.

"Then I'll get the information against his will," I replied. "I don't care what I have to do."

"I don't think that will be necessary," said Matthew, shaking his head. "Yvette saw the license plate of the car used to kidnap Sylvia. I'm having it traced right now. They're looking up the owner and finding the address. I was just about to call them back when you came in."

Matthew dialed the number and spoke to someone on the other line, writing down the name, number, and address as they spoke. Unknown to Matthew, I listened to the entire conversation even though I was not next to the telephone. Another CIA agent had not only tracked down the name and address of the registered owner—he had driven out to the house. He now waited, parked across the street for further instructions.

Matthew thanked the person on the other line, then immediately dialed the cell phone of the agent parked at the house. I heard the information on the phone before Matthew repeated it for us. The Mercedes that Yvette had identified was in the driveway. A Rolls Royce was pulling up in front right now.

"That's it!" Matthew said to us. "Let's go." He told the other man to wait there for us. After hanging up the phone, he opened one of his drawers where he had a miniature armory inside. Several handguns of different sizes, holsters to be worn on the shoulder, on the hip, behind the back, along with boxes of ammunition. He pointed at the drawer. "Pick your weapons," he said to Yvette and me.

As he said this, I realized that I had left Sylvia's silenced automatic at the house, not bothering to get it out of her purse, which now lay in our bedroom.

"This may come as a surprise," Yvette said to him, "but guns really aren't that necessary for me or Mark. Remember, they can't kill us by shooting us, at least not at night. You're the one who's in danger."

"Perhaps you're right," he admitted. "I'll put on a bulletproof vest underneath my jacket."

"That's a good start." Yvette nodded her head.

As Matthew slipped a bulletproof vest on underneath his sweater and then put on a sports coat over that, he added, "But I'd still like both of you to carry guns. You may have powers I lack, but without a gun you still can't kill them unless you are able to reach out and touch someone."

"I'm real angry about Sylvia being kidnapped," I admitted. "If I can kill the ones who did it with my bare hands or drink their blood, I think that would be more satisfying than shooting them."

"Yes," agreed Yvette. "Guns are so impersonal."

Matthew handed a 9mm automatic to Yvette and one to me. "There are fifteen rounds in the magazine," he explained, ignoring what we had just said. "You have more than three times as many bullets in this as a snub-nose revolver. You probably won't even find it necessary to reload, unless they have a private army out there. If you want to kill these people with your bare hands or if you want to drink their blood that's fine with me. If you can disable them without killing them and hypnotize them afterwards to get information out of them, that would be even better. But regardless of what you do, carry these damn guns. Better to have a gun and not need it than to need a gun and not have one." He handed each of us two extra magazines, already loaded.

"You must plan on us spending some time on this," I remarked.

"I certainly hope not," he answered. "The less time, the better. I don't want any complications. If you can use your hypnosis so that no one has to fire a shot, that's even better."

Yvette put her gun in her purse. I tried tucking mine in my belt, but it kept slipping around. Matthew gave me a holster, which clipped onto the back of my belt, so that with a jacket on, I appeared unarmed even with the jacket opened. The only disadvantage was that the holster could not be worn comfortably while sitting down. I carried the gun and holster inside a paper bag as we left. I would put it on my belt once we arrived at the house where I would be spending my time standing up.

Since Matthew's Jaguar seated only two people, I followed in Sylvia's Aston Martin. Matthew kept in contact with the other CIA agent as we made our way over. We had to drive through Central London and head back towards Highgate.

I drove with the Sylvia doll in the passenger seat next to me. Right before we left, I took the doll out of the box and held it in my hands gently as I stared into its eyes. As I did so, I could feel her eyes staring back—Sylvia's eyes. Her eyes pleaded with me to find her, to save her.

I addressed Sylvia through the eyes of the doll with my mind: *Just a few more minutes. I'll be there in just a few more minutes. We'll be together again. Forever.*

The road became narrower, the area more isolated, hidden within the darkness of tall trees. The Jaguar pulled up behind a BMW parked on the side of the road.

Facing us stood a large house, not quite as large as the mansion, yet this was also in Highgate, though an even more sparsely populated area at the edge of a park, which appeared to be more like a forest.

Matthew and Yvette exited the Jaguar, and it was at this point that I had to leave the Sylvia doll behind in the Aston Martin. I first carefully placed it inside its box, then locked it in the trunk where it would be safe.

Matthew introduced us to the driver in the BMW, who had been sitting in the car with a high-powered unidirectional microphone aimed at the house. Connected to this was a set of headphones that amplified the sound. Both of the men put on bullet-proof vests under their jackets.

"I can't hear very much," Matthew's partner admitted. "I heard the men talking in the front room when they first went in. The ones who came in the Rolls Royce."

"How many were there?" asked Matthew.

"The driver, a tall man with blond hair. Two very large men from the back seat, probably bodyguards by the looks of them. The man in the passenger seat was elderly, and they brought him in on a wheelchair."

"A wheelchair?" Matthew questioned. "Who would he be? The bodyguards would have to be for him, not for Ronald."

"Let me see those headphones," I said. "Maybe I can hear something."

Matthew nodded, and the man handed the apparatus to me. I put the headphones on and aimed the microphone at the house. This amplified my already sensitive hearing to an extraordinary degree. I pointed it at the front door. "There are two men in the hallway past the front door. By their accents, I can tell that they're both American."

The man in the BMW looked at me, surprised. "I couldn't even hear what they were saying. It sounded garbled."

"They're talking about how much money they'll make

because of tonight. They're also saying that they have to keep their eye out for any rescue attempt from the outside or any betrayal from the inside."

Yvette nodded. "If they're dealing with Ronald, they certainly have to worry about betrayal from the inside."

I pointed the long microphone towards other parts of the house. On the third floor, inside a lit room, which stood out among an otherwise dark floor, I heard other voices. An elderly man, who was obviously American, said he was ready to wire all the money to Ronald's bank account. I relayed this information to the others.

"Who else is there?" Matthew asked.

"I'm not sure," I admitted. "He could be sitting in a room alone talking to himself. Or he could be addressing ten suicidal terrorists with Uzi machineguns. No one else is talking. I guess they're just listening to him. He does have a certain air of authority in his voice. He sounds like someone who is used to telling other people what to do."

"That's about to come to an end," Matthew said.

His partner from the BMW got out of the car. He placed the headphones in the trunk and drew a pistol from his shoulder holster, as did Matthew.

"We have to go in very fast," Matthew explained. "I have a glass cutter so we can get in the window, but we must do so without being seen or heard."

The four of us walked as quietly as possible towards the large mansion. I kept my ears trained on the voices near the front door. Hearing that they still guarded the front, I motioned to the others to follow me to the side. We found a large window. Matthew silently cut out a pane of glass, then we climbed through, into what appeared to be a study with a well-stocked library. We stepped carefully across a carpeted floor in the darkness to the door, which was closed. I could hear the two men in the hallway talking to each other.

"I thought I heard something in the study," one of

them said.

"Better check it out," the other one replied as their voices came closer.

We waited in the darkness. The door opened. As the first one walked into the room, I grabbed him by the wrist that held his gun. My other hand clapped over his mouth, so that when I crushed his wrist, only a muffled scream escaped between my fingers.

Yvette grabbed the other bodyguard in the same manner as he stumbled through the door. She immediately bit into his neck and began drinking his blood.

Matthew stood transfixed, watching this scene in the near darkness, his eyes wide open. Though he had said he knew that Yvette was a vampire, or so she had told him, he had apparently only believed this on an intellectual level. Now he was seeing the reality; the woman he had professed his undying love for an hour earlier was consuming a man before his eyes as one might consume a refreshment to satisfy a thirst on a hot summer night.

My victim had lost his grip on the gun. I looked him in the eyes. *"I will take my hand away and you will not scream. You will whisper to us about who is upstairs."*

He told us what we wanted to know as well as he was able. His boss was up there in a wheelchair along with several men, but he did not know everyone's names. He did not even know why they were there, except that they came with the man in the wheelchair to protect him. He did not know anything about a woman in the house.

When I determined that he knew nothing else of value and would be of no further use to us, my canine teeth immediately grew about half an inch in length and sharpened to two fine points in anticipation. I bit into his neck and drank his blood until he collapsed. As his life force flowed into mine, I became renewed and strengthened. Even as my fangs retracted to their normal

273

length afterwards, I felt the power surge through my veins—power which I would now use to save Sylvia.

We slowly exited the room into the dimly lit hallway. A small elevator could have provided us a swift passage upstairs, but we opted for the slower but quieter stairway.

At the top of the stairs, we silently stepped to the door where the voices came from.

I put my hand on the knob and slowly turned it, to find that it was unlocked. With one swift motion, we burst into the room. Everything happened so fast, it was a blur.

Matthew immediately shot the closest person to him who pointed a gun in our direction. The bullet struck the man in the head, killing him instantly.

Only a split second later, another man across the room pointed a sawed-off shotgun at us and fired. The main portion of the blast struck Matthew's partner in the chest and face, slamming him against the wall where he left a large stain of blood before bouncing off onto the floor, dead.

The shotgun blast also struck Matthew in the chest and shoulder. His gun flew out of his hand. Blood oozed from his shoulder down to his chest. Yvette knelt down beside him, screaming.

My eyes took in the entire room with a single glance. There was the elderly man in the wheelchair. Standing next to him was a man pointing a gun at us.

Next to them stood Ronald triumphantly. "Don't move!" he yelled. He pointed just beyond where I stood, to the right and behind me.

Sylvia stood weakly, barely able to support her weight on her feet. Her hands and legs were in shackles attached to the wall. Her sad eyes filled with hope as she saw me. "Mark," she said softly, as if my name were a magical chant.

"She's been given the antidote," Ronald said,

relishing his complete control of the situation. "Until I decide to make her a vampire again, she's temporarily human. That means that she can be killed. Take one more step and she will be killed. Just like your friend over there."

Ronald pointed at Matthew's partner, now nothing more than a crumpled pile of clothes on the floor soaked in blood.

The man with the sawed-off shotgun aimed the barrel at Sylvia's head and waited for my next move.

Chapter Twenty

Behind Sylvia's outer look of despair, there seemed to exist the slightest glimmer of hope in her eyes. As I glanced around the room, there did not seem much cause for hope at all. Although Matthew had killed one of the men, his own partner had been killed, and he appeared to be seriously wounded. One of the gunmen had his gun trained on Yvette, Matthew, and me, while the other had his sawed-off shotgun pointed at Sylvia's head.

"Do not move," Ronald repeated, "or Sylvia dies."

"If she dies, you die," I told him.

"You're not in a good position to make any threats." Ronald sneered. "Sylvia is temporarily human and can be killed just as easily as your friend."

"Don't believe him, Mark," Sylvia said. "I'm worth more to him than your friend. He needs me to make the antidote worthwhile."

Ronald shook his head. "Not anymore." He pointed at several beakers on a table. One appeared to be filled with about a cup of blood. Another contained a clear liquid that could have been water. "We have everything we need to make my rich friend here a well man—a man who can throw his wheelchair away, who will never get sick, and who will never age. But unlike a vampire, he will be able to live a normal life. He'll never have to drink blood or kill people."

"Never kill people!" I said. "What do you call this?" I pointed at the dead CIA agent, and at Matthew bleeding in the arms of Yvette, and at Sylvia shackled to the wall.

"I call this a fair trade," Ronald said. "My friend here gets health and immortality. I get one hundred million American dollars."

"He's traded us for money," Sylvia said.

"Yes," Ronald agreed. "But look at the bright side. You weren't traded away for some paltry amount.

Absolutely not. Despite what you think, Sylvia, I've always liked you. I find your superiority complex amusing. You have been useful in ridding me of my enemies. Your magical power has been a help in our rituals. I wouldn't sell you for a million dollars." Ronald leered with a gleam in his eyes. "But one hundred million dollars! Well that's another story, isn't it? Never let it be said that I betrayed you for nothing."

Yvette looked down at her arms, covered by Matthew's blood, as she cradled his head. She could not stop the bleeding. She turned to Ronald. "You bastard! Look what you've done."

Ronald shrugged his shoulders. "You killed my girlfriend. I kill your boyfriend. I'd say that makes us even, wouldn't you? "

"Your girlfriend?" Yvette asked.

"Yes, the one who died in your new Ferrari. She and I were going to be married."

"Married? You're still married to me," Yvette pointed out.

"That's why it was necessary to get rid of you. I knew you'd never agree to a divorce. And after you got involved with a CIA agent, well what did you expect me to do? Stand by and watch you tell him everything about us? I had you followed when you left the house the other night. It was a simple matter of matching his license plate to the one that Mark and Sylvia saw in the parking lot at the Heathrow Airport. Then I knew who he was and realized you both had to be killed."

"But why did you try to have Sylvia killed in the Atlantis Hotel last week?" I asked. "Why did you send Father Callen after us?"

"Because I knew that once she brought someone new to the house, she'd want a bigger share of the money. Of course, that's exactly what happened. Sylvia immediately wanted a larger cut of the money for you because of her murder of Graystone. Why should you get some of my money just for sleeping with Sylvia? But worst of all, you had to meet Father Clifford and Brother Phillips at Highgate Cemetery and try to interview them. I knew you would soon find out who gave them the information that enabled them to kill the couple from our house last year and who sent Father Callen after Sylvia in Reno. I couldn't take the chance of you getting the truth out of them. And I knew you would have gotten the truth out of them."

"But you changed your mind about killing us after you burglarized the lab and discovered the antidote," I said.

"Yes," Ronald admitted. "I realized that Sylvia and you would be worth more alive than dead because your blood is needed to be mixed with the antidote. The antidote alone turns a vampire into a human temporarily. There's not much of a market for that. I don't know any vampires who would be willing to pay for the penalty of becoming human again. However, mixing the antidote with the blood of either you or Sylvia creates a new compound—one that conveys immortality to a human without the disadvantages of becoming a vampire. Now, that is something with profit potential."

"But if you were to kill Sylvia and me, you wouldn't be able to make that formula anymore," I pointed out.

"By giving both of you the antidote, I can keep you here as long as I need to, but if you cause trouble and have to be killed, well—" Ronald shrugged his shoulders. "At least I will have made the one hundred million dollars from my friend here. That's enough for right now. After all, I'm not greedy."

"Wait a minute," I said. "If you're mixing Sylvia's blood with the antidote and she's now human, then why would our blood be worth more than any other human?"

"Ah, that's where Jack and Helen really outdid

themselves." Ronald smirked. "The antidote soon wears off, and when it does, the subject goes back to being a vampire and the blood changes back to the way it was before the antidote was given—even when it's just sitting in a test tube." Ronald poured some of the antidote into a glass, then added some of the blood and handed it to the man in the wheelchair.

"To long life." The elderly man raised his glass to us in a toast. He slowly drank the contents. "The most expensive drink in the history of the world," he remarked.

We all watched him to see a change, but nothing happened.

"You won't feel anything different until the antidote starts to wear off," Ronald explained. "At the same time that Sylvia starts to become a vampire again, you will feel the change." Ronald turned to Sylvia. "Of course, before that happens, I'll give you some more of the antidote. I certainly wouldn't want you to get all of your special abilities back, now would I?"

"Your friend may be in for an unpleasant surprise," Sylvia told Ronald. "Did you mention to him what happened to the other men who drank my blood?"

The elderly man looked alarmed. "What happened to them?"

"My blood killed them," Sylvia explained, enjoying the look of horror on the man's face as he stared at the now-empty glass.

Ronald shook his head. "Mark didn't die from your blood."

"That's because Mark and I are both inhabited by the same demon. The demon lives in both of us—and lives inside our blood. I don't think it's going to like being inside someone else's body. I don't think it will like that at all."

Ronald waved his hands, dismissing this notion. "Don't listen to her," he told the man. "The scientists who discovered this know a lot more about it than she does."

"They know about science, but not about Satan," Sylvia said.

"Perhaps," Ronald agreed. "However, you know about Satan and not about science. But you're now going to see the greatest scientific feat in history, the creation of immortality." He pointed at the man in the wheelchair, as if Ronald were some sort of carnival barker introducing someone in a freak show.

Everyone stared at him, waiting for something to happen, but he still looked the same.

"The first thing that will happen is you will get the feeling back in your legs," Ronald promised. "Then you will be able to stand up and walk again. At the same time, the cancer in your stomach will get smaller and smaller, until all of it is gone and you are completely healthy." As Ronald gave this little speech, he did it with the emotion of a preacher at a religious healing.

"You don't have the power to do such a thing," I said. "Only Sylvia does. She healed Lilly."

"And I did that with the spiritual power within me," Sylvia said, "not with my blood."

"No," said Ronald. "It's the blood. Just as your blood gave special abilities to Mark, it will now give the same special abilities to me." With that, he picked up the beaker filled with Sylvia's blood and drank some of it. "Now I will have all the abilities that the two of you have. Once my blood has changed, I will no longer have any need for either of you."

"When does the antidote wear off?" I asked.

"Very soon," Ronald said. "That's why I must give Sylvia some more right now. We wouldn't want her getting her special powers back right now, would we?" He put a small amount of the clear liquid into a glass, then a small amount into a second glass. "But before we have Sylvia drink some more of the antidote, I would like you to have some."

He walked over to the man who was holding a gun on Yvette, Matthew, and me, and handed him the glass, then went back to the table and picked up the other glass. He held it up in the air in our direction. "Shall I propose a toast? To wealth and long life—for me and my friend, of course." Ronald turned to the gunman. "Would you be so kind as to offer our friend, Mark, a drink. Don't worry. He won't turn you down. After all, Sylvia could still be killed by this gentleman here with the shotgun, and it makes such a mess, don't you think?"

The two men nodded in agreement with Ronald. They were like two robots, totally devoid of emotion. The man with the shotgun didn't even blink when Ronald alluded to shooting Sylvia. My whole body filled with rage.

Then I saw the man with the gun pointed at me start to walk towards me with the glass in his hand, to take away the only hope I had of saving Sylvia.

I looked at the man with the shotgun, but he would not look back at me. He stared only at Sylvia as he pointed his sawed-off shotgun at her head.

"I'll pay you more money than they will," I said to him.

Having heard the phrase "more money," he suddenly looked away from Sylvia and towards me.

Our eyes met for only an instant, but it was long enough.

"*You will shoot that man holding the gun and the glass,*" I ordered him.

He immediately trained the barrel on the other man. The other man froze for a second, not understanding what was going on. An instant later, the shotgun went off, hitting the other man right in the middle of the chest, killing him instantly. The man landed on top of Matthew's partner. The amount of blood almost made it difficult to tell that there were two bodies, not one.

"*Listen,*" I said, and the man with the shotgun immediately looked back at me like a puppet. "*You will put the barrel inside your mouth —*"

"No!" yelled Ronald, but the man could not hear him.

"*You will put the barrel inside your mouth,*" I repeated, as he followed my instructions precisely, the shortness of the barrel making it easier to do as he was told, "*and you will pull the trigger.*"

Boom! The blast scattered his head in a hundred bloody little pieces over half the wall. The headless body fell forward as the shotgun slipped from his grip.

I rushed towards him, broke the shotgun in half, then snapped the shackles around Sylvia so that she was free. Taking one of the sharp pieces of metal, I cut my wrist and held it bleeding to Sylvia's lips. "Drink," I said. "It will counteract the antidote."

"No!" Ronald screamed, as he tried to grab me.

My free hand balled into a fist and struck him as he reached for us. It only pushed him back slightly for a moment, then he grabbed for me again. My fist struck him harder this time, almost knocking him down, but he was on me instantly. I had to pull my bleeding wrist away from Sylvia's lips to stop Ronald.

But as we struggled, he seemed to grow weaker, and when I struck him a third time, the blow slammed him against the wall, where he had to rest for a moment to catch his breath.

It was then that we noticed that the elderly man in the wheelchair and Ronald both began to change.

The elderly man screamed in horror as he stared down at his stomach, which actually expanded before our eyes.

The cancer inside him grew with incredible speed and he clutched his stomach in pain as he screamed as loudly as he could. His hand clutched his heart, and his

282

body froze like a cold hard statue.

Ronald still leaned against the wall, but instead of rushing towards me, his hand grasped the table for support. He looked down at the floor as if examining something, but his actions were slow, as if he had forgotten what his next move was to be. When he looked up at us, the face was a different one, lined with age. With each passing second, another year would go by. He watched this progression by staring at his changing hands in horror and seeing the shocked reaction in our eyes.

Yvette gasped and turned away with a shudder. In the middle of the room, a withered man, appearing to be well over a hundred years old, cast a bitter look in her direction, then fell to the floor, face down.

As Sylvia and I approached the form in the middle of the floor, all that was left was a crumbling skeleton inside a new set of clothes.

Yvette stared at the empty pile of clothes, the bones inside them falling apart into dust. Then she stared at Matthew cradled in her arms, his blood oozing from his neck, his eyes flickering, and his breathing growing weaker every moment. "No!" she screamed. "No!" She cried loudly, as if that might somehow save Matthew from dying as well.

I put my arms around Sylvia and we held each other. In the face of so much death and uncertainty, she became even more precious to me because I realized how close I had come to losing her. We held each other tightly for several seconds, but then let go of each other, feeling self-conscious about our luck at surviving together while Yvette seemed to have lost everything at once.

"I won't let you die," Yvette said. "I'll save you."

Matthew's eyes barely registered a reaction to her words, though he seemed to take some comfort in being held by her as his eyes began to close.

"I'm not going to die," Matthew gasped. He undid his

jacket, which showed that the shotgun pellets were stopped by the bulletproof vest he wore, protecting his chest. "I just need my shoulder bandaged, but I'll be fine."

"Perhaps we can finally put all this trouble behind us," I said to Sylvia.

She smiled at me. "Oh, I wouldn't be too sure about that. With a CIA agent at the house with Yvette, I'll bet trouble will find us again, unless he resigns his job." She then phoned Joseph and Susan to pick up the Rolls Royce and drive it back, leaving nothing behind to link the incident to us.

Just then, I noticed Ronald's laptop computer on a table, with the screen showing a transfer of $100,000,000 to a bank account. "Take a look at this!" I yelled to Sylvia and Yvette.

Sylvia's eyes opened wide as she and Yvette both walked slowly to the computer.

"The money Ronald was going to be paid," I said. "One hundred million dollars! It seems the transaction went through, probably to a secret bank account."

Yvette looked over at us, then stepped up to the computer and began typing on it. The screen changed as another transfer occurred. "I had the password, so I just transferred the money to our joint account for the household. Ronald's 'secret' account now will be empty."

The three of us helped Matthew out and put him in the Jaguar, so that Yvette could drive him home. Sylvia and I took her Aston Martin. Susan and Joseph drove the Rolls Royce. We set fire to the house, then called the Fire Department, so that the house and all inside would burn, without spreading to any neighboring homes.

As the three cars pulled into the driveway at the Highgate mansion, Sylvia and I rescued her doll from inside of the Aston Martin, then looked over our shoulders at the gate closing behind us, the well-manicured grounds with the wolves running over the lawn to greet us, and up ahead, the mansion—where things had not always been what they had seemed.

When we went inside, we cleaned Matthew's wounds, which turned out to be much milder than we had originally thought. Apparently, much of the blood on him came from his partner, who was hit by most of the shotgun blast.

Susan and Joseph took some time to explain to Jack and Helen all the details of what happened. They were shocked and angered that Ronald would have used their formula to betray everyone.

Susan looked at all of us, bewildered by what had occurred. "What do we do next?"

"Good question," replied Sylvia, as she pointed at Matthew. "He knows all about us, but works for the American government. We can't have them knowing everything about us." She looked at Yvette. "What do you plan to do about it?"

Yvette stared at Matthew while she thought. "Well, let me ask you. What do you want to do? Are you ready to quit your career with the CIA and become one of us?"

Matthew hesitated. "I can't do that. I have an important job to do."

Yvette winced. "Oh yes, business. I know how important that is. I've heard that excuse."

Sylvia looked around at all of us. "If Matthew is not going to join us here, then there's only one thing we can do to protect ourselves from what he already knows."

Matthew's eyes showed the alarm in his thoughts.

"I will have to use a trance to erase the parts of his knowledge he gained here that could be used against us later." The others nodded their agreement. Matthew sighed as he realized he wasn't about to be killed. But Yvette just looked angry and rejected.

"Listen," Sylvia began, and then once she had Matthew in a trance, she found out everything he knew

about us, and had him forget much of what he discovered about us while in London. He forgot that Yvette was a vampire or what happened at the house with him and his partner fighting Ronald. He forgot about the $100,000,000 that Yvette pulled out of Ronald's secret bank account. He would leave London knowing about the same as what he knew when he arrived. But in keeping with Yvette's wishes, his memory of having sex with her would still be intact.

Everyone followed him out to the driveway as he drove off in his Jaguar to his hotel.

Sylvia and I paused for a moment with our arms around each other standing outside in the moonlight.

Sylvia tried to explain all about how the demon who inhabited us entered the bodies of Ronald and the other man, accelerating Ronald's aging and the other man's cancer.

"I'm not sure I understand," I said to Sylvia. "You mean the demon that killed them was the same as Satan?"

"Yes, the same."

"And you said the demon is part of us or that we are part of the demon?"

"Not just a part," Sylvia answered. "The demon is us, and we are the demon."

"So if you and I are a part of each other, then we are part of Satan," I replied.

"We are not a 'part' of Satan nor 'apart' from Satan," Sylvia explained. "We are all one."

"All?" I asked.

"Yes," Sylvia beamed. She gazed into my eyes, as if I were her mirror. "You and I are more than just a part of each other. We are each other. Soulmates. Forever."

THE END